THE THREE HARES
THE TERRACOTTA HORSE

THE THREE HARES

HARES

THE TERRACOTTA HORSE

SCOTT LAUDER
AND DAVID ROSS

SEVEN SEAS
COLLECTION

NEEM TREE PRESS

Published by Neem Tree Press Limited 2022

Neem Tree Press Limited
95A Ridgmount Gardens, London, WC1E 7AZ
info@neemtreepress.com
www.neemtreepress.com

A catalogue record for this book is available from the British Library

ISBN 978-1-911107-19-4 Paperback
ISBN 978-1-911107-20-0 Ebook

Printed and bound in Great Britain

CONTENTS

PART 1

LONDON,
UNITED KINGDOM
THE PRESENT DAY

CHAPTER 1

—

Salma Mansour climbed the stairs to the first floor, placed her hand on the door of the dojang, and pushed hard. The door, creaking like a giant frog, slowly swung open, revealing the same bare neon lights, blue mats, and leaky, iron-framed windows. Nothing was new—except the dead silence and the startled eyes of fourteen people locked on her.

"Just me!" she beamed.

As though a spell had been broken, everyone unfroze and returned to what they had been doing before she entered.

She wasn't the one they were all waiting for.

Still grinning at how tense everyone had looked—like mice watching a cat—she swung her bag off her shoulder. Her instructor, 4th Dan Lee Arnott, standing in front of the mirrored wall, raised his head and caught her eye in the reflection. Straightening her face and quickly tightening the yellow hair tie around her short ponytail, she gave a solemn bow, which Lee returned. Stepping up to the mat, she slipped off her birthday present—straw zori sandals her mother had bought last month. Her mother had acknowledged that they were Japanese, not Korean, but no matter: Salma loved them. They were pale golden, with light-blue straps illustrated with a dragon motif in dark blue. With care, she placed them together, making sure the edges of each met heel and toe. She wanted to take her time and enjoy every minute. Because tonight was a big deal: tonight was the night she got her red-black belt.

Bare feet on the cold, hard mats, she bowed again, as was the custom. When she raised her head, Lee Arnott was standing next to her.

"Are you ready?" he asked.

"Absolutely," she said. And she was.

Lee Arnott, who had been Salma's taekwondo instructor since she had walked into the dojang five years ago, smiled. "Well…good. There's no reason not to be, but…"

Salma nodded as Lee talked, but her eyes had found the clock over Lee's shoulder whose second hand was creeping closer and closer to eight o'clock.

"Salma?"

Her eyes snapped back to Lee.

"Stay focused," he said. "Remember: this isn't just a test of your physical skills." He held her gaze.

Duh! thought Salma. Of course, the exam was not just about physical strength.

"You should start your warm-up."

Salma nodded. As Lee made his way to the front of the class through the other candidates, arranged at neat intervals on the mat, she began her warm-up, grinning when Alison, in the second row in front of her, turned and gave her a thumbs up, which she returned. There were eleven others taking their grading exams, not including Alison and her. Some, like Alison, were trying to get their blue belts, some their brown, and just two, their black. She was the only one who was trying for the red-black. To get it, she would have to perform a series of regulated moves, spar with a partner, and do various kicks, such as a spinning heel kick. Breaking boards— otherwise known as the destruction—was the last part of the exam. The destruction didn't worry her. In fact, it was probably the part of the exam she was looking forward to the most. She loved the sense of power, of achievement that smashing through the boards gave.

Grabbing both ends of her current red belt, she pulled hard. She wanted the next belt, red and black, so much. The red signified that the belt-holders were aware of their skills and recognised the need for self-control. She had that! As for the black, it represented indifference to darkness and fear. Well, she wasn't afraid of anything, least of all this exam.

She breathed out slowly, forcing the air through her slightly parted lips, and thought about her uncle and her father. They would be proud. Her Uncle Sameer, her father's brother, had been a taekwondo champion in Aleppo. She'd never been to Syria, but she'd heard plenty about it from her father: about his home city, one of the most ancient in the world, and his brother and the rest of his family there. The news that a shell had destroyed Uncle Sameer's apartment, killing him, her cousins, and her aunt, as well as her grandparents, came when she was at primary school. She could still hear the cry of grief her father had given when he got the news. The doctors at Hammersmith hospital said he died of a heart attack. It wasn't true. He died of a broken heart.

Two rows in front of her, the new boy, Kofi, was frowning, listening intently to Lee Arnott, who, she guessed was giving him advice about his first grading exam. One of the things she loved about taekwondo was that nationality, origins, religion—all of those things were secondary. What counted was how well you could deal with an opponent who was trying to knock your head off!

She began bouncing forwards and backwards on her toes. Any moment now, the promotion exam would begin. *Think of your chi*, she told herself as Lee went to the back of the room where the concrete blocks were kept. *Think of the energy that flows through all things*. In the mirror, Lee's image picked up a dozen or so boards and began carrying them to the front of the dojang. She changed exercise and swung her arms in big circles. She had a lot of schoolwork to do, which meant she didn't get to the dojang more than once a week. So, not really often enough to progress through the ranks quickly. But still, it had annoyed her that she had been made to wait so long to take the red-black exam. She'd asked Lee twice before if she could take it. The third time, he'd agreed. Great. But why not the first time?

A sudden gust of wind rattling the dojang's tall windows interrupted her thoughts. The dark grey light pressing against the glass made it seem like winter, yet it was July and only 8 pm!

Brr! British summertime! She could almost feel the rain sweeping across the streets. She looked at her reflection, the light-brown hair pulled tightly over her scalp, the almond eyes, the slim shoulders. Her mother was always saying she was too skinny. Perhaps she was right. An image of the last time she had visited her aunt's house in Chelsea and its dining room table groaning with food came to mind: yabrak, hummus, fattoush, kibbeh, mahshi, muhammarah, kebab halabi. She loved visiting her aunt's place. Besides her aunt being a great cook, there were always loads of people there talking, laughing, offering plates, filling cups, discussing…

As she smiled at the memory of the last visit to her aunt's house, the top of a bus, about six metres away with an advertisement covering the space between the upper and lower deck, filled the dojang's windows. The advert, she noticed, was for a company called Bai Lu, which she'd never heard of. The upper deck was empty apart from an old man halfway along it, whose head was leaning against the bus's window.

A strange coldness crept over her as she gazed at him. Suddenly, the man twitched violently as though someone had jabbed him, his whole body jerking with the spasm. Straightening his hunched shoulders, he sat bolt upright and slowly twisted his head towards her. As he turned, he began to change: his hair becoming darker and longer, his jowls disappearing, his skin tightening…A boy with intense eyes and dark, scraggly hair was staring at her, a mocking grin spreading across his face. Salma staggered backwards as she gazed in horror, unable to look away as the boy's face began to change. Like watery slime, his skin and muscles were melting, sliding away until all that was left was the white, shiny bone below. The skull's two deep, dark, empty sockets stared at her. Salma had the sensation she was underwater; she was drowning, her lungs pressed and squeezed, unable to breathe. Revolted, rooted to the spot, she watched as the thing raised a bony, white finger and pointed at her. A scream rose in her throat, but just as it was about to escape, the bus's engine roared, the bus lurched forward, and the old man was back again, snoozing like nothing had happened...

"Salma?"

She swivelled around. Lee was staring at her, a quizzical look on his face.

"Are you with us?" he asked.

All she could manage was a weird grunt. Her heart was pounding, her palms sweaty.

Lee's eyes held her for a moment longer; then, addressing the whole class, he clapped his hands and said, "Good luck, everyone." A moment later, the door to the dojang creaked open. Salma turned as a small, stocky man with snow-white, close-cropped hair entered, bowed low, and stepped onto the mats.

Grandmaster Cho had arrived.

CHAPTER 2

—

As she turned into Mill Road, a gust of wind barrelled towards her. She grasped the edges of her hood with both hands and held on to it. Beyond the maisonettes at the end of Mill Road, a section of Tower Block Four's twenty-five floors rose into the gloomy night, a smattering of the windows on the upper floors lit. She wondered if her mother was back yet. Their apartment was on the 18th floor but on the other side of the block.

The grading exam.

Ugh! Talk about pathetic! She had never felt so…weak and unfocused. Lee had been disappointed. He hadn't said anything, but she could tell. *And what about that…thing she had seen on the bus? What was that all about? It seemed like something out of a Netflix show!* Nothing like that had ever happened to her before. But even if it had freaked her out—and it definitely, *definitely* had—it wasn't an excuse: she should have been able to concentrate.

Salma could see through the small frame of glass in her front door that the lights inside her flat were switched off. Her mother hadn't yet returned from the lecture she was giving at the British Museum, where she worked as a curator for the Middle Eastern galleries. Salma was almost glad.

Inside the flat, she opened the kitchen door slowly, so as not to bang it against the fridge. The kitchen's fluorescent light blinked five times and finally shone down. Apart from the fridge, she and her mother had managed to cram in a tiny table, a sink, a cooker, a microwave, a washing machine that also dried clothes, and four kitchen units. She saw the note immediately, folded with her name on it, leaning against the microwave door.

Should be finished around 10. See you when I get back.
Dinner in the microwave.

With her elbow, she popped open the microwave. The smell of fish, ginger, paprika, and cinnamon from the heaped plate of Sayadieh wafted into the air. It was the remains of a larger portion her mother had made the night before. Salma didn't mind eating it for the second night in a row: Sayadieh was one of her favourites. And anyway, beggars couldn't be choosers.

Her mother's job with the British Museum was well-paid, but everything in London was so expensive. After her father's death, they'd been forced to leave their rented house in Fulham near the dental practice her father had worked at and move to the tiny flat they were in now. As her mother always said, life goes on and we adapt, simple as that.

Ping! The microwave announced two minutes had passed. Salma flicked the door open and pulled out the plate. Mechanically, she began shovelling the food into her mouth.

The destruction! That had been the worst. She had failed to connect with the board properly three times. *How? How was that even possible?* She had done jumping sidekicks—twimyo yop chagi—hundreds of times before. *Why had her technique failed her now?* Head down, gathering her thoughts, she had been preparing to try again when Grandmaster Cho had clapped his hands and cried, "Enough!" It was over.

The rest of the dojang had gone very quiet. She had stood, bowed, and sat down. Lee Arnott had fixed his eyes on the ground. But Grandmaster Cho had stared straight at her. She had met his eyes and held them. She might have failed the grading, but she wasn't ashamed. She wanted him to know that. She felt angry with herself that she had allowed whatever she had seen on the bus to affect her so much. Unexpectedly, Grandmaster Cho had smiled and, in a quiet voice, said, "Not every failure is a defeat; not every success is a victory." His words had instantly made sense to her. She had failed, but she wasn't going to crawl away and feel sorry for herself. No way.

What had annoyed her was Lee Arnott. After Grandmaster Cho's departure, he'd taken her aside and told her he wasn't surprised. Confidence, he'd said, was good. But over-confidence was not. *What!? Was that how he saw her? Over-confident?* She'd been too astonished to reply and instead had given him a cursory bow, quickly changed, and left the building. What was over-confident about believing in yourself? She'd practiced hard every day at home for a half-hour, even if she'd only made it to the dojo once a week. She could do the destruction; she could do it in her sleep! That wasn't over-confidence. It was a fact. OK, so she'd failed. But there was a reason for that.

Finishing the last of the Sayadieh, she ran the hot water and washed her plate. She was drying it when she heard the key in the front door and, a moment later, her mother's voice. Her mother, who had been almost as excited about the grading as she had, would want to know all about it. How would she explain not getting the belt?

The door opened and her mother, panting, squeezed into the kitchen. "Those stupid elevators…" she grumbled. Smiling, leaning down and dropping the small bag of groceries at the foot of the kitchen table, she hugged Salma, "Salaam habibti," she said as she took off her pristine white hijab and baby-blue cardigan.

Salma returned the cuddle and greeting.

"Well?" her mother said, releasing her.

Salma looked into her mother's hopeful eyes, the same shape and colour as her own.

"Don't keep me in suspense. How'd you get on?"

Salma shook her head. Her mother's shoulders immediately slumped.

"Oh," she said, pulling out a chair and sitting heavily. "I'm so sorry." She rubbed Salma's hand. 'What happened?'

Salma paused. *An old man on a bus turned into a boy who turned into a hideous skeleton, and I lost concentration? The examiner, Grandmaster Cho, has always hated me? I didn't take the exam seriously enough because I was "over-confident"?* She could imagine the billions of questions that each of those answers would summon. There was only one thing to do.

"I don't want to talk about it."

Her mother's delicate eyebrows rose sharply, the same sandy colour as Salma's hair. "You don't want to talk about it?"

"I don't want to talk about it."

Her mother let out a long breath. "Well, if you don't want to talk about it, you don't want to talk about it." She held Salma's eye. Salma refused to blink, and her mother, looking faintly puzzled, shook her head, and stood. "Have you had something to eat?" Before Salma could reply, her mother said, "I bought some ice cream. Salted caramel: your favourite."

Salma could practically hear the unspoken words: *to celebrate you getting the red-black belt.*

CHAPTER 3

—

"Turn to page 46, everyone," Mrs Green said as she zipped around the over-warm, stuffy classroom. "Quickly, please."

"What's this?" Kaylee asked, looking up as a copy of *Collected English Poems* landed on her desk.

"It's a book," replied Mrs Greene as she hurried past. "An object whose pages we read."

Tuyen snorted and Salma grinned at her: Mrs Greene had some wicked retorts. Tuyen was Salma's best friend and totally on her wavelength.

"Very funny," Kaylee muttered darkly.

"Right," Mrs Greene said, standing at the front of the class, hands finally empty, "today we are going to look at—"

"What's a Viking?"

Salma, Tuyen, Hazel and everyone else turned in their seats. It was Kaylee again. She was holding the book in the air and pointing to page 46, where there was an introduction to a poem called 'The Battle of Maldon'. "'The first recorded Viking raid,'" Kaylee said, reading from the book, "'was at Lindisfarne in 793 CE.'"

"Indeed, it was," replied Mrs Greene. "Now, does anyone know what a Viking is?"

A few hands went up. "Yes, Anita."

"It's someone from Scandinavia. They were—"

"Scandinavia? Where's that?" shouted Kaylee, struggling, it seemed to Salma, to keep her face straight as Elaine, seated next to her, giggled.

Mrs Greene's eyes narrowed; nevertheless, she turned back to Anita. "Anita? Do you know?"

"Isn't it like Norway and Sweden and…er Denmark?"

Mrs Greene smiled. "That's right. Vikings were people from these northern countries who began raiding Britain, and other places, around the 8th Century or perhaps even earlier. The book that Kaylee just read from says that the first recorded Viking raid was in Lindisfarne. What does 'first recorded' mean?"

Salma put her hand up.

"Salma?"

"Written down for the first time?"

Behind Salma, Kaylee whispered something and Elaine smothered a laugh.

"That's correct. The raid was discussed in a letter written by someone who lived at the time, Alcuin of York. And why do you think the Vikings raided Lindisfarne?"

"'Cause it was easy?" someone said.

"Well, yes, I suppose so. Not many places at that time were prepared for attacks by people on ships," replied Mrs Greene. "So—if you were a raider, what kind of place would you look for?"

"A rich one!" shouted Kaylee.

"Absolutely right!" Mrs Greene said, "And monasteries were rich: they had lots of gold and silver. They also had lots of people who could be taken and sold as slaves. The poem we are going to read today is about a Viking raid in modern day Essex in 991 CE. The Vikings weren't just raiders though: they were also settlers. At this time, some of them were living all the year round in some places such as parts of Scotland, Wales and Ireland—"

"What's Byrh…tnoth?" Kaylee asked, struggling to say the word.

"It's a name—of the East Saxon leader at the Battle of Maldon. 'Beorht' means bright and 'noth' means courage. Most of the Anglo-Saxon names meant something. 'Aldred' meant 'old advisor';

'Godric' meant 'by God's power'; 'Seward' was 'guards the coast'. They..."

As Mrs Greene continued to talk and Kaylee continued with her regular interruptions, Salma suddenly smelled a waft of breeze, her hair ruffled, and rays of sunlight warmed her skin. She heard the roar of waves, the squawk of seagulls, tasted the salt on her tongue, and steadied her feet in the sand against the surf that lapped and tugged at her ankles...

Except she was in a London classroom and not at the seaside. *What on earth was happening to her? Did she need to see the school psychologist? Should she say something to Tuyen?* Salma felt a deep unease settle over her.

After class, Salma rushed outside into fresh air. She was in the middle of untying her sweater and wrapping it around her waist when the security door swung open and Tuyen stepped through it. Unusually for Tuyen, who usually wore her straight, dark hair loose, today she had it in a ponytail. Salma guessed her new earrings were the reason. "Nice earrings by the way," Salma said.

Tuyen leaned her head sideways. "Thanks!" Each was a little golden cat whose eyes were made of tiny diamonds. "Present from my uncle. He's visiting from Vietnam."

"So why cats?" asked Salma.

"I'm 'Year of the Cat.' In China, it's the 'Year of the Rabbit,' but the Vietnamese have cats instead. Cats are better. People who are cats are good artists and doctors. They have supple minds and they—"

"Enjoy a little mouse meat?" Salma suggested.

Tuyen gave a squeal of laughter. Some of the other students streaming out of the doors turned and stared at her. What they saw was Tuyen clutching her stomach and sliding down to squat on the floor, her whole body shaking with laughter. "Mouse meat!" she said, almost choking.

"And lucre!" Tuyen cried, brandishing two rolled-up twenty-pound notes as she stood up again. Grinning, she smelt the rolled-up notes.

Salma laughed, her mood clearing in Tuyen's presence. "Someone's rich today!"

"Also, from my uncle. He's here for my cousin's wedding. Gave it to me this morning and told me to spend it wisely."

Salma smiled. "VeeGees would be a very wise spending decision…"

Tuyen suddenly rested a hand on Salma's arm. "Oh! I'm so sorry! Just realised I haven't asked you about your grading. How did it go?"

"Not good," Salma said, her tone flat, hoping Tuyen would take the hint and not ask for details. Maybe she'd talk to Tuyen about that and her crazy imagination later. But right now, all she wanted to do was enjoy her lunch.

"Sorry to hear that," Tuyen said carefully like she knew it was a touchy subject. "But…you'll get another chance, right?"

Salma nodded. Her mother had said the same thing when she had told her last night.

The rest of the way they didn't speak, and Salma was grateful. It was one of the many things she liked about Tuyen: she knew when to ask questions and when not to.

As they walked side-by-side in silence, Salma thought back to Kaylee's annoying interruptions. Recently, she and a few of her friends had been giving Salma hard stares, muttering about "refugees", "immigrants" and "scroungers" and how they were ruining things for decent people—whoever they were supposed to be. It made her mad: especially scrounger. Her mother worked full time every hour she could, just to pay for council tax and food. What right did Kaylee and the rest of them have to call anyone names? The refugees she met at the centre wanted to work too: they wanted a job, a chance to earn money for themselves and their families. Did Kaylee's mother or father work as hard as her mother?

Arriving at VeeGees interrupted her thoughts—as did Tuyen's smile.

"I told you already: it's my treat!" Tuyen was saying, pushing away Salma's money and insisting that the cashier take her notes, not Salma's. Veegees was their favourite vegetarian café.

Salma had no option but to accept. "That's kind of you."

"No, it's kind of my uncle," Tuyen replied, grinning.

As they sat eating on tables in front of the restaurant, Salma's mind wandered to the strange experiences she had had over the last two days.

"You seem a little quiet, are you ok?" asked Tuyen.

"Yeah, fine, just thinking about the homework from Mrs Greene's class." Normally Salma discussed everything under the sun with Tuyen, but something held her back this time. Something told her nothing good would come of her telling Tuyen about the bus incident.

CHAPTER 4

That weekend, Salma's Saturday morning began with the sound of her mother creeping quietly, but not silently, into her room.

"Sorry, I've woken you," her mother whispered.

"That's okay," Salma, sitting up slowly.

Her mother smiled and sat next to her on the bed. Above the turned-up collar of her coat, she had wrapped a silk scarf around her neck. Her hands swept back loose strands of Salma's hair from her face.

Eyes half-closed, feeling groggy with sleep, Salma said, "What time is it?"

"Nearly 8.30. I'm giving a lecture at 11. Remember?"

"Oh, yeah. Yeah. That's right. What time will you be back?" Salma was so tired that she was practically slurring her words. She gave a huge yawn.

"It'll finish around 12.30. What time is your class?"

The yawn stopped Salma from answering immediately. When she was able to speak again, she said, "Sorry—at 10."

"Are you going to the centre today?"

Salma knew she meant the Finsbury Refugee Centre. She nodded. "After class."

"Okay, so do you want to meet me in the museum? We can have lunch and you can go to the centre afterwards. You're doing your volunteering today, right?"

Salma nodded and grinned. "Can we go to…you-know-where?"

Her mother stood up. The London Review of Books' Cake Shop was just a few minutes' walk from the British Museum and was one of Salma's all-time favourite places for a treat. Leaning over, her mother kissed Salma on the head. "We'll see. OK, I must dash."

A few moments later, the front door closed, there was the noise of a key being turned, and Salma was alone in the flat. She lay warm and comfortable and thought about the rest of her day. She had some maths and English homework—algebra and a typed essay on the old English poem about the 'Battle of Maldon', which the class had eventually read after Mrs Greene's little talk with Kaylee. The essay was due at the end of the month, so she still had some time.

The maths homework was for Monday morning. And right now, she needed to get up and get a move on if she didn't want to be late for taekwondo. She hesitated. A minute later, she was opening her laptop, newly repaired after she had accidentally dropped it and broken the screen. Five minutes checking Instagram; then she'd get up, make some breakfast, get her kit together. Just five minutes.

With the laptop sitting on top of her thighs, she waited for the locked screen to appear, fingers ready to punch in her password. Nothing happened. "Aw, you're kidding!" she groaned. *What was the matter now?* She folded the screen down and re-opened it. Still, the screen was dark. She pressed the on/off button. Then pressed it again. It made no difference: the same dark, empty screen stared back at her. "They were supposed to fix this," she grumbled and raised it from her lap, ready to put it aside when the screen suddenly flickered and a bright box appeared. *What...?* She stared at the box which contained a conversation between two people. One of them was named the "First Hare" and the other "Second Hare". She scrolled up. There were pages and pages of it! They had been chatting for ages, and now, she could see every word they had written, for some reason. All the pages had the same title, "The Three Hares". She frowned. As far as she could see, there were only two people. She scrolled to the end of the page she was on. A little shiver went through her. A cursor blinked, and next to the cursor was a name: "Third Hare".

She was the Third Hare.

*

How was that even possible? For a moment, she debated what to do. If her mother were here, she would probably tell her not to do anything: she didn't know who she was talking to; it could be anyone—some weirdos playing a trick or…well, something worse. Her mother was always worried about that. Not that she needed to be. Salma knew the dangers of chatting online with anyone she didn't know. Her hand wavered over the keyboard. She should probably not write anything…but it was a private conversation. It didn't feel right that she should be able to see what these two people were writing without telling them that…Her hand continued to hover. Was there any harm in warning them that their conversation wasn't private?

Her fingers punched in the message.

> **Third Hare:** Hi—sorry, but I've been added to this conversation. Don't know why. Just thought you should know.

Leaning back, resting her head on her pillow, she waited. She didn't feel right about scrolling up and reading more of the conversation than she could see on the screen in front of her. But from what she could see, it was clear that the other two were in different countries—there was talk about flight times, hotels, their parents' plans, and where they should meet once they arrived. It also seemed they were both around her age—they had discussed their end of year exams, which were coming up soon. The First Hare was nervous about those, and the Second Hare was, too—especially geography. It was really tempting to read more…But, no. It wasn't any of her business. *How would she feel if someone did the same to her?*

She stared at the slowly blinking cursor. But nothing else happened: no one answered and nothing appeared. Her stomach rumbled. She waited a few more seconds. She glanced at the time. She would need her computer later in order to prepare for the class she was teaching and needed to escape from the current screen. She pressed Ctrl+Alt+Del. Nothing happened: the conversation and its flashing cursor stared back at her. She tried again. Same result. She pressed the power button. Still, the cursor blinked at her. She pressed it again. And again. And again. Nothing. "Whatever," and slapped the laptop onto her bedside table. She didn't have time for this.

*

Still feeling annoyed about her laptop, Salma walked quickly out of the lift, which was—*thank goodness!*—working again. Bright sunshine greeted her. She took a deep breath. It was already 9.15. She would have to hurry if she wanted to be on time for taekwondo.

CHAPTER 5

—

The tallish, narrow-shouldered boy staring at the top of the museum's South side entrance had his back turned to her. But Sara immediately knew it was him. She recognised the checked shirt and the curly, black hair. But that wasn't all. The weird part was she could feel it: she was being pulled towards him as though there was an invisible sail above her and the wind had suddenly caught it. As she closed the distance, something else began to happen. The air around him began doing something. It was like tiny sparks—or maybe intensely bright fireflies—had launched themselves and were circling above his head. Wait! They were above her head, too! They were small, round, and sparkly—sort of like tiny beads or pearls. Quicker than she expected, she was within arm's length of him. She reached out to tap him on the shoulder, one eye still on the things floating around her, but he was already turning around.

"Sara!" he cried. His eyebrows shot up above the frame of his glasses, and a beaming smile lit up his face.

"Sanjeev!" Sara said.

For a moment, he regarded her with his shining brown eyes and Sara wasn't sure if she should hug him or not. But she leaned forward and did. It seemed silly not to. After all, they had been chatting madly since all of this started and she had probably sent more text messages and emails to him than all her other friends, Lily included.

Their brief embrace ended and they separated. Looking a little flustered, Sanjeev stared at the space above her head, his eyes darting all over the place.

"You see them, too?" Sara asked. "When did it start?"

"Soon as my feet touched British soil!" Sanjeev replied.

"Yeah, me too. I started ducking and diving. My mother thought I'd gone nuts."

Sanjeev grinned and reached up; he swiped a hand back and forth. It passed straight through the lights. "Some sort of localised luminescence that no one else seems to be able to see…"

"I'm not surprised," Sara said.

Sanjeev's brow creased. "Not surprised that there are specks of light circling our heads?"

"Correct. I mean, think about it—you're a bright spark and so am I!"

Sanjeev grinned. "Neat joke."

Sara inclined her head. "But seriously, is it any weirder than any of the other weird stuff that's been happening to us?"

"I suppose not," Sanjeev admitted. "It's so good to see you in the body…Er, I mean in the flesh…in real life, not on a screen."

Sara suppressed a laugh. She had discovered it wasn't difficult to tease Sanjeev. And she couldn't resist doing it now either: "What do you mean?" she asked, a mock edge to her voice, "What's wrong with my pixels?"

Sanjeev pushed his glasses to the bridge of his nose. He opened his mouth, but nothing came out. Instead, he stared at her like a goldfish from inside its bowl. This time, Sara laughed. "I'm kidding!" she cried.

"Oh yes. Right! Cool," Sanjeev replied. He looked up again and frowned. "Some sort of geostationary orbit."

"Eh?"

"These things," Sanjeev said, pointing above their heads. "They're stationary above us—like satellites above the Earth in an orbit that matches the rotation of the Earth so that the satellite stays in one place."

Sara grinned. "I don't think my head is spinning at 1,000 miles an hour."

"Er…no. Right."

"By the way," Sara said as they climbed the steps together, "what were you looking at—before I arrived?"

"Oh…it was that," he said, pointing a slender finger upwards. "It's a story."

Sara scrunched up her eyes. "What is?"

"The frieze. It's the story of civilisation. At the far left-hand side is primitive life," Sanjeev was pointing to the top of the columns that supported the building's roof. A large triangle, the pediment, was filled completely with stone figures. "It's a crocodile," continued Sanjeev, "which makes sense—cause reptiles are pretty primitive beasts. But…" his voice trailed off.

"But what?" Sara asked.

"But it should have been a fish—or maybe an amphibian— because these are more ancient than reptiles. Though, of course, they are all part of the phylum chordata."

Sanjeev, Sara thought, knew an amazing amount of stuff; he was like a walking encyclopedia. But sometimes he lacked… common sense? Once, he'd asked her how to stop his dog, Jigsaw, from slipping in the tub while he bathed him. *Ummm…use an old towel and lay it flat in the tub while you wash him?* Didn't take a genius to work that one out. Another thing about Sanjeev was he loved to mansplain. Annoying, but sometimes she liked it because watching him squirm when she caught him at it was fun. "So," she said, "in your opinion, Sir Richard Westmacott should have carved something like a toad and not a crocodile?"

Sanjeev blinked. "Sir Richard Westmacott…He's…the guy who made the sculptures?"

Sara nodded, trying not to look gleeful.

Sanjeev cringed. "So, you know the story already?"

"Yup."

Sanjeev started to open his mouth.

"Come on!" she said, weaving her arm through his, pulling him through the massive doors at the museum's main entrance and into the cool interior.

Inside, it took a few moments for Sara's eyes to adjust to the lack of bright sunshine. When they had, she said: "How long do you have before you have to be back?"

"About an hour," Sanjeev replied. "My parents are having a nap at the hotel: they don't even know I'm gone. How about you?"

"My dad's here—in the museum."

"Oh!" Sanjeev said, and releasing her arm, he glanced left and right.

Sara couldn't help but smile. *Was he expecting to see her father rushing angrily towards them?* "I'm meeting him at the bookshop in the Great Court at 3 pm. I wouldn't mind finding a quiet place to have a chat." In front of them was a large donations box on top of which someone had left a map of the museum. Sanjeev was about to take it, but Sara said: "No need. I had a look online. There's a cafe on Level 3. We can go there."

Sanjeev nodded and swiped at the specks of light circling his head. "They're kind of bugging me."

"Is it because you can't explain what they are?"

Sanjeev pondered that, biting the inside of his cheek. "Maybe…"

"Don't you think there are lots of things happening to us that we can't explain?"

Sanjeev thought about that for a second. "I guess you're right."

They reached the stairs leading to the first floor. The laughs, shouts, and chatter of people climbing the steps along with them filled the stairwell.

"You know," Sarah said, nodding up at the lights still following them, "I think they're beautiful. It's like…it's like we have our own stars."

Chapter 6

—

It happened during her sparring with Theo. She'd had injuries before: a torn ligament, a broken finger. These things happened all the time. You just had to deal with it: Taekwondo was a contact sport. But the annoying thing was, Theo's Spear Hand Strike was one of his favourites, so it shouldn't have surprised her. But it had. Totally her own fault; she'd been distracted. Theo had lunged forward, arm outstretched and—*wallop!* —the Pyong Sohn Keut Chigi had caught her on the cheek bone just below the eye and knocked her flat.

Theo, who was taller and older than her, immediately began apologising, asking over and over if she was alright. It was the first time she had seen Theo look so serious, and it almost made her laugh. "I'm fine," she said, but her eye was throbbing. Theo slipped the head protector off. Others were gathering around. With Theo's hand supporting her neck, she raised her head, but a wave of pain forced her to put it back down again. She touched her nose. No blood. At least it's not broken. Her eye was watering. She wiped it with the back of her hand and heard Lee Arnott tell someone to get the Coolbox. A moment later, she heard the box being opened and Lee's face appeared above her. Silently, he handed her an ice pack. Grimacing, Salma slowly sat up and put the ice on her eye. It felt like her eyeball was on fire!

"Are you okay to stand up?" Lee asked. Salma took a deep breath and slowly got to her feet. Both Theo and Lee were watching her carefully. Around her, the crowd had thinned. She guessed they thought her injury wasn't that interesting.

"Do you feel sick?" Lee asked.

Salma didn't.

"How about dizzy?"

"No, I'm fine."

Theo raised his hand. "How many fingers?" he asked.

"Twelve." Salma replied and grinned.

"Seriously," Lee said.

"Four," Salma said. "I'm fine, honestly."

"Come on. Let's go and have a seat," Lee said.

Even though her head was much clearer and the ice was numbing her face, Salma didn't argue. The fact was the class was almost over. She may as well sit down and think about what she was going to say to her mother. She sighed. Her mother had never been very keen on Taekwondo. Not that she ever said Salma shouldn't do it, but Salma could tell. The last injury—the torn ligament—had prompted her mother to ask whether there wasn't another activity she could try instead. But Salma wasn't interested in stamp collecting or pony trekking. She loved Taekwondo, even if it meant getting injured once in a while.

Lee and Theo guided Salma to the only chair in the dojang and told her to sit. "Can't believe I didn't block you," she said to Theo.

"I'm lightning fast, man! No way you can block me!"

"Don't make me laugh!" Salma grimaced, and Theo chuckled. He knew it was quite a fluke he'd managed to make contact with Salma's body at all! She was normally so fast and light on her feet.

"Let me see," Lee said.

Salma took the ice away and showed him the eye, which felt hot and swollen. Lee drew in a breath. "It's going to look worse before it looks better."

"You've got a Theo souvenir!" cried Theo.

Salma snorted. It made her head throb. She winced and replaced the ice pack.

"Shouldn't we get the girl to the hospital?" Theo asked. "A Theo Spear Hand Strike is leeeethal!"

Salma punched Theo's arm lightly.

"Okay, Okay. The girl still got strength. She is fine," Theo said, rubbing his arm.

"Are you going to be OK getting home?" asked Lee.

"I'm actually supposed to meet my mum for lunch. I'll be fine, honestly."

Lee glanced at the clock. "Stay till the end of class, please. I need to make sure you're going to be OK."

"Sure," Salma replied and for the next twenty minutes, she sat in the chair as the class finished and the students gathered around her, forming a tight huddle. Salma batted away their worries. She was fine, she told them and when the last one had filed out of the dojang, Theo left too, winking and smiling at her. When he was gone, Lee asked Salma to stand on one leg—to see how her balance was. He also checked her pupils and whether she was experiencing any blurred vision. When all of that was done, Lee's pinched face relaxed and he said, "Doesn't seem like you have any concussion, but you have to promise me that you'll see a doctor the moment you feel dizzy or—"

"—I will," Salma said. "I promise."

"Where are you meeting your mum?" Lee asked.

"The British Museum. She's at work today."

*

The sun blazed down as she walked along Aldersgate Street, the sky cloudless except for some high, wispy-white cirrus clouds. According to her mother, "cirro" meant "curl of hair". It made sense. Way above everything else, these clouds looked just like strands from an old man's beard. Salma knew they were made of ice crystals which meant the weather would change soon. But for now, it was fine, in fact, better than fine.

The nearest tube station to the dojang was Farringdon or Barbican, but she walked towards St Paul's and the Central line, which would take her to Holborn. From there, it was a short walk to the museum. Salma had decided to go to St Paul's—she needed some air. She was at the end of Aldersgate Street in a few minutes and entered St Martin's-le-Grand. In front of her, the sleek, pale dome of St Paul's rose above the boring, modern buildings around it. Huge and outlandish amongst these rectangular boxes, it hovered like an alien space-ship—not a saucer, but a giant, upside-down cup. *I have come from the Planet Wren to give you great architecture!* Salma smiled.

On the concourse, there was the usual scrum: at the back of the platform, people flowed towards the exit; at the front, they stood lumped together, eyes forward, waiting.

In the thick of the crowd, Salma had her backpack on but clutched the plastic bag with her zori sandals so they wouldn't get bent and squished in with everything else. She glanced at the announcements to see when the next train was due—still a 6-minute wait…

As she stood, plastic bag dangling at her side, shoulder-to-shoulder with the others who were waiting with bored expressions on their faces, she idly wondered which cake she'd have at the London Review of Books' Cake Shop. *Lemon drizzle? Victoria sponge? Banana and walnut?* She chuckled to herself. *Who was she kidding?* Every time she went there, she ended up choosing the same thing. *Chocolate gateaux, all the way!* And she was picturing her fork slowly pressing its way into the gateaux's dark, rich moistness when someone behind her barked: "Mind where you're going!"

She twisted around to see a tall man staring down his nose at a woman who was trying to manoeuvre a huge suitcase nearer the front of the platform and out of the way of the people trying to get past her. "Ridiculous!" the man spluttered.

The woman, looking flustered and hot, began apologising— *Why?* Salma thought. *If anyone should be sorry, it should be him for being so rude.* The woman squeezed the suitcase as close to her body as she could, but still, the man wasn't happy. Shaking his head, he pushed away from her but there was really nowhere to go and like dominos being toppled, the person he bumped shoulders with bumped the next person and the next…

Her whole body shunted forward, Salma bent at the waist and threw her arms back to counteract the force driving her forward. She wobbled…and regained her centre of gravity just centimetres from disaster. But not before the bag slipped from her fingers and disappeared from view onto the track below.

"Idiot!" someone cried, meaning the tall man, Salma presumed. She couldn't have agreed more! Feet planted, she leaned over and looked down. Between the two shiny rails, lying on a filthy wooden sleeper, the plastic bag was open, the pale toe of one of her beautiful zori sandals peeking out. She turned and stared daggers at him, her emotions in turmoil, rising anger along with a deep sadness. Nose in the air, he was pretending that nothing had happened. She lifted her eyes to the announcements.

NEXT TRAIN: 3 minutes.

She could jump down and get them. *No, that would be really stupid. But look at her beautiful sandals!* Three minutes. *There was time. It would take her seconds to drop, grab the bag and be up on the platform.*

"There *is* time," a whispered voice said. "Get them."

Salma look to her left and right. Disinterested expressions and slack faces met her startled gaze.

"Slip onto the tracks. Won't take a minute. Get them," the voice, now louder, repeated.

Salma reeled. The voice was in her head! As she struggled to absorb this fact, the feeling that a weight was pressing down on her, squeezing her brain, making her thoughts fuzzy, her eyes unfocused, grew and grew. She shook her head. Through the haze, the announcements changed.

NEXT TRAIN: 2 minutes.

"You will never find zori sandals exactly like these again. So beautiful, aren't they? Such a *gorgeous* present. You are so fit, you know you would be so quick. Go on now, get them," the voice continued. Salma felt her legs twitch, her foot shuffle just a little.

She blinked hard, trying to clear her mind. It didn't work. Her other foot, of its own volition, inched forward so that it was parallel to the another. She looked at the black trousers she was wearing and tried with all her might to lift her legs, push her heels backwards, do *something*, but couldn't.

"Wouldn't want those lovely sandals destroyed, would you? Shredded to bits. You'd regret it forever."

A surge of panic; her eyes flew to the announcements. *The voice was so right, it would take her seconds…*yet her sensibility was screaming not to do it.

NEXT TRAIN: 1 minute.

"Get them!" the voice commanded; its tone suddenly harsh. "Get them, *now!*" And in horror, Salma watched her leg start to rise.

"No!" she said aloud. "No!" And with all her focused concentration, she fought the force moving her body as a rumble that had been distant a second ago grew louder and louder.

No! No! No!

With a blast of hot, sweetened air, the train swept into the station, the wind hitting those closest to the platform's edge and making them stagger backwards. Lights blazing, brakes screeching, hauling carriage upon carriage full of bored passengers, it hurled past Salma, its convex steel body just a nose-length away from her plate-shaped eyes.

She stared at the space where her zori sandals were. It was now occupied by the train which, brakes still complaining in hard metallic screeches, was slowing to a dead stop.

She was actually shaking, her heart pounding against her ribs like a blacksmith's hammer. *What or who had spoken to her?*

In a shocked daze, she managed to find a seat next to an older woman wearing an all-white trouser suit. The doors closed and a moment later the train was rushing out of the station.

Her mind in turmoil, she sat open-mouthed and uncomprehending, barely aware that her gaze had landed on the adverts above her as the train entered the tunnel.

CHAPTER 7

━

For a moment, she wondered if she had closed her eyes as the train entered the tunnel and had somehow fallen asleep. She was positive she hadn't, but just to be sure, she blinked hard. No. They were definitely open; she was definitely awake.

"What the...?" she whispered into the dense blackness and the equally dense silence. *Why was it so quiet? Had everyone gotten off?* "Hello?" she said, hating how tentative, how *scared* her voice sounded. No answer.

She cleared her throat; tried again, this time louder: "Hello? Is anyone there?" Again, no answer. It didn't feel like she was alone. *Was there someone next to her? Either side of her? In front of her?* She dared not reach out. *What if she touched someone? What if they could see her but she couldn't see them?* A shard of fear, small but sharp, stabbed at her heart. She was still sitting: she could feel the seat's cushioned fabric below her, the weight of her body on it, her feet against the metal floor of the passageway. But there wasn't the slightest tremor, not the faintest hint of steel wheels travelling over steel rails. *Had the train stopped? If so, why? Had the power failed? Was the train in the depot?*

Be calm, she told herself and took a deep breath. Looking down at where her arms were supposed to be, she saw nothing. Nothing at all. She raised her hand—so close, it touched her nose—and waved it back and forth twice. Not even the slightest hint of movement. She sat very, very still and listened, slowly turning her head one way then the other. Again, nothing—except the thrum of blood pounding in her ears. Her breaths, she realised, were coming in little shallow gasps. *Should she stand up? What if she made a noise? Was it safe to make a noise?*

My mobile! The surge of joy she felt almost made her laugh until she realised she had no idea where her backpack was. Reaching down, she padded around with her fingers and touched something metal: the zip on her bag. Pinching it between her two fingers, she unzipped, cringing at the loud rasping sound it made. Her breathing quickening, she delved, pushing through the mass of tangled clothes. Where was her phone? Panic swept through her. Had it been stolen? Had she dropped it?

Her fingers touched a hard, rounded edge. Pinching its corner, she began easing it out. The worry of dropping it made her tighten her grip. She tapped the screen. Nothing. She tried again. Nothing.

What's the matter with you? she screamed in her head, shaking it, but stopped when the train's neon lights suddenly buzzed, spluttered, and sparked into life, filling the whole of the empty carriage with their dull, eerie light. She was alone.

Dropping the mobile back into her rucksack, she was pushing to her feet when the door at the end of the carriage flew open with a crash that made her jump. She froze. Seconds ticked by. The doorway remained empty. *Could she hear something?* A soft, padding sound, very close: footsteps. And just as she recognised the sound, to her astonishment, a boy, head down, wearing rags and no shoes, stepped into the carriage and the doors slammed closed behind him.

Fighting not to stand and flee, she clenched her fists, staring at the boy who came to a halt fifteen metres away: his thin legs and arms, dark, shaggy hair, bare and cold-looking feet. A sudden realisation hit her: it was the same boy she had seen on the bus; she was sure of it. As though reading her mind, the boy's head jerked up and his black eyes locked on hers. A grin began to spread across his face. As it did so, a tide of dark water—as dark as the boy's eyes—crept up behind him. Momentarily, it swilled around his feet, hissing, covering his toes; carrying on past, it raced towards her.

Scrambling to pull up her knees, she leaned back on the seat, eyes on the water as it silently and rapidly deepened in the passageway, already above the boy's ankles. She looked up and gasped. Somehow, the boy was now standing over her. Raising a hand, he pointed to Salma's legs and all by themselves, they slowly straightened, and her feet, ankles, and calves plunged into the freezing liquid which swallowed them with barely a splash as if the liquid were not water but an oilier, more treacle-like fluid.

Furious, terrified, shivering, Salma stared at her legs, then at the boy. A sound whispered all around her: "Shaaaaaaaaaaan Wuuuuuuuuuu."

"So, you are her," the boy said sneeringly. "Ha!" His face was so close to hers that his exhalation struck her cheek and a smell of... spent matches, rotting seaweed, filled her nostrils. It was a voice she recognized: the same one that had commanded her to get onto the tracks. She tried to speak—tell him that his breath stank, to back off, get lost—but the words stuck in her throat and the boy sniggered.

The numbing dark tide was still rising. Having climbed above her knees, she watched it flow towards her waist, gasping at its icy coldness, struggling in vain to stand.

A hand reached under her chin and yanked her head up. She stared into the boy's eyes: two bottomless pools of hate.

"Very soon, you will be called upon to join them. You do not know who they are or what they will ask of you, but that will change. You are one of three. Thus far, two have been recruited, one a boy, one a girl—both mere children. They know little of the dangers that await them. They did not volunteer to fight, yet their participation was guaranteed the moment they brought a piece of the triskelion out of their adventures and into the world of things— this world. Had they not done so, they would have been free to refuse the Eight's...demands. And did the Eight tell them this? Did they honour them with the right to make a choice about being soldiers in a war?" The boy laughed scornfully.

The liquid, which had submerged her thighs and waist below its flat, unperturbed surface, was half-way up her torso. Shivering uncontrollably, teeth chattering, she fought the thought that it would reach above her head very soon. The boy, also partly submerged along with most of the carriage, gave no sign that this sub-zero, midnight liquid bothered him. On the contrary, he seemed to be at home, enjoying himself as he watched her suffer.

"What do you want?" she shouted.

He flicked a strand of hair away from his face. As his hand moved, Salma caught a glimpse of a tattoo—Chinese characters perhaps. Licking his dry lips, he continued: "So now their fates are yoked to those of the Eight and though the Eight's two soldiers do not know it yet, they will soon be fighting for their lives." The boy paused and drew even closer to Salma. "Let them fight their own battles. You will be spared the pain that will follow their certain defeat. All you have to do is refuse the triskelion." A smile revealed his teeth, though his eyes remained cold. "When the Eight approach you, you must not leave your adventure with the triskelion in your possession. Follow my wishes, and I shall not harm you—or your mother."

Salma grunted in anger, desperately trying to speak. The boy wafted a hand. Suddenly, though her body remained rigidly immobile, her throat loosened: "Who are you? How dare you threaten my mother or me!"

"My name is Shan Wu and—"

"What do you want?" she repeated. The water, lapping at the top of her neck, offered up a smell—something overpoweringly sweet and rotted—which almost made her gag.

"I've already told you: you will not bring back your portion of the triskelion; you will not join with the other Hares; you will not help the Eight!"

Out of sheer frustration, she felt a tear trickle down her cheek: she'd never wanted to land an elbow strike on anyone as much as she wanted to land it on this thing in front of her. But she needed to think strategically. "If…" she said, waiting for the words to catch up with her thoughts, "…if we are such a danger to your plans, why haven't you killed the others? Why haven't you killed me?"

The liquid, daubing at her mouth, reached up and stroked her lips. She pressed them together, hard.

"I was so close with you—such a shame you didn't rescue your sandals…" he hissed.

The boy's face took on the appearance of thoughtful amusement. "I almost destroyed the First Hare on a mountain in Scotland," he said, as though it were a fond memory. "The Second, well, he was trickier—by that time, the Eight knew my plans. But I almost got him, too. The Eight have made sure I am unable to kill any of you directly at present. But—" The boy's chest swelled and his eyes, dark as pits, darkened further "— when I win, I will kill every last one, including you, if you do not do what I ask."

Salma had heard enough. Tilting her head back so that it brought her mouth out of the liquid, she yelled: "Get lost, moron," and closed her mouth again. Hardly clever, but definitely heart-felt. If those were to be her last words, then good!

For a moment, she thought the boy was going to hit her. But he chuckled mirthlessly. "Remember," he said, raising a finger and pointing it in her face, "I'm giving you a choice."

She wanted to laugh in his face, tell him to go jump in front of a bus, but the liquid was past her nose, almost at her eyes. She stretched her neck, and managed one last, desperate breath. Then she was under, head made light by the buoyancy of the liquid, a muffled roar in her ears. She wanted to scream. But instead, she held onto the last, precious lungful: a strange calmness replacing the fear and anger she had been feeling.

She knew she couldn't hold her breath forever: her lungs were already screaming at her, telling her they wanted air. Was there any point in delaying the inevitable? This was her fate. She began saying a prayer. If this was the end, she would go reciting the testimony of faith all Muslims hope to die uttering: *La illaha illallah*…and then she began counting down. Five, four, three, two, one. She was ready. Her last thoughts were of her mother.

CHAPTER 8

—

Salma blinked—and blinked again. Bright neon lights and a melange of faces whizzed past the window. She felt her body lean to the side, succumbing to the force of deceleration. A sign slipped past, too fast to read; then another and another. On the fourth attempt, she caught the name: Holborn station.

Salma surreptitiously felt the legs of her trousers. Bone dry. She gazed at the faces of the other passengers. Not a hint of anything out of the ordinary. The old woman in white next to her was unfolding her arms, preparing to stand up. On the faces of the other passengers, there was boredom, sleepiness, and indifference. A normal, everyday scene.

"What the..." she said, which immediately earned her a side-long glance from the woman. Salma coughed, pretending she hadn't spoken while her mind replayed the waking nightmare she had just been through. She'd gotten into the carriage, sat down, the train had approached the tunnel, she had glanced up...

The answer hit her like Theo's Pyong Sohn Keut Chigi. The advert. It was the advert! She had seen one on the side of the bus—a picture of a man in a white lab coat with the words "Bai Lu" above it—when the boy, Shan Wu, had taken over the old man's body on the top deck of the bus. And she'd seen the same one a moment before Shan Wu had appeared in the carriage. *But...but people didn't get waking nightmares every time they looked at ads! Of course, they didn't! So...what was going on?*

That question dogged her brain as she exited the carriage and the station. Now, as she strode quickly along Southampton Row, the pavement barely able to contain all the people on it, dodging and swerving between its human-shaped projectiles, the same question continued to niggle.

She paused to cross a busy intersection while an endless stream of buses roared past. Her mother had once told her about Leó Szilárd, the Hungarian physicist who was crossing the road on Southampton Row when he realised that splitting the atom was a way to make an atomic bomb. The history of the world had changed that day. Her own life, it seemed to her, had changed pretty dramatically today, too: though exactly how, she wasn't yet sure. Once again, the boy's threat echoed in her head. Was he a jinn, a creature of fire and smoke created after angels but before humans? Salma knew of a hadith that divided jinn into three types: one that flew through the air, one that took the form of snakes and dogs, and one that looked like humans. Had she seen the third kind? The thought made her shiver. Supposing he was a jinn, what should she do? There were some things she could recite to protect her...

She stopped what she had been reciting since the crossing at Southampton Row. Because there, on the right, looking glorious as usual, was the British Museum, a Union Jack snapping back and forth at the top of its pediment. It momentarily lifted her spirits. But as she stared at the sun-brightened building and the fluttering flag, the knot in her stomach, a mix of fear and puzzlement, crept back and tightened. "All you have to do is refuse the triskelion," he had said. *What did he mean? What did any of it—the Three Hares conversation on her computer, the skeleton on the bus, the thing on the Tube—mean?*

As she set off again, she realised she had completely lost her appetite. *No wonder! And was it possible Theo's accidental thump on the head temporarily knocked something loose in her brain?*

It was comforting to imagine it had.

CHAPTER 9

—

Behind the cafe's crescent-moon shaped counter, two assistants were working hard making teas and coffees, bringing plates of sandwiches, and taking orders. In all, there were about twenty tables in the little cafe: some in front of the counter; others scattered around the edge of the room. All of the tables were taken—except one. It was next to a tall doorway that led to another gallery, Room 41.

"Quick! Grab that." Sara said, pointing. Sanjeev was about to scurry over but Sara grabbed his arm. "Wait. What would you like?"

Sanjeev surveyed the vast array of cakes. "What do you suggest?"

"English tea and a scone with cream and jam? It's traditional."

Sanjeev looked at the massive scone Sara was pointing at and grinned. "That sounds great!"

When it was her turn, Sara ordered a tea pot for both of them. She wasn't feeling hungry, so she didn't have a cake—though they did look good.

After paying, Sara brought the tray to the table where Sanjeev was seated, waiting.

Sanjeev's eyes jumped greedily to the scone and the little pots of cream and jam accompanying it. "Didn't you get a cake?" he asked in a tone that suggested Sara must be crazy not to.

Sara shrugged. "Not hungry. Must be the huge breakfast I had this morning."

"It's about 8 am in New Jersey and I am starving!"

Sara poured the tea into both their cups. "You know…I just realised something," she said, picking up a cube of sugar and dropping it into her tea.

Sanjeev added milk to his and stirred. "What's that?"

"How many of those tiny lights are above my head?"

Sanjeev put down his spoon, looked up, and counted. He opened his mouth. But before he could speak, Sara said: "Eight. Right? And there are eight above yours too…"

"The Eight Immortals!" Sanjeev cried.

Sara nodded.

They both looked up at the sparkling, glowing orbs.

Sara sighed. "I want to know why they chose us. Don't you?"

"Yeah, I sure do. I mean, okay, they chose us—for whatever reason—but tell us why!"

He paused, unsure what to do with the scone. Should he dip it in the jam? Break pieces off?

"Slice it through the middle," Sara told him, "then spread the jam and cream."

Sanjeev nodded and Sara continued: "I just wish we could get on with it: whatever it is the Immortals want us to do,"

"I don't think we can do anything until the third hare appears," Sanjeev said, layering cream and strawberry jam onto the scone's surface.

"So where is he or she? There's not been a single word from this person on the Three Hares chat thingy, right?"

"I checked my computer before I left New Jersey, and there was nothing," Sanjeev said and crammed in a huge piece of scone into his mouth.

"So, what's going on? Who is this person? Where is this person?"

Sanjeev shrugged and mumbled something as crumbs from the piece of scone he had stuffed in his mouth tumbled from it. Sara frowned, waiting while Sanjeev chewed. Taking a gulp of tea, he washed down the scone and said: "By the way, did you bring it?"

"Oh yes. You?"

"Sure did. Wanna see it?"

"Go on then."

Glancing nervously about the room, Sanjeev extracted two objects from his pockets and slowly opened his hand, hunched over as he did so, as though he expected someone to snatch them away. And there they were: the silvery piece of the triskelion and the gold key, both of which Sara had seen before, but only as pictures.

"Nice," Sara said, taking the key and examining it close up. The gold monkey's face stared back at her. The expression on the monkey's face looked…mischievous. Handing it back to Sanjeev and reaching under her seat into the satchel she had with her, she pulled out her piece of the triskelion and the silk dagger, which of course, was just a piece of highly decorated silk cloth. Dropping the silk onto Sanjeev's hand, she took her piece of the triskelion and fitted it into the piece that belonged to Sanjeev so that the triskelion was two-thirds complete. "It's beautiful, don't you think?"

Sanjeev nodded. "Yeah…and such an ancient symbol for so many peoples…"

Sara held up her hand.

Sanjeev got the message.

"Are you seeing what I'm seeing?" Sara interrupted.

Puzzled, Sanjeev followed Sara's pointed finger. "Oh!" he said. "Oh, that is awesome!"

Now both of them were looking at the tall girl who was standing next to the counter and peering at the little globes of light above her head, a totally amazed expression on her face.

"Seems like we might be about to get some answers after all." Sara whispered, raising her cup.

"Is it my imagination," Sanjeev asked, the rest of his scone in his hand, "or does she have a black eye?"

"Yeah," Sara said, half-smiling. "What's the story behind *that*?"

"Punch up?" Sanjeev suggested.

Sara smirked. Somehow it seemed the most likely explanation. It was the way the girl carried herself: as though she was arguing with gravity, friction, and anything else she thought was impeding her.

"I think she's not enjoying this much," Sanjeev chuckled as the girl ducked and bobbed only to find the satellites still orbiting as closely as ever.

"We've tried that," Sara said under her breath. "It doesn't work."

"I guess she's seen our satellites," Sanjeev said, placing his half-eaten scone on the dish and slowly getting to his feet.

"I guess she has," replied Sara, pushing her chair back.

The girl with the black eye, yellow hair tie, and ponytail glanced at them and like a switch had been flicked, the scowl disappeared, and her look of astonishment returned.

PART 2

MALDON, ESSEX, UNITED KINGDOM
AUGUST 991 CE

CHAPTER 10

━

Having gone through the double row of columns at the museum's grand entrance, Salma turned left and climbed the South stairs to Level 3 and the cafe outside Room 41. Around her, excited, squealing voices from a group of fifteen or twenty kids all wearing identical yellow hats bounced off the stone steps and high ceilings. They were walking in twos, climbing the stairs as fast as they could in front of her. Amongst the chatter, she heard the words "mummies" and "gladiators" more than once. Obviously, on their way to Level 5. She patiently followed behind, realising suddenly how dry her mouth was. Her favourite cafe in the museum was at the top of the stairs. She would get some water there. It would tide her over until her mother finished work. Though right now, she didn't exactly feel ravenous: far from it, in fact. Still, maybe a cup of tea would do her good.

At the top of the stairs, the cafe outside Room 41 came into view. She joined the short queue, dug in the pocket of her trousers, and pulled out what she found. Her eyes widened. In her hand were two small, silver coins, each raggedly circular with some kind of stamped image on them, too faint to see clearly. She blinked and blinked again. The coins disappeared, and instead, she was gazing at two ordinary pound coins, one heads, the other tails.

She was really starting to wonder if her brain was a bit loose from Theo's strike when her eye was caught by something moving above her. She looked up and instinctively ducked.

Just centimetres from the top of her head, like a crown of bright jewels, a dozen sparkling, spinning, ball-shaped things bobbed silently in the air.

"Oh!" she yelped, shoulders hunched, and bending her knees, she crouched down. As though they were attached to her by unseen strings or powered by invisible motors, the sparkly things dived down so that a millisecond later, they once again crowned her.

Rising slowly, ignoring the puzzled looks of the woman behind her in the queue, she leaned to one side, then the other. Whichever way she moved, the things instantly adjusted, keeping a constant distance. Hesitantly, she reached up. She felt nothing as her hand passed straight through several of them. She took a huge step to the right; the things went with her. She leapt back; the things instantly did the same. She stared at the woman behind her who was watching Salman's antics with increasing alarm on her face. But the woman's eyes were on *her*, not the globes. *What was going on? Didn't she see them? How could she miss them?*

A creeping sensation, the feeling that she was being watched, made Salma freeze. She turned. Like an arrow, her gaze went straight across the room to the two sets of eyes that were locked on her. Her chin hit the floor. A boy and a girl, both about her age, were seated to the right of the door that led to Room 41. The boy's dark brown eyes peered at her through black-framed glasses. The girl, whose long black hair was thick and shiny, had eyes that were even darker than the boy's. They were both watching her with unblinking intensity: the boy with his mouth open, crumbs dotted on either side of his lips, the girl with a cup in her hand as if frozen enroute to her mouth. They both had the same shiny things circling their heads.

"Now what...?" she whispered, gaping at the boy and girl as they gaped back at her. The strangest feeling that she had seen them before flickered but died. No names came to mind; no recollection of who they were or where she could have possibly met them...

"Next, please," the woman behind the counter said and served the person in front of Salma.

Reaching over and picking up a small bottle of water, Salma placed it against her forehead, pressing its cold glass against the side of her eye. To the right, she could see the boy and girl were getting slowly to their feet. *Could they see the things above her head?* She stepped forward in the queue and staggered a little. Suddenly, she was feeling really warm. She wiped a hand across her head. She was sweating. Had Lee Arnott been right to fuss about the smack on the face she got from Theo? Were the things above her head…a symptom of concussion? She'd never heard of such a thing, and she'd never suffered anything like it despite being hit and punched many times.

She swallowed, realising the cakes, sandwiches, and tables were beginning to blur at the edges, softening their lines and spreading themselves as though they were melting. Panicking a little, she took a deep breath. *Should she tell someone? Get medical help? Or was she just dehydrated? Was her blood sugar low?* The ceiling was probably 6 metres high, but Salma felt it was rising and falling, and the whole building was breathing.

As she sucked in air and emptied her lungs, the room seemed to darken and then lighten again, over and over and over. *What was going on?*

"Can I help you?"

Just the cashier. Salma showed her the bottle, deciding she wanted water and not tea.

"One eighty-nine," the woman said.

Darkening, lightening, darkening, lightening.

Salma gave her the coins. Without waiting for change, she opened the bottle and took a sip of water and felt better. But only for a moment. She glanced at the pair who were gazing silently at her. She wasn't sure what to do. It seemed too strange to just walk up to them and start talking about how they seemed to be the only people who had little globes circling their heads…She hesitated. The other two watched. She went past, eyes fixed on them, and entered Room 41.

Darkening, lightening, darkening, lightening.

She didn't need to look around to know the boy and girl were following her. A few metres more and she took another sip of water. She felt as light as a mote of dust. Around her, visitors wandered quietly, mulling the exhibitions. No one was paying the slightest attention to her.

Darkening, lightening, darkening, lightening.

She looked up. In the ceiling, sunlight flooded through the skylights in one blink of the eye; the next, there was darkness, over and over again. She took another sip. The cold liquid tumbled down her throat. In front of her, in a tall, rectangular glass case, the Sutton Hoo burial mask's empty eyes glared at her.

Darkening, lightening, darkening, lightening.

Swerving past the mask, she entered another room: the Viking collection. She staggered over to a large display in which a hoard—coins, ingots, brooches, rings—was laid out.

Darkening, lightening, darkening, lightening.

Leaning against the display, she searched for and quickly found the boy and girl. They were walking straight towards her, looking determined, ignoring everyone and everything else. With a huge effort—because it felt like every muscle in her body had been drained of strength—she lurched towards a different display case. She had just time to see the object in it: a small, silver-coloured hare. Her eyes glued themselves to the information tag next to it:

Hare-shaped fitting
Finnish/Baltic region
ADs 900s-1100s
This exquisite silver belt buckle is shaped like a hare.
No other object exactly like it is known to exist.

She heard herself repeat the words "no other" over and over, until they lost all sense of meaning. The light in the room disappeared one last time.

CHAPTER 11

—

The heavy scent of damp soil and…sap? pine? filled Salma's head. Slowly, her mind reached out and found her arms, legs, head, torso, and she realised she was lying on her back, head to the side. Her cheek rested on something cold. Below her, the ground was lumpy but yielding. She groaned. Above that sound, there was another, rising in intensity, becoming a gentle, pleasant roar. "Leaves," her mind told her. "The wind blowing through leaves."

A moment later, her eyes flickered open. She took a deep breath and, raising a hand, rubbed her face. More noise: this time, distant, running water. A river. Not close, but not far away either. But where exactly, she had no idea: darkness surrounded her. Blinking, she stared into it. Inky, gloomy shapes lurked. *Where was she? What had happened?* She was thinking of standing when she froze.

Voices, murmuring voices, were coming from somewhere in front of her, the words strange at first. She strained her ears. Slowly, the sounds began to make more and more sense. Two men were speaking. One, his voice softer, was telling the other of the dangers he had faced in coming to the meeting. The other voice was rough, contemptuous. It replied that they understood each other well and that money was their only god and reward. They continued to talk, but the wind rose and swishing leaves washed away the words.

She felt a sudden itch all over her body. She ran her hands over her arms and legs, rough material—cotton? hemp? She scratched and shivered. One minute she was in the British Museum; the next minute, she was here: wherever "here" was. The faces of the boy and girl who had followed her into Room 41 floated into her mind. And the shiny things that had bobbed about above all their heads, but no one else's? *What was that all about?* She looked up. Nothing there now; no sign of the little orbs, just the night sky and thousands of tiny sparkling pins of light. Hyperventilating, she struggled to push the rising panic down.

"Focus," she told herself. *Focus, breathe deeply and slowly.* First, how did she get here? No. Wait. That wasn't what she needed to think about. She had to deal with what was in front of her. Right here, right now. She started again. First, she couldn't stay where she was, in the middle of a forest, in the dead of night. But she couldn't just walk up to complete strangers and ask for their help either. That would be mad. She needed to get closer to whoever was speaking. That way, she had a chance to find out who they were, where she was, and what was going on. Not much of a plan, but it was the best she could do.

Waiting until the breeze was once more rustling the trees, she slowly got onto her hands and knees. She could see more now: tree trunks, leaves, fallen branches. She was in a hollow in a forest, the ground rising up all around her. On all fours, she crept forward, moving upwards, her hands landing on leaves which were cold and damp and made little noise. *Is it autumn here?* As she reached the lip of the hollow, the wind died. Flattening her body, she held her breath, raised her head, and peeked over.

Next to a crooked, ancient-looking tree whose thick limbs touched the ground, two men stood, darkly silhouetted against the starry night whose moon shone on the sea behind them. Although the moon was bright, she could not see either of their faces. As she watched, their words floated to her once again.

"...is agreed. A share for your...services," the harsher voice said. His dark form was larger than the other man's. A deep laugh sounded. "So, by God's power, we shall win. Eh?" he roared. "Eh?"

"Very funny," the other said. "One more thing."

"What's that?"

"How will your men recognise me? After all, I don't want to be the victim of one of your sea wolves, do I?"

"Very true. What do you suggest?"

As Salma listened, the wind rose again and all she could catch was a fragment of what the man said: "Byrhtnoth…Northey Island…red cap…"

Salma frowned. Byrhtnoth…The name echoed in her head. *Byrhtnoth*…It sounded familiar. She tried searching her brain, but its meaning stayed just out of reach, lost in a tangle of hazy thoughts. Well, no great surprise that the battery in her brain wasn't at full power! All of this was a dream. Had to be! She was dreaming. Her brain was busy recharging! That's why she couldn't remember.

And yet…she couldn't deny what her senses were telling her. Everything was so *real*: the scratchiness of her rough woollen clothes against her skin, the wind rippling through the trees and her hair, the cold ground beneath her body…If it was a dream, it was the most realistic one she'd ever had. *And if it wasn't? Had she time-travelled? Tumbled through a wormhole?* The wind brought back the men's words, interrupting her thoughts.

"You need have no worries," the one with the harsher voice was saying. "I'll be sure to let all my men know."

"I'm glad to hear it. Now—"

But Salma never did find out what he was about to say. Hearing something move next to her, she turned, saw a pair of eyes staring at her, and yelped—the sound escaping her lips before she could clamp a hand over her mouth.

Two things immediately happened. First, the fox, which had been minding its own business while she crept about her territory, bolted, terrified by the yelp Salma had given. Second, the smaller of the two men drew his sword and began charging towards her.

Salma jumped to her feet and faced the top of the opposite side of the hollow, where she paused a second, peering into the deep darkness that lay in front of her.

"Come here!" the voice behind yelled.

Hands outstretched, blind, she plunged forward. She'd barely gone ten paces when her shoulder struck a tree trunk, and she crashed to the ground. Picking herself up, ignoring the pain, she ran on but almost immediately tripped over hidden roots and hit the ground again.

"Hey!" the man cried; his voice closer. "Stop, I tell you."

She struggled to her feet. She had to get away. But the forest was merciless. Its branches tugged and tore, its roots tripped and snagged. Her shoulder was aching. She had no idea where she was going. She dared not look back. But the noise of him crashing through the undergrowth behind her was so loud, so close. *Should she stop? Should she turn and fight? Did she have a choice? She had to. She had to—*

Suddenly, the forest released her. The ground had opened and she'd stepped off the edge of the Earth, The surprise caught her scream, held it in her throat, and immobilised her arms and legs as she tumbled through the emptiness. *Splash!* She hit freezing cold water and sank in a frenzy of noise and confusion. Down she went, down and down. Would it ever stop? The pressure of its deepness squeezed her head, her eyes, her ears. She felt her descent slow. As hard as she could, trusting her sense of where the night sky might be, she kicked with all her might. The weight of the water was enormous. It wanted her. It pressed and it pushed and refused to give her up. But she fought for the surface until suddenly, unexpectedly, her head was free and she was taking gasping, grateful breaths.

Boom! Her shoulder, then her head, struck the boulder. Water surged around her, roaring, slapping, thrashing. Recovering just in time, she threw her hands onto the rough stone, dug in her nails, and desperately tried to hold on. Her fingernails scratched along it and slid off. Water swamped her. She threw her hands above her head, broke the surface, and took another gasping breath. Somewhere below her, an object struck her legs as twigs scratched her face. A heavy branch, she realised, just in time to grasp it, wrap her arms around it, meld with it as the river twisted, churned, and swept along…

CHAPTER 12

—

Memories washed over her. In one, her father was still alive: talking about the port of Tartus, a place he used to go as a boy. She was sitting next to him, listening as he talked about the yellow rocks that formed Tartus's harbour, its restaurants, its glistening blue water and soft, lapping waves. She could almost smell the sea…

"Tartus," she whispered and opened her eyes. She was expecting to see her father. Instead, what she saw was…strong sunlight and… pointy ankle boots? She blinked. Her head was aching and sand clung to her face. Eyes crusted; she looked up. There, in dazzling brightness, a boy—tall, fair-haired, puzzled-looking—was standing above her, staring down. She let out a sigh of relief. She had fallen into a river; floated away on a branch; escaped the man who was chasing her. She was safe.

"Get up!" the boy said, and before Salma could move, he kicked her, the blow thumping into her side and knocking the breath from her lungs.

"Get up!" the boy cried again, swinging back his foot and preparing to deliver a second kick.

Salma sucked in air and raised a hand, "Wait! Just wait!" she cried.

The boy lowered his foot.

In her head, she made the words: "I'm Salma. Who are you and why are you kicking me?" But when she opened her mouth and spoke, something very different came out: "I'm Embla. Who are you?" Salma gasped. She tried to say her name again. "I'm Embla. I'm…Embla. I'm…Embla. I'm—"

"I'll tell you who you are," the boy replied fiercely, "you're a Viking. And around here, we hate Vikings."

Sitting on damp, grey sand and clutching her side where the kick had landed, Salma straightened up. She felt her head. A huge bump had risen above her left ear and her eye hurt thanks to Theo. She brushed away some grains of sand that had stuck to her temple and shifted uncomfortably in her damp clothes.

Groggy, aching, she shielded her eyes and looked up at the long, blonde, scraggly hair falling into the narrowed, suspecting eyes watching her, the sharpened-metal point of a spear levelled at her, the small, rounded shield poised in the boy's other hand, ready to fend off an attack.

"Where am I?" she croaked.

The boy jabbed the spear's gleaming tip at her. "I won't tell you again. Get up."

"Okay, okay!" she replied irritably and gathering her knees, her shoulders in pain, she pushed herself to a standing position. "Now what?"

"Now I take you as my prisoner."

She stared at him. He was wearing a brown tunic with a rough hole cut in the fabric for his head to go through. The tunic was long, almost to his knees, and was tied around his waist with a leather belt. Over his shoulder, there was a square-cut cloak, held in place with a circular brooch.

"What are you looking at?" he asked angrily. "You act as though you've never seen an East Saxon before!"

"Well, I...I don't exactly see one every day of the week," she spluttered

The boy pointed to her waist. "Give them to me."

Salma looked down. She was wearing a long sort of pinafore made of wool on top of another dress made of softer fabric, both soggy and damp. Her eyes widened. She was wearing a belt made of red and white strands of fabric woven into a kind of rope and on the belt was…a small, silver hare, identical to the one she had seen in the British Museum.

"Hurry up!"

Her eyes moved from the silver coloured hare to a broad leather pouch that was tucked into the belt—and a knife. Slowly, because the boy was crouched and looked ready to stab her any second, she pulled out the knife and handed it to him, hilt first. The boy darted forward and snatched it away.

"Open the pouch," he said.

The belt was threaded through a loop on the pouch. Holding the pouch in one hand, she unpicked the knot and reaching inside, grasped what looked like a piece of folded paper. But when she touched its soft, waxy surface, she realised it wasn't paper; it was some kind of animal skin. "Ewww," she cried and with the tips of her fingers holding it by the edges, she pulled it free.

As soon as she did so, the thing doubled and then quadrupled its size, stretching Salma's arms as she struggled to keep hold of it.

"What…what kind of trickery is this?" the boy cried, jumping backwards and pointing his spear at her.

Salma, eyes on what was before her, shook her head in amazement. "I've no idea," she half-whispered.

At the very centre of the broad rectangular object she was holding, an impressive swirl of lines congregated in an elongated vertical shape. It took her a second to realise it was a drawing of a tree. She leaned in and read the name written next to it. "Yggdrasil." More shapes began to make sense. She realised that the lines extending to the top map were not just random squiggles but Yggdrasil's branches and the lines running to the bottom corners were, she saw now, Yggdrasil's roots.

But it was what she saw around Yggdrasil that really astounded her. Rings, like the rings of Saturn, circled the great tree, each tilting back and forth as the map gently swayed in her hands! And the rings weren't the only things moving. Other stuff was, too. There, next to Yggdrasil, water was actually falling in a waterfall; over there, a dragon—a tiny dragon! —was prowling around breathing fire. Not only that, above Yggdrasil, an eagle was circling, and near a rainbow bridge, stags were bounding and a snake was slithering.

"What strangeness is this…?" the boy whispered, having edged close enough to see what Salma was seeing.

What she was looking at, she knew, was a map of the Viking cosmos, its nine worlds on each of its rings, the sacred tree, Yggdrasil, at its centre. "I think it's a map," she said flatly, not wanting to elaborate or mention the word "Viking" again.

"Put it away!" the boy cried.

"But—"

"Away! Away!" he repeated.

Reluctantly, she folded the map towards its centre, and as she did so, it shrank in size so that it became no bigger than a phone.

A mobile phone! What she would give to have one of those right now!

She slipped it back into the pouch and tied it. "Happy now?" she asked.

In reply, he jabbed the spear towards the woods. "Go!" he commanded.

She raised her hands. "I'm not going to do you any harm, OK? Just take it easy." The boy stood at least three metres away, his stance firm, his spear ready.

The boy's face twisted, and he gave a bitter laugh. "Do no harm? Like you did no harm to the folk of Ipswich? Move. And don't talk!"

Reluctantly, she dropped her hands and turned to face the wood as he scuttled around and stood behind her. The point of the spear prodded her lower back.

"Move," he commanded.

"Keep your hair on," she snapped. She was angry about being his prisoner, but at the same time, she knew that now wasn't the time to start anything. Instead, she needed to wait for a better opportunity. And when it arose, when he was least expecting it, she'd pounce.

She'd take that spear off him and break it over his stupid head!

Chapter 13

—

Speckled sunlight fell through the branches and leaves, spotlighting pinecones, ramsons, and honeybees dipping and rising in clumps of clover at her feet. The path she and the boy were on was well-trodden. *If only I'd been able to find it last night!* She glanced up. Beyond the green canopy, the sky was a cloudless blue. *What a lovely stroll this would be—if she were in Bloomsbury walking towards her favourite cafe with her mother next to her.*

"Where are we going?" she asked, directing the question over her shoulder.

"You'll see soon enough. Stop talking."

They walked on in silence for perhaps ten or fifteen minutes, during which time she wondered about the other two who had been in the British Museum and had followed her into Room 41. Those weird satellite things had been floating around their heads as well. *Were they in this dream, or whatever it was, too? And what about the freaky map in the pouch she was carrying? What was all that about? But the biggest question was: why was she here?* Replaying what the boy had said in her head, it seemed that the Vikings had—in this world at least—recently attacked Ipswich. If that was true, no wonder the boy wanted to take her prisoner: after all, she looked like a Viking; she talked like a Viking; she was even carrying a Viking map. *But why was she here? That was the question. What was the meaning of all this?*

After they had been walking for another five or ten minutes, Salma sniffed and sniffed again. *Woodsmoke?* Yes. Definitely. Meaning the place the boy was taking her had to be nearby.

She gazed at the path in front of her. Up ahead, it turned to the right, swinging behind a huge oak and disappearing. Suddenly she realised this was the chance she had been waiting for. The tree would hide her for a second as she turned the corner. If she was going to escape, this might be the only chance she would get. Heart pumping, she walked the last few steps leading to the oak. Get ready! She inhaled; exhaled; tensed her arms and her legs.

The tip of the spear jabbed her lower back. "Don't even think about it. I've taken prisoners before. I know what I'm doing."

Salma wanted to kick herself: her body language must have alerted him. *Grrr!* She followed the path as it led around the gnarly old oak and through bushes higher than their heads. "Where are you taking me?" she asked, still annoyed by her own stupidity.

"You'll find out when you get there."

"What's your name?" she asked, suddenly aware that she had no idea who had captured her.

"None of your business."

"That's a funny name," she muttered.

"What?"

She turned but continued to walk. "I said: it's a funny name. I asked you what your name was, and you said, 'none of your business,' so, your name is 'None of your business.'"

"Are you trying to be funny?"

"Are Vikings allowed to be funny?"

Another prod in the back.

"Hey! Take it easy. I'm walking, aren't I?"

The boy gave her a funny look—not apologetic, but not quite as angry as it had been.

As they walked, they continued in silence, the path growing broader and more distinct. Clearly more feet had trodden it. A small hillock rose in front of them, and the path, she saw, traced a meandering route up its flank. With the boy four or five metres behind her, Salma climbed. As she climbed, she noticed that smoke from unseen cooking fires had greyed the air on the other side of the hill. The settlement was very close. She had lost her chance.

When she finally reached the top, she paused, drawing breath and taking in the view spread out below her. Surrounded by open fields whose wheat rippled like a golden sea, the settlement consisted of a hundred or so wooden huts, each topped with a roughly thatched roof and a curl of smoke. The wooden huts appeared identical. But on the edges of the burgh, several larger buildings rose, two or three times the size of the others. A moat circled the biggest of these, around which sharpened tree trunks, sunk into the ground, pointed like timber rockets at the sky.

"Why did you come here?" the boy suddenly asked.

Salma spread her hands. "Your guess is as good as mine." The frown on his face told her he was definitely *not* happy with that answer, but what else could she say?

"Look," Salma said, "I'm not a hundred per cent sure." She pointed to her swollen eye. "Maybe this knock on my head has scrambled my brains a bit. All I remember is I was in the woods and heard two people talking. It sounded like they were up to no good. But I didn't hear much because I made a noise and one of them chased me. I fell into a river. And the next thing I know, you're kicking me. That's it. That's all I have."

Deep in thought, the boy gazed at her for several more moments. He brushed a strand of his fair hair from his eyes and nodded slowly.

"Who were they?"

"The men who were speaking? I don't know."

"What did they say?"

"It didn't make much sense."

"Tell me."

Salma puffed out her cheeks. "OK, well, there was something about somebody getting a share of something. And…er…sea wolves and Byrhtnoth—"

"Byrhtnoth!" the boy cried.

Suddenly the fog in Salma's brain cleared. Now she knew where she had heard the name before. *Duh!* It had been in Mrs Greene's class: Byrhtnoth was the leader of the East Saxons who fought the Vikings in the Battle of Maldon near Northey Island. The Battle of Maldon near Northey Island in…in 991 CE! She was in the year 991 CE! *The year 991 CE!* She closed her mouth, which she realised had fallen open and saw that the boy was waiting for an answer to a question she hadn't heard. "Sorry, what?"

"I said, did you see who was talking?"

Salma shook her head. "Only that one of them was a big guy and the other was smaller." She shrugged. "I was trying to stay out of sight."

She gazed down on the settlement. "It's Maldon, isn't it?" she drew her nails through her hair trying to loosen a leaf that had been caught there.

The boy nodded curtly.

For what seemed like minutes, the boy, his brows furrowed, said nothing. He was staring at her, but it was clear his mind was somewhere else.

"We should go, speak to Byrhtnoth, tell him what happened," he finally said. "It could be important."

Did she have any option not to go with him? She doubted it.

"So, do you believe me?"

"Do I have any reason not to?"

"No."

The boy nodded. Slowly, he changed his stance, raising the spear's tip until the shaft was vertical and the spearhead was pointed at the sky.

"Nice to know you don't plan to stab me," she said. "By the way, you still haven't told me your name."

In a softer voice than the one he had been using until now, he said: "I'm Wistan."

"OK. Good," she said.

"Good?"

"I like to know whose prisoner I am."

Wistan opened his mouth to say something, but just then, her stomach gave a loud growl.

"You are hungry?" he asked.

Salma hadn't been thinking about food at all. But now, suddenly, it seemed like she would faint if she didn't have something to eat. Wistan stopped walking and Salma did the same. Her stomach thundered again. Reaching into the pouch he carried tucked into his belt, he handed her something. Salma examined it. It was a piece of bread. So, okay, it didn't look very fresh and it didn't feel very fresh. But she was starving. While Wistan watched, she devoured all of it.

"Thanks," she said when she had finished.

Wistan nodded.

"I suppose we should continue?" she asked.

Wistan nodded. A strange look had formed on his face—as though he had done something clever.

She shrugged. Whatever this was all about—crazy dream, time-travel, alternate universe—at least her stomach didn't feel quite so empty.

CHAPTER 14

The first person to see them enter Maldon was a boy aged about eight or nine with thick, dark hair and a filthy face. Standing outside a hut with a bowl in his hands and chewing what to Salma looked like thick porridge, the kid stared at her through huge, surprised eyes. Did I just turn into a unicorn? Salma wondered, smiling to herself…until the boy dropped the bowl, picked up a clod of earth, and heaved it as hard as he could in her direction.

"Hey!" both she and Wistan cried as it sailed narrowly past Salma's ear.

The boy took no notice. "Viking! Viking! Viking!" he screamed over and over, running beside them and pointing at Salma.

It didn't take long before others—men, women, and children— came running, gathering around Salma, and jostling to get a better look. Some were just curious, but one or two groped at Salma, and Wistan, better dressed and stronger-looking than many of them, had to warn them to stay back.

"Where are we going?" Salma asked, shoving away a face that got too close for her liking.

Wistan pointed to the biggest building. "Over there."

They strode on, the crowd thickening around them. As Salma and Wistan crossed the muddy ground, the faces in the crowd began to change; curiosity gave way to anger. People leaned in, and some shouted in her face. The noise rose—boos and hisses and vicious words. Blows landed on Salma, hitting her arms and her back. She struck back. Wistan turned and began throwing punches too, telling people to get away, but there were too many people, too much anger.

A pair of strong hands grabbed her by the throat. Salma smashed her fist into the man's face. Another tried to grab her hair. Wistan brought the shaft of his spear crashing down on the man's head. But others took their place, screaming and jostling to get at her so that it felt like a sea of hatred surrounded her. More blows landed heavy kicks and punches. She had to stay on her feet. If she fell now, she knew she would never be able to get up again. But she was fighting with quicksand: the more she struggled, the worse it became. Her knees started to buckle. She was on the verge of collapsing when:

"BE STILL I COMMAND!"

Like the flick of a switch, silence fell, and everyone stood still except Salma. Arms still protecting her head, crouched on one knee, she opened her eyes. On a platform above the stockade's moat and sharpened logs, a tall, broad, and white-haired man with a thick white beard, dressed in dark colours—was standing, legs apart, arms in the air, gazing down at them. "Now," continued the man in his deep, calm voice, "what is going on?"

It was Wistan who spoke first. "I have captured a Viking. She was on the shore of the River Blackwater when I found her."

The man's snowy eyebrows rose. "A Viking you say? Very well, bring her to me."

Wistan stood and the crowd around them stepped back, making a corridor. He motioned for Salma to come past him. As Salma did so, she whispered: "Who's he?" and Wistan, whispering too, replied: "He is Ealdorman Byrhtnoth."

With Wistan behind her, Salma walked between the line of people. On either side, faces—old, young, scared, angry—stared. When she met their eyes, some looked hurriedly away; others held her gaze. All were silent.

A few moments later, the gate of the stockade swung open and Ealdorman Byrhtnoth appeared, arms folded across his broad chest. Three other men were standing behind him watching as Salma and Wistan entered. All three of the men behind Byrhtnoth wore similar clothes—heavy, black tunics, black trousers, and deep brown cloaks, and all were white-haired except one whose dark, greasy-looking hair clung to his skull. As Salma watched, Byrhtnoth reached up and fitted a red cap on his head. A red cap! Salma suddenly remembered what she had heard last night. She had to tell Wistan!

Byrhtnoth's cry echoed around the stockade "A Viking! You have done well, Wistan," and reaching forward, he clapped a hand on Wistan's shoulder. "Tell me," he said, eyeing Salma head-to-toe, "what should we do with her?"

Wistan, adjusting his feet, a determined look in his eye, said loudly and clearly: "We should treat her as our guest."

"Should we now? And why is that?" Byrhtnoth asked sternly.

Wistan glanced at Salma and back at Byrhtnoth. "Because I fed her."

"You fed her? You fed the enemy?"

Wistan nodded. "So now she is our guest."

Silence. The four men stared at Wistan. It was the custom and they all knew it.

Suddenly there was a roar of laughter, from Byrhtnoth and the other two standing nearest him. "Wurstan, one day your son will make a great ealdorman," Byrhtnoth cried. "Is that not so, Dunnere?"

Dunnere, the third man nodded. "Indeed," he said. He looked at the fourth man, who made no comment and whose expression was not just unsmiling but positively hostile. Godric, looking pencil-thin compared to Dunnere, shrugged his boney shoulders and gave Salma a look that would have curdled cream.

Obviously not a fan, thought Salma. She gave him a fake smile and wondered briefly how he got the scar that ran the length of his cheek.

Wurstan, shorter than Byrhtnoth but just as broad and white-haired, had clapped a meaty hand on Wistan's shoulder and looked into his son's eyes. "He will make a great ealdorman…but only if I don't murder him first!"

It brought more gales of laughter from Byrhtnoth and Dunnere and nothing from the scar-faced man.

"Come," Byrhtnoth said to the other men when he had stopped chuckling. "Let's go inside and talk more."

Wurstan, Dunnere, and Byrhtnoth turned towards a large, open door. "Come Godric," Byrhtnoth said over his shoulder.

Salma's eyes stayed on Godric, who had not moved. His gaze met hers. Suddenly, his face gave several violent twitches, and to Salma's horror, the bones began to realign themselves, the skin tightened and slackened, the irises switched colour, the mouth broadened, and the hair lightened. And Lee Arnott's features surfaced out of the twisting, morphing flesh! Salma let out a stifled gasp. The next second, in a blink of an eye and a shake of the head, Lee's features disappeared completely, and in their place, the dark, moody face of the gaunt, skeleton-thin Godric returned. His eyes drilled into her. Godric's scar twitched, his mouth twisted, and his eyes drilled even deeper into hers.

"What are you looking at?" he asked sourly.

Wistan, she noticed, was waving, trying to get her attention and gesturing for her to follow him. She nodded and as she strode past Godric, a hand reached out, grabbed her wrist, and pulled her close.

"Watch yourself," Godric snarled, his stinking breath almost making her gag.

"You grab me like that again, and you'll be watching my fist smash your face," she fired back. Having snatched her arm away, she proceeded to catch up with Wistan who had already turned his back on them, meaning he had missed the confrontation. As she closed the distance between herself and Wistan, she tried to imagine what he would have done if he had seen the clash. Somehow, she felt sure Wistan would be on her side, not Godric's. The thought made her smile.

Nevertheless, as she continued to walk away from Godric, her smile faded. Questions were piling up, one on top of the other.

Why was Godric being so nasty? Why had he turned into Lee Arnott? Why was she a Viking? Who was Embla? What was it she had heard last night? Who were the men who had been talking? What was the importance of the map she had found in her pouch? And of course, most important question of all: what was she supposed to do next?

CHAPTER 15

—

Salma stepped into the room and blinked as her eyes struggled to adapt to the semi-darkness and stinging wood smoke. In front of her, two long tables and a short one formed a U-shape around which maybe a hundred people could sit. She guessed this was where they celebrated and ate their feasts. She glanced up. High above, heavy ceiling timbers spanned the room's wooden interior, making a roof whose shape reminded her of a ship's hull turned upside down. She returned her eyes to the three ealdermen who were making their way to the top table. Although sunlight streamed through several small windows on one wall, the room was too large to be well-lit, and gloom reigned behind the top table.

Grunting, Byrhtnoth and the two other older men sat down on heavy wooden chairs, Byrhtnoth in the middle, Wurstan and Dunnere on either side of him. To their left, on a stone hearth, some logs smouldered, the blue-grey smoke filling the room making everything hazy. Godric slithered next to the hearth and continued eyeing her with daggers. *What exactly was his problem?*

"So," said Byrhtnoth, leaning his elbows on the table in front of him, "you are a Viking—a sea wolf—yet you have come to Maldon. Why is that?"

Salma glanced at Wistan who was standing directly behind Byrhtnoth. He nodded as if to say: just tell them what you told me. She took a deep breath. "OK, well, the thing is, I have no idea."

Byrhtnoth frowned. "No idea?"

She shook her head. "I was somewhere else. And…er, I hit my head. Next thing, I was in the forest, and I heard some people talking. They heard me and started to chase—"

"Why did they chase you?"

"I guess they didn't want me to hear what they were saying."

"And what were they saying?"

"Something about—" From the corner of her eye, she saw Godric take a step forward. She glanced at his face and tensed. There was only one way to describe the expression he wore: murderous. Suddenly, everything made sense. It was him! It was Godric she had heard last night. That was why he seemed to hate her. She turned back to look at Wistan, who was gazing expectantly at her, as were Byrhtnoth, Dunnere, and Wurstan.

"Well?" Byrhtnoth said. "What did you hear?"

And yet…was she absolutely sure it was Godric? She hesitated, remembering what Lee Arnott had said. She had been too confident, and it had cost her the belt she had coveted. What if her over confidence leads her to accuse people wrongly? Was Godric turning into Lee a sign?

Just then, out of the darkness behind the top table, a skinny, dark-haired boy appeared carrying a huge silver platter. The boy excused himself, apologising in a grovelling manner for disturbing his "mighty lords and masters", and Salma, eyes on the boy's face, had the feeling that he and Godric might be relatives. Something about the long, pointed chin and the length of his nose made her feel sure they were.

"Ah, Alwin!" Byrhtnoth cried, "some morsels at last."

Salma scoffed silently. Morsels? Alwin was carrying what looked like half a roasted cow. It smelled delicious, she had to admit, but she doubted it was halal.

The boy, his grin revealing twisted teeth, came further forward and set the platter down in front of Byrhtnoth.

"Thank you, Alwin," Byrhtnoth said, his eyes locked on the food.

"Welcome, my lord," Alwin replied and raising his head, looked Salma in the eye.

Salma gasped and shook her head, not willing to believe what her eyes were telling her. It was happening again! Alwin's mouth was stretching. His teeth were straightening and whitening. His face was swelling; his chin was shrinking, and his eyes were losing their nervousness. And there he was! Lee Arnott! Staring straight at her with a stern look on his face.

"What," Salma hissed as she backed away, "is going on?" But no sooner had the words left her lips than the features on Alwin's face shimmered like a mirage in the desert and Alwin, the mini-me of Godwin, was back in the room, wiping his greasy fingers on his tunic and grinning his twisted-tooth smile.

Was she going completely nuts?

"Food," Byrhtnoth said. "That's what's going on. What else?"

"Er, right," Salma replied.

"So, you were about to tell us what you heard."

"What I heard," Salma said slowly. "Right. Yes. Uh-huh."

"And?" Byrhtnoth said.

Again, Salma saw the dojang, the look of disappointment on Lee Arnott's face when she had failed her test when according to him, she had been too confident.

"I'm-I'm…not sure," she stuttered.

Byrhtnoth frowned. "You're not sure?" he asked, irritation rising in his voice.

"I…No, I'm not sure," she stuttered again. Because the fact was, she wasn't 100% sure that she had seen or heard Godric last night. It *could* have been him. But it could also have been someone else.

Byrhtnoth tore off a piece of meat and bit into it. "Nothing?" he cried angrily as Dunnere and Wurstan helped themselves to fatty chunks of beef and Alwin disappeared into the darkness from which he had come.

"Nothing," Salma replied, careful to avoid Wistan's gaze.

"Huh!" Byrhtnoth snorted. "Huh!" he said again, holding Salma's gaze.

From the corner of her eye, she saw Godric retaking his place closer to the fire.

"Very well," Byrhtnoth said, clearly not convinced. "And what name shall we call you?"

At least I can answer that. "My name's..." But suddenly, Salma had the same horrible feeling as before: that her mouth and lips were not hers. "My name's...my name is...Embla." She held up a finger. "Gimme a second." She cleared her throat. "My name is ... Embla!" *Argh!*

"What?" she said, aware that everyone was staring at her like she had gone mad.

Byrhtnoth, who like the rest had stopped chewing, was gawping at her. "Your name...is Embla?"

Salma shrugged. "Seems like it, yeah."

Byrhtnoth swallowed. "And...are you Olaf Tryggvason's *daughter*?" he asked, sounding incredulous.

Who is Olaf Tryggvason when he is at home? She gazed back at the ealdormen. The way they were behaving, this seemed like a *very* important question. She hesitated. If she said yes? What would happen then? The East Saxons and the Vikings weren't exactly best friends. But what if this Olaf was important? Wouldn't that be a good thing if she were supposed to be his daughter? Head bowed, she fiddled with the pouch that contained the map. No, she decided. Best to tell the truth. And if they didn't like it? Tough! Raising her head, she pointed to her eye. "Maybe the blow has muddled my brain. The fact is, I honestly don't know. But what I *do* know is—"

"Perhaps she *is* Olaf Tryggvason's daughter; perhaps she is her father's messenger come to negotiate with us," Dunnere said.

"Or perhaps she is a nobody," Wurstan muttered. "A lunatic who will say anything if she thinks there's a reward to be had."

As if imitating one another, the three men regarded her, mediative looks on their faces as they stroked their beards.

"Is your father nearby?" Dunnere finally asked.

If that was supposed to be a trick question, thought Salma, *it wasn't a very good one.*

"I already told you: I don't know if he is my father or not."

Byrhtnoth's face clouded. The men put their heads together and began conferring in whispers, glancing now and again at Salma. She looked at Wistan, who was making a What-on-Earth-are-you-up-to? face.

Byrhtnoth, straightening in his chair, cleared his throat. "You are our prisoner."

"What? Hold on! I was your guest a minute ago!"

"Your father and his sea wolves threaten many communities. We are lucky—we have the men to fight him—"

"Whoa! Who says I'm Olaf Tryggvason's daughter?"

"You might be!" Wurstan cried triumphantly as if it were a clinching argument.

"I might be, and I might not be!" Salma retorted. "Where's your evidence?"

"Olaf Tryggvason has a daughter called Embla, and your name is Embla!" Wurstan replied, banging the cup he was holding onto the table.

Salma snorted. "So what? If I have a dog called Godric, does that mean he—" she pointed to Godric "—is my dog?"

Roars of laughter from the three elders and Wistan greeted her remark, as a furious-looking Godric squirmed momentarily. With a sly grin spreading across his face, Godric said: "What's in the pouch?"

The question, drowned out by the ealdormen's hearty chuckles, went unheard. He repeated it, louder this time: "What's in the pouch?"

The ealdormen's laughter died to nothing as all eyes turned to her.

CHAPTER 16

—

"A map," Salma said, touching the pouch as her eyes flicked to Wistan.

Godric's eyes locked onto Wistan. "You've seen the map, haven't you?"

Wistan nodded reluctantly.

Godric swivelled. "Let's see it," he said to Salma. "Let's see this Viking map of yours."

Reaching into the pouch because there was nothing else she could do, Salma pulled out the map and began unfolding it. And just as it had done before, it suddenly multiplied in size—doubling, trebling, quadrupling—until her arms were barely long enough to hold it by its edges. All five men immediately shrank back, which was kind of amusing: fierce Saxon warriors afraid of a piece of parchment!

It was Byrhtnoth who finally spoke. "What is that?" he asked, a tremble in his voice.

"I think it's a map of the Norse universe. See," she pointed to the different rings, "one ring is for where the gods stay, the next ring is where humans—"

"Enough!" cried Godric. He pointed a bony finger at her...

"Witch! The girl is a witch!"

"Oh, oh," Salma thought, biting her cheek as she surveyed the expressions on the faces of those staring at her which were, apart from Wistan's, a mixture of fear and horror. She had no idea what Saxons did to witches, but she guessed it wasn't nice things like make them new brooms or feed their black cats.

As the silence lingered, her mind returned to the dojang and the red-black test. She had failed it because she had allowed her performance to be affected by what happened with the strange boy on the bus. She couldn't let that happen again. She had to focus. She had to go for it.

"Alright," she said, straightening her shoulders, "If I make a good case for why you should keep an open mind and give me a fair hearing, I'll—"

"We don't bargain with witches," Godric spat.

"Who says I'm a witch?" she fired back.

Behind the ealdormen, Wistan grinned.

"It's obvious! Just look at her!" Godric cried, directing his words to the ealdormen.

"He's got no proof," she said, pointing to Godric. "I might look a bit strange but you can't judge a book by its cover."

The reaction on the ealdormen's faces told her they hadn't understood what that meant. *Of course not!* She opened her mouth to explain, but Godric got there first.

"She'll pour magic words in your ears!" Godric said melodramatically. "She's a witch!"

She faced Godric, "Really? Again?" She turned back to the ealdormen. "As I've already said, it has not been established that I am witch, so," she jabbed a thumb at Godric, "—can't be believed until he proves I'm a witch—which he won't, because I'm not."

"We saw with our own eyes what your map did. No normal map can do such a thing." Godric replied.

"No normal *Saxon* map…"

Godric eyed her suspiciously.

"You said it yourself," she continued. "This is a *Viking* map!"

"And?" he spat.

"And maybe it's a special map for you, but not for Vikings. Every Viking has one!

They're as common as…as apples."

"We've seen Vikings before and none of them had a map like that."

"Well, there are different sorts of Vikings! Duh! There are Vikings from the far north. There are Vikings from the far, far north. There—"

"We get the idea," Byrhtnoth interrupted.

"Burn her!" Godric suddenly cried. "If she's a witch doing the devil's work, we'll all be safer with her committed to the flames. If she isn't a witch…" he shrugged. "Well, who's going to miss one more silly girl?"

"Oh, that's nice," Salma said, her words dripping with irony. "Do you have kids?"

"What has that got to do with—?"

"Just answer the question."

"As a matter of fact, I do."

"Boy or girl?"

"Girl."

"And would it matter to you if she were wrongly accused? Wrongly called a witch? Wrongly committed to the fire?"

Godric said nothing, just stared back fiercely.

Salma turned to the ealdormen. "Of course, it matters whether I am a witch or not—his refusal to answer my question tells you that. But the fact is I am not a witch—"

"Prove it!" shouted Godric. "Prove you're not a witch!"

Salma's anger, which she'd managed to keep under control until now, finally flared up. "If I was a witch, do you think you'd still be a human and not a fat, croaking toad?"

Godric's mouth flapped open and the ealdormen roared with laughter once more.

"Look," she continued, trying to regain her composure, "if I am a Viking—and let's face it, my clothes and the fact that I'm carrying a Viking map suggest I am—and if I am Olaf Tryggvason's daughter, which I could be, the last thing you should do is not treat me well."

"How so?" Byrhtnoth asked, but Salma could already see that he had understood.

"You believe Olaf Tryggvason is out there getting ready to attack you. You also believe you have his daughter—me. If all of that is true, you should tell him that if he gives you his word that he will sail away and never return, you'll give his daughter back safe and sound. That way, there needn't be any bloodshed and everybody gets what they want." She glanced at Godric, who looked deflated.

Putting their heads together, the three ealdormen conferred in whispers, glancing now and again at Salma and Godric. Finally, Byrhtnoth straightened. "We have decided," he announced. "For now, Embla will remain our...honoured guest. You will tend to her," he told Wistan. "Is that clear?"

"Yes, Byrhtnoth," Wistan replied.

"Take her to the far barn. There is still straw for a bed and the lock is strong."

"Yes, Byrhtnoth." Walking around the table past Godric, Wistan came towards Salma and pointed towards the door.

Salma sighed. She was still their prisoner, but at least they weren't planning to light a fire under her—for now! It was no small victory, and she felt good. And to show it, she gave Godric a little wave with her fingers. The vicious look he gave in return made her feel even happier.

Following Wistan into the fresh air again, she was soon clomping through the burgh between the huts whose roofs reminded her of birds' nests. As she walked, dragging one muddy foot after another, the burgh's people watched her from their doorways with a mixture of incredulity and suspicion, their mouths open, some eyes narrowed, some goggling. A few children skipped and laughed behind them as they walked, and although Wistan tried to shoo them away, they never went far, buzzing around them like flies.

As she continued to walk, tiredness gnawed at her. Her shoes were heavy: sodden and caked in mud; her clothes were still damp, and she smelled smoky and sweaty. Ugh! What she would give to have a shower! It was also becoming clearer that Wistan was taking her to the edge of the settlement, where a tallish building with no windows and one large door stood. The barn: her prison.

She glanced at Wistan. He seemed lost in his own thoughts. They continued on in silence. The children drifted away and the barn grew taller until finally, they were at its door. A heavy bolt was drawn across it. Propping his spear against the barn door, Wistan slid the bolt away and tugged the door open.

The sweet, stale smell of straw wafted out from the dark interior.

"Seriously?" Salma said. "You want me to go in there?"

Wistan squirmed.

"Can we at least chat with the door open for a while?"

Wistan looked back at the stockade as though trying to figure out what his father or Byrhtnoth might say. "I guess that would be okay," he said finally.

Gathering a bundle of straw at the doorway, Salma sat down while Wistan stood. She was glad to get a rest. The sun was warm and the straw surprisingly comfortable.

"Here," Wistan said, reaching into his pocket and pulling out another piece of bread. "I took it from the table when no one was watching. And here's something to drink."

"Thanks," she said, accepting a roughly torn, dark-crusted chunk the size of her hand and a small wooden flask with some liquid inside.

"Good?" he asked.

She nodded. It wasn't chocolate gateaux from the London Review of Books' Cake Shop, but it was good all the same. And she was so thirsty she had barely registered the taste of the liquid.

"What you said about the map. Was it true? Does every Viking from Lapland have such a thing?"

Salma was pretty sure at least some Vikings came from Lapland in Finland. She was also pretty sure there wasn't another map like hers in existence. She grinned and after a moment, Wistan grinned back.

"Tell me truly: are you Olaf Tryggvason's daughter?"

Salma puffed her cheeks. "Honestly, I have no idea."

They fell into a short silence. It was interrupted by the appearance of an old woman carrying a bundle of sticks on her back.

"Be thou healthy!" the old woman called.

"Be thou healthy!" Wistan replied.

They both watched as the woman, eyes gaping at Salma, continued past, walking at a snail's pace. "Is she the oldest person in the village?" Salma asked.

Wistan laughed. "Of course. Some say she's sixty-three."

"Oh…OK." To Salma, she had looked a hundred and sixty-three.

As Wistan watched the old woman continue towards one of the huts, Salma's eyes found the spear. Leaning against the barn door, its spearhead pointing to the sky, it was as close to her as it was to Wistan. In a moment or two, Wistan was going to follow Byrhtnoth's orders and lock her in the barn. Once she was in there, she would be completely at their mercy—while Godric was still out there, presumably still pouring poison into the ealdormen's ears about her. What if he convinced them she was a witch? What then?

One word echoed in her head: *escape.*

Wistan would be no pushover, that was for sure. But if she took him by surprise? Was that crazy? Was it crazy to think she could overcome a Saxon warrior? And what about attacking him without any warning? Was that dishonourable? Lee Arnott and Grandmaster Cho would certainly think so. But they weren't in the situation she was in, were they? They weren't more than a thousand years in the past, stuck in a Saxon village, about to be locked in a barn…All the same, she knew she couldn't do it. She knew she couldn't attack Wistan. He had been kind to her—the only person who had.

"You think it was Godric you heard talking, don't you?" Wistan suddenly asked, breaking into her thoughts.

She frowned as she met his eyes. "Why do you say that?"

"Nobody likes him. If someone was up to something, it would be him."

"Is there any way to prove it?" she said, mouth half-full.

Wistan shrugged. "I don't see how. People are free to come and go as they please. He could have crept out of the settlement last night and nobody would have known."

"And what about Alwin?"

Wistan burst out laughing. "You don't suspect Alwin, do you?"

"Why not?"

"Why not? Because Alwin wouldn't hurt a fly. And he's not the smartest hound in the pack."

"Right, well...just thinking out loud."

Wistan wiped away the smirk that had formed and his face slowly took on a more thoughtful look. "Maybe you should have said something to Godric. To see how he reacted."

"Well, I wanted to," she admitted. "But accusing him just because I don't like him? No, it wouldn't have been right."

"I suppose so," Wistan conceded. He grinned. "Would have been good to see his face if you had though."

Salma grinned too. "It was tempting, believe me. By the way, I remembered what one of the men said. It was something about a red cap."

"Like the one Byrhtnoth wears?"

"Yeah. What do you think it means?"

Wistan shook his head slowly. "No idea," he admitted as his eyes moved away from Salma and landed at the open the door to the barn.

Salma finished the bread and gulped the rest of the drink. She looked up at Wistan who gave her an apologetic smile. "I should..." He motioned towards the door.

"I suppose you should. But promise me you won't let Godric change the ealdormen's minds about me."

"I promise," he replied.

Reluctantly, Salma stood, kicked the straw she had been sitting on back into the barn, and stepped over the threshold.

"I'll come later with more food," he told her, and avoiding her eyes, he slowly swung the door towards her. As he did so, the sunlight shrank and shrank until there was a *clunk* and a rasping sound. The bolt was in place.

"Great," she muttered angrily and pressing an ear against the door, she listened as Wistan's footsteps grew fainter and fainter until they were no more. She stepped back, raised her leg and kicked. The door hardly budged. Apart from slivers of light peeping through the edges of the frame, she was in darkness. The sound of her own breathing filled her ears. All she could do was make herself as comfortable as she could. Who knew how long they would keep her here? Suddenly, somewhere behind her, something rustled. Salma's heart stopped beating. A rat! She was locked inside a pitch-black barn with a rat scurrying about. But a second later, there was the sound of wings flapping—rapid beats—and a chirp. She dropped her shoulders and breathed again. Not a rat, most likely a sparrow. Nevertheless, she banged at the door. "Wistan! Open the door. Please. There's a bird trapped in here." She waited. She banged again. Called out. But Wistan did not return.

Salma turned to face the interior. The sparrow fluttered unseen above her head, chirping, flapping its wings, and moving from perch to perch. Gathering a bunch of straw, she piled it against the wall of the barn nearest the door and sat, staring at the gloom above her head. Salma turned to her side, her gaze shifting to the cracks of daylight around the frame of the door and was reminded of the prayers for protection her mother had taught her as a child. "Say, I seek refuge in the Lord of Daybreak," Salma whispered the Qur'anic verses to herself. She felt the agitation within be soothed. "From all the evil that has been created; from the evil of Darkness as it overspreads; from the mischief of those who practice Secret Arts; and from the mischief of those who envy."

The small bird's chirps quietened, the flapping less frequent. And Salma's eyes grew heavy…

*

Salma woke as though she were swimming towards the surface of a treacle lake: her eyelids flickered but refused to open; her mind told her she was awake, told her she had arms and legs and a body, but only very, very slowly. She took a deep breath, shifted, stretched, feeling the straw move beneath her, the ends poking into her arms and legs. Now she remembered. A barn. In East-Saxon territory. In the year 991…She groaned. *Great. Just great.* She opened her eyes, rubbed them, and sat up to look around. Same old darkness. How long had she slept? No idea, but there was still daylight seeping through the doorframe spaces, so not that long. She stood. Apart from the rustle her feet made, there was complete silence…which somehow felt strange.

Ignoring the feeling of unease that had crept over her, she shuffled to the door and listened with her ear against it. Nothing. She sat back down. When would Wistan come with food? Sitting quietly, she listened to her own breath for a while. She frowned. Something wasn't quite right; something didn't add up…What was it? Before she could figure it out, she heard footsteps—someone was running, getting closer with every step. Suddenly, there was a loud *thunk* and the door crashed open. Salma covered her eyes, blinded by the flood of light.

"Embla! Come! Come!" Wistan's voice.

She stumbled forward, still covering her eyes. "I'm here. What is it?"

"The causeway. Come with me!" Wistan said, grabbing her.

"Hey! That hurts. Let go!" Salma shouted, jerking her elbow away.

"Sorry! I'm sorry," Wistan shouted, dodging other men who were also running and carrying swords, axes, shields, and arrows. "You must come with me."

"What's going on?" Salma shouted as more men jostled past her, running in the direction of where she had first entered the burgh. Now that her eyes had adjusted, she could see the whole place was in turmoil.

Wistan took her arm again and began dragging her forward, a look of panic on his face. "Olaf Tryggvason—he's at the causeway!"

CHAPTER 17

—

Running through the woods behind Wistan, Salma could only ask questions between gasping breaths. "What is…so important… about…the causeway?"

Wistan, as nimble as a deer and hardly breathing, replied, "It connects Northey Island to the mainland. Olaf Tryggvason's men are at one end—on Northey Island. My father, Byrhtnoth, and Dunnere are at the other end."

"When…did…they arrive?"

"Olaf's fleet? We saw it sail up the River Blackwater only a short time ago. We went to the River Blackwater to look for signs of the sea w—I mean, Vikings. Men from Maldon were searching the whole coast, but we found them. As I was leaving to bring you and our army, your father's fleet was disembarking. I have never seen so many…" Wistan's words trailed away. He dodged through the trees in silence, and Salma asked no more questions. Soon, the salty smell of the sea grew stronger. The path led them to a hollow. They leapt down into it, leaves tumbling at their feet. *Was it the place where she had found herself after Room 41?* she wondered. But not for long: she was more focused on not tripping over the branches that lay strewn across the ground. Racing to the other side, she launched herself after Wistan who was already on the slope that rose five metres above them. A strange noise grew louder—like rolling thunder or crashing waves. Salma, scrambling on all fours, digging her nails into the soft ground, finally reached the top. Wistan was already there, standing motionless. Panting madly, she joined him. Standing shoulder to shoulder with the East Saxon boy, she gazed over the estuary. The scene before her made her gape.

"Dragon ships," she whispered.

Perhaps a hundred dark, low-lying ships—sails billowing, oars raised, carved heads at their prows bobbing and turning—were crammed together around Northey Island.

Like ants, men were swarming off them and onto the island, their faces turned towards the causeway, swords, spears, axes, and shields raised above their heads. Every Viking was roaring, screaming at the heavens, demanding battle, demanding blood. That was the noise she had heard. But the strip of land that connected the island to the mainland—the causeway—was only broad enough for two or three men at one time, which meant there was complete and utter gridlock. Thousands of Vikings standing on Northey Island could not move. It was like a huge traffic jam with a massive tailback—and all because on the mainland side of the causeway Byrhtnoth, Wurstan, and Dunnere were standing, swords raised, faces hard, ready to strike down the first Viking who came within reach. Salma had never seen anything like it: three East Saxons holding back 3,000 Vikings!

"Come on!" Wistan cried, rushing down the other side of the embankment and onto the shore. Salma followed. They pelted along the soggy sand towards the island and the causeway. As they grew closer, more East Saxons arrived, pouring out of the woods and forming a ragged crowd behind Byrhtnoth, Wurstan, and Dunnere, still standing with swords poised.

As soon as Wistan and Salma reached the causeway, they joined the crowd of men from Maldon. Somewhere in front of her, horses were neighing—Byrhtnoth, Wurstan, and Dunnere's, she guessed, their high-pitched cries sounding like they were calling the word "no" over and over. She was peering over someone's shoulder—a huge, sweaty man with tangled hair who smelt like dirty socks—trying to see what was happening. The chants and bellows from the Vikings grew steadily less until there was complete silence. Even the horses grew quieter and quieter until all that could be heard was the soft lapping of waves on the shore. Slowly, Byrhtnoth, Wurstan, and Dunnere lowered their weapons and cast quizzical glances at one another. A moment later, the two huge Vikings nearest the three East Saxon leaders grunted and turned to the side, making space to allow a man, shorter than the others but just as powerful-looking, to slip between them. The man, bald headed with a scraggly yellow beard and an amused expression, flashed his eyes across the army from Maldon and then smiled at Byrhtnoth. Salma realised that the dark marks on the man's bald head were tattoos, their curling lines extending past his ears and meeting at the top of his head. Salma's eyes widened. The man's incisors were filed to a point and as sharp as cats…

"Who's he?" Salma whispered to Wistan.

Wistan shot her a funny look. "Olaf, of course!"

"Oh, right," Salma said, giving an apologetic grin.

She and Wistan turned their attention back to the causeway. As they watched, Olaf planted the point of his sword between his feet; leaning down, he rested his chin on the sword's pommel. "Greetings, men of Maldon," he said.

Wurstan and Dunnere glanced at Byrhtnoth, who kept his eyes on Olaf.

Olaf sighed contentedly, "So, here we are, eh? Is it not a beautiful day for battle? The water is so blue. The clouds," he lifted his chin and looked up, "are so white. The sky is so clear."

"It is indeed a beautiful day; if battle, there must be," Byrhtnoth replied.

Olaf's eyes crinkled. "You sound a little doubtful about whether you want to fight me—if you don't mind me saying so. Perhaps you are worried your men cannot defeat mine?"

"No," Byrhtnoth said firmly. "The only doubt I have is how many minutes it will take."

Olaf chuckled and wagged a finger. "I'm not so sure. Maybe you want us to go away? Maybe you will pay for us to go away? Then your men of Maldon can return to their homes and collect their crops—I saw your golden fields. Such a wealth of wheat."

"Yes, our harvest is ready. But the gold in our fields is the only gold you shall see."

"Ah…" Olaf said. He bit his lip and nodded. "I see…"

Byrhtnoth held up his hand. "But I have something more precious than gold," he said. Olaf eyed him suspiciously. "You see," Byrhtnoth continued, "I have your daughter.'"

Olaf took a step forward; all amusement wiped from his face. "Embla's alive?"

Salma could feel Wistan's eyes on her.

Byrhtnoth nodded. "She is safe and well."

"She fell from my ship last night, though no one heard her fall. When we couldn't find her, we thought she had drowned. Is she here?" He leaned on either side of Byrhtnoth, peering over his shoulders. "Show her to me!"

"You are his daughter," Wistan said in a fierce whisper, eyeing her bruised face.

"Seems like it," Salma muttered.

"All in good time," Byrhtnoth replied. "First, we must talk."

Chapter 18

The August sun shone brightly while Byrhtnoth and Olaf talked. Sweat ran down the neck of the man standing in front of her and Salma stood like everyone else, silent and watchful. Would there be a battle? No one was sure. Byrhtnoth was listening calmly as Olaf made his demands. He wanted Embla—Salma—returned to him, and he also wanted 8,000 ingots of silver. Salma had no idea what an ingot weighed, but 8,000 of them sounded like an awful lot; the expressions of the other East Saxons told her she wasn't wrong. Olaf swore he would sail away in return for this payment, "Give me my daughter and the silver and you will never see my men or me again."

"Forgive me, but what guarantees do we have?" Byrhtnoth asked. "How do we know you won't forget about your promises when you have spent all the silver? How can we be certain you won't attack us again next year?"

"It is a risk. But nothing in life is certain," Olaf grinned, "except death."

Byrhtnoth shook his head. "No. I am certain I would be a fool to give you all of the money. Instead, we will pay you some now. After a year or two, you will get more—if you keep your promise and do not attack."

Olaf's face broke into a smile. He sighed. "You don't trust me."

"You are right," Byrhtnoth. "I don't."

"And yet I must trust you? I must trust that you will pay me later—a year from now? Two years from now?"

"Yes," Byrhtnoth said. "You must."

The two men stood, feet planted far apart, staring at one another. It was Olaf's chuckle that finally broke the silence. "I tell you what," he said, wiping a hand over his bald head, "give me back my daughter. I will be in a better mood to talk."

Byrhtnoth glanced at Wurstan and Dunnere. Each gave the tiniest of nods. Turning around, Byrhtnoth faced the East Saxon men. "Wistan? Where are you? Bring Embla to us."

Salma's eyes widened.

Wistan caught the look of horror on her face. "What's the matter?" he whispered.

"I…I…" Salma stammered, backing away.

"What are you doing?" Wistan said, reaching out, trying to catch hold of her arm.

Salma brushed his hand away. "I can't…He isn't…"

"Wistan! Bring Embla—NOW!"

"You have to come," Wistan said, catching her arm, he pulled her towards the front of the East Saxons.

"No!" Salma cried.

"Here she is!" Wistan shouted, pointing at Salma as the rows of men around them cleared. "She's right here!"

"Embla!" Olaf cried. "I hope you haven't killed too many East Saxons!" He grinned and his men roared with laughter. Olaf's eyes shifted away from her, and the smile on his face disappeared. "And the silver?" he asked. "How much do we get now?"

"Three thousand now and the rest later."

Olaf shook his head. "Five now; the rest next year."

Byrhtnoth's deep voice did not waver. "Four now. Two next year. Two the year after."

Behind Olaf, there was a murmur of approval from the rest of the Vikings. Olaf shrugged and gave a big, theatrical sigh. "Very well," he said. "Four now. Four over the next two years." He smiled and rubbed his hands together like a child. "So, where is it?"

"Do you think we carry 4,000 silver ingots in our pockets?" Byrhtnoth asked.

Olaf shrugged as if to say: "Why not?"

Byrhtnoth shook his head. "No. You will have to be patient and wait."

"But I am not a patient man," Olaf replied as Salma, edged forward by Wistan's hand on her back, reached the end of the causeway where Byrhtnoth, Wurstan and Dunnere stood, blocking the Vikings' path.

Olaf peeked between the three East Saxon leaders. "Ah, child. We thought you had drowned."

"Do we have an agreement?" Byrhtnoth asked. "You shall have your daughter and the silver. In return, you swear to leave?"

Olaf opened his arms wide. "I swear."

"Go," Byrhtnoth told Salma. "Be with your father."

Salma could not believe this was actually happening. She was about to be handed over to a 10th Century Viking she'd never laid eyes on who was supposed to be her father! But…if her pretending to be Olaf's daughter was going to stop a battle then she had to do it! Fixing her eyes on Olaf as Byrhtnoth stepped to one side, she stepped onto the causeway.

"Surprise! I'm alive!" she said, trying her best to sound cheerful.

Grinning, Olaf gathered her in his arms and pulled her close.

"Are you ill, my daughter?" Olaf asked, releasing her and looking anxiously into her face.

"No," Salma replied, still coughing at the fishy stink that clung to him. And his breath! It was even worse! "No. It's just the…er… Nothing. I'm fine. Honestly," she said, wafting a hand back and forth.

Olaf gave her a puzzled frown. Thinking no more of it, he drooped a chunky arm around her neck and eyed Byrhtnoth. "I'm waiting," he said.

"I suggest we bring the silver to Northey Island by boat. It will be there in a few hours."

Olaf looked up at the blue sky. "By my estimation, it is undorn. I will give you until mid-evening to bring the silver."

"That's not enough time. You shall have it before nightfall."

Olaf thought for a moment. "Very well," he said and removed his arm from Salma's shoulder. *Finally!* thought Salma. But as Olaf regarded her, a frown slowly darkened his face.

"What?" Salma asked.

"The map," Olaf said. "Where is the map?"

Salma glanced down. The pouch was open; the map gone.

CHAPTER 19

—

"It was…I had it…" Salma spluttered, but Olaf wasn't listening.

"Where is it?" he hissed, his narrowed eyes on Byrhtnoth.

"I have absolutely no idea," he replied.

"Don't play games with me, Saxon. Where is it?"

Byrhtnoth's face hardened. "I'm telling you I have no idea."

Olaf's lip curled. "No idea?" he repeated in a mocking voice. "No idea!" He turned to his men. "Did you hear what he said? The Saxon said he doesn't know where the Map of Nine Worlds is. Yet," he cried, pointing to Salma, "it was in my daughter's safe-keeping when she fell overboard."

A cry of anger exploded as the Viking army stabbed the air with its spears, swords, and axes.

Salma, struggling to be heard above the cries, shouted, "The Saxons didn't take it off me. I had it when I went into the barn, so… so it might have fallen out when I was running here."

Olaf brushed her words aside. "The Saxons talk about trust," he said, addressing his army. "They want us to trust them, yet they steal our most precious possession? Is this the way to behave? Is it? Is it?"

"NO!" the Vikings roared. "NO! NO! NO!"

Suddenly, a Viking as big as Byrhtnoth lunged past Salma. She turned just in time to see the Viking's axe rise in a great arc and come swishing down towards Byrhtnoth's head. Nimble as a cat, Byrhtnoth slipped to the side and the Viking's axe tore into the ground at Byrhtnoth's feet. Byrhtnoth immediately swung his broad sword, bringing its blade down on the axe's wooden handle and slicing through it as though it were a twig. Raising his foot, he pushed the Viking into the water where he landed with a huge splash. For a moment, nothing happened until the Viking broke the surface, spluttering and coughing. As though it were a signal, the other Vikings nearest the causeway's end surged forward. Suddenly, the air was filled with the sound of Viking and East Saxon spears and swords clashing.

A pair of strong hands grabbed Salma by the scruff of the neck and pulled her away. "Come!" Olaf cried, dragging her through the mass of Vikings baying for East Saxon blood.

"Get off!" Salma shouted, pulling at Olaf's hands. But he was too strong, and Salma could do nothing to prevent him from taking her away from where the three East Saxons were fighting the Vikings, dragging her more than half the length of the causeway before releasing her.

"Stay out of the way!" he shouted in her face, and before Salma could say a word, he plunged back into the crowd. Salma scrambled to her feet and saw that Byrhtnoth, Wurstan, and Dunnere were still at the end of the causeway. Swords were swinging, preventing the whole Viking army from getting onto the mainland. As she watched, she saw Olaf pushing his way through the Vikings, getting closer and closer to the end of the causeway. When he reached there, he took something from his pocket, put it to his lips, and blew. A horn or a shell? He was too far away for Salma to be sure. It didn't matter. The long, deep note echoed across the estuary and slowly, the Vikings stopped attacking the three East Saxons. For a moment, nothing happened except that one of the horses behind Byrhtnoth, a huge, silvery beast, rose onto its hind legs and pawed at the air. Olaf stepped into the no-man's-land between his Vikings and three East Saxons. "Byrhtnoth," he cried, opening his arms wide, "is this the way honourable men conduct themselves? First, you steal our map; then you act like scared dogs, too afraid to allow my army to get off the causeway and fight your men on the mainland. Let my men come off the causeway. Ready your men. Then we shall fight."

Byrhtnoth, Wurstan, and Dunnere lowered their swords and gathered together. Salma couldn't hear what they were saying, but it was clear they were considering Olaf's words. She looked at the rest of East Saxons, standing beyond where their leaders were talking. A distant face caught her eye: Wistan. He was staring at the Vikings, his expression grim like everyone else's. Her eyes moved on. She frowned. She brought a hand to her brow, peered across the water, trying to focus on the face of the man standing next to the three horses belonging to the East Saxon leaders. As she stared, a creeping horror slithered up her spine. There were three or four thousand East Saxons about to fight and maybe die but one man—just one— looked like he was enjoying himself: Godric. Standing on a hillock overlooking the ground between the armies, his smile made Salma shiver.

Why was Godric smiling? Only a lunatic would do that—only a lunatic would want there to be a fight...Salma looked at the pouch attached to her belt again. The large and shiny buckle was strong, and she had definitely fastened it after she had put the map back inside. If the map hadn't fallen out while she was running to the causeway, that meant only one thing: someone had taken it while she slept in the barn.

The barn...what was it about the barn? Something had puzzled her. *What was it...?* "Oh no!" she groaned and slapped her forehead hard. *How could I have been so stupid?*

It was the sparrow that had puzzled her, but now she understood. Someone had opened the barn to steal the map. And while the door was lying open, the sparrow had flown out. That's why there had been silence inside the barn after she woke up: she hadn't heard the bird because the bird was no longer there. But who would want to steal her map? And if the map had been stolen, why wasn't that person admitting it now—so that a battle could be avoided? The answer was clear: someone—an East Saxon—wanted the East Saxons and the Vikings to fight.

"Get out of my way," she screamed, beating at the backs of the Vikings who were standing in front of her. "Move!" she cried, and shoving and kicking and punching, she began squeezing her way through the hundreds and hundreds of tightly packed men. *Who wanted the Vikings and Saxons to fight?* She had no idea. She had to speak to Olaf and Byrhtnoth; tell them what she thought had happened. There was still time for peace.

"Stop!" Salma was crying at the top of her lungs, "Stop! Stop! Stop!" Around her, a few puzzled Vikings turned and stared, shuffling away to make room. But just as a little space opened up and she dodged into it, she stepped on a piece of seaweed, lost her footing, and fell sideways into the water lapping at the causeway.

Splosh!

Like a stone, she felt herself plunge down. She didn't know what had happened or where she was for two or three dizzying seconds. Her eyes blinked open. The swirling salt and sand stung them. Somehow, she kept them open. Above her, through the dark water, there was light. She pushed up until she finally broke the surface. Chin in the air, legs kicking hard, she stared. Where was everyone? But then she understood: she was facing Northey Island. Paddling with her arms, she turned herself around and gasped. The Viking army was streaming off the causeway and onto shore of the estuary, lining up in front of the East Saxon army: Byrhtnoth and the other East Saxon leaders had agreed to allow all the Vikings to get off the causeway, and now the two armies were about to fight.

As hard as she could, she swam towards the edge of the causeway, but the current was strong and it was pushing her away. She kicked and thrashed her arms. She wasn't getting anywhere! In fact, she was being carried away from dry land! She screamed in frustration. She realised she was being carried down the coastline towards a small outcrop, its grasses dipping in the water. She twisted around to look behind her. Two hundred metres away, the armies were standing on the beach, silently facing each other. She couldn't beat the tide, it was too strong, and if she kept this up, she'd exhaust herself and drown. *Go with the flow* she told herself. Swimming furiously in the same direction she was being taken, she aimed for the outcrop.

As soon as she was close enough, she grabbed a handful of grass and heaved herself out of the water. Dripping wet, she scrambled along the beach towards the armies, shouting as she went. "Someone came into the barn while I was sleeping. That's why I didn't hear the sparrow when I woke up. Listen to me! The person who took the map opened the barn door and the sparrow escaped! Do you hear me? The map was stolen when I was sleeping—Byrhtnoth knew nothing about it. Listen to me. It wasn't Byrhtnoth."

But no sooner had she said the words when a mighty roar filled the air and men from both sides charged at one another. Weapons in hand, they raced across the sandy ground, faces twisted in hatred, mouths screaming in anger, until—*crash!* —the Viking and East Saxon warriors who had run the fastest met in the middle, quickly followed by the rest. Salma stopped running. Arms hanging at her side, she watched in horror as men hacked, lunged, and tore at one another. "No," she whispered. But there was nothing she could do. A barrage of arrows from the Vikings; then from the East Saxons, shot into the air. Like slender, dark birds, they rose to their peak, hung momentarily in the blue sky, and plunged down, their razor-sharp tips skewering, piercing, killing. Screams of pain and pleading filled the air. Tears rolled down Salma's face. The slaughter continued, and soon it was clear that the Vikings were losing ground, retreating as the East Saxons pushed more and more men against them.

Right at the front of the two armies, she caught a glimpse of Olaf. Surrounded on all sides, his sword swinging left and right, his bald head gleamed like a strange, polished egg. Her eyes continued to scan the battlefield. Where was Wistan? He had to be there somewhere…Through the mass of bodies, she saw Godric. Still standing on the hillock next to where the three horses were, he pulled something out of his tunic and put it on his head. Even though he was just a small figure in the distance beyond the battling armies, Salma felt he was staring straight at her, his eyes drilling into hers as the discussion she had heard in the woods last night came rushing back. The man betraying his fellow East Saxons was him! Godric had just put on a red cap. The same colour of the cap as Byrhtnoth wore. Godric was pretending to be Byrhtnoth!

And now everything she had heard while she lay in the hollow listening to the two men talking suddenly made sense. "By God's power, we will win, eh?" God's power! It was the meaning of Godric's name: God's power. Godric had been talking to Olaf. Godric had been planning to help the Vikings all along!

"You!" Salma cried furiously and leapt off the causeway. At the same time, Godric climbed onto the largest of the horses, the huge silvery grey one, and pulled on the reins. The massive horse reared up on its hind legs, its front legs pawing the air three, four, five times. It landed again lightly. As soon as it was on all fours, Godric dug his heels deep into the horse's side and tugged the horse's head violently. The great horse spun around and leapt forward, galloping away, forcing Godric to lean down and hold on to it with all his might.

The effect on the East Saxons near the back of their army was immediate: they froze, watching in horror as the great silver horse rode further and further away. It was as if all their courage and fierceness had galloped away too. Instead of pushing forward, they began to step backwards.

A cry went up—"Byrhtnoth has ridden away. Byrhtnoth has left!"

Suddenly, all over the battlefield, East Saxons were dropping their weapons and fleeing, leaving a shrinking number to continue the fight.

Racing towards the front line of the battle, Salma was knocked over several times by fleeing, terrified East Saxons. But she picked herself up and carried on, her eyes pinned to the hundred or so East Saxons still on their feet, desperately fighting and huddled around a body.

As she ran towards them, she realised with a jolt that the man on the ground whose white hair was partly covering his bloodied face was Byrhtnoth. Her heart leapt as she saw that one of the East Saxons standing over Byrhtnoth was Wistan. He had survived. But in the next instant, her smile was gone: a Viking, who was carrying a shield and a double-headed axe, was charging towards Wistan. Too late, Wistan turned. The Viking crashed into him and Wistan was thrown backwards. He landed heavily, the impact knocking his sword from his hand.

The Viking gave a huge, toothless grin, raised his axe, and aimed it at Wistan's head.

Salma launched herself. "Hey!" she cried.

Boom! Her feet struck the Viking in the chest and knocked him down like a bowling ball hitting a pin.

Whump! She landed on the soft sand and rolled—once, twice, three times—and grabbed Wistan's sword which was lying where it had fallen. Scrambling to her feet, she raised the sword, preparing herself to battle with the Viking, who had picked up his axe and was stomping towards her with a murderously dark expression on his face.

And the world ended.

CHAPTER 20

—

With a gasp, Salma sat up, wide-eyed, heart pounding.

Her gaze was met by gentle waves a few metres in front of her lapping onto the shoreline.

She looked down. She was sitting on wet, sandy ground. She jumped to her feet. Hand sheltering her eyes from the sun, she peered along the shore, searching as far as she could see. She turned. In the thick forest, nothing moved except leaves blown by the wind and the occasional small, dark form of a bird fluttering from branch to branch.

"Wha—?" she whispered.

Rooted by confusion, she continued to stand and the sun continued to shine while the scent of pine, twinkling bird song, the gentle swishing of leaves, the soft tumble of waves, and the sparkle of sunlight filled her senses.

And that was all.

There were no dead. There were no injured. There were no dropped weapons. There were no cries, no screams, no pleas. There was no blood. There was no gore. There weren't even any footprints aside from hers. Nothing. It was as if the battle had never happened.

Her thigh, she realised, was hurting. Perhaps she had landed on a stone after she had delivered the two-footed kick on the Viking who had attacked Wistan. But had that really happened? How could it be when there was no evidence of it now?

The wind blew again, ruffling her hair. This time, from the direction of the forest, it brought a sound. A human sound: laughter. Jovial, happy laughter.

Moving as quickly as she could, she climbed the sandy dune that lay between the estuary shore and the forest. At the top of it, she stood and gazed into the wood. Another shrill peel of laughter and the tang of woodsmoke greeted her. She climbed down the embankment and limped across the hollow and moved further into the wood. The smell of smoke grew stronger, the laughter louder with each step. As she walked, she tried to make sense of the snatches of conversation reaching her. Were they chatting and laughing about the battle? Sometimes the wind brought words; sometimes, it drowned them in the rustling treetops. She was concentrating on catching the words when movement caught her eye. She stopped and crouched. In front of her, a short distance away through the trees and bushes, stood the great oak tree where she had thought about fighting Wistan.

Someone's elbow was sticking out from behind it.

Holding her breath and moving as lightly as she could, she padded to the lush hawthorn bush in front of her. Even though she had walked carefully, she had still made a lot of noise: the leaves around her feet were dry and crunched when she stepped on them. Breathing in little gasps, she waited. The talking had ceased. Had they heard her? What was happening? Craning her neck past the hawthorn's twisty branches, spikes, and small leaves, she leaned as far as she could without moving her feet. No sign of anyone. But she still couldn't see far enough to know who was behind the oak. She straightened. She looked at the dried leaves around her. If she moved, she'd make a noise. *How am I going to…?* A sudden gale of laughter exploded.

Go! Like a deer, she darted across the leaf-littered ground towards a clump of trees standing to the oak's left. Panting, she leaned back against the knobbly trunk of an elder tree. The laughter ceased. The sound of her pounding heartbeat grew louder than the wind in the trees.

"Have you quite finished running around?" a deep voice boomed. Salma gasped. *Did someone just say—?*

"We've got other things to do, you know." A different, younger-sounding voice.

Salma remained crouched. Was it a trick? Maybe they had no idea where she was? Maybe—

"You're behind the hawthorn bush," a deep voice said. There was a clanking sound as if someone had struck metal against metal. "We've got hot tea. I'm sure you could use some."

Salma straightened. She looked behind her. No one was sneaking up on her. If she ran, they, whoever they were, might chase her. But she still had a chance to get away. *I should run! I should—*

"Your name's Salma Mansour. You're fifteen years old. Your mother works for the British Museum…"

Swallowing hard, she whispered: "Salma Mansour…"

How strange it was to hear her own name again. How fantastic it was to hear it again! She wasn't Embla and Olaf certainly wasn't her father anymore. A great wave of happiness swept over her. Was this craziness about to end? She sniffed, laughed, sniffed again. In her mind's eye, she saw her mother's face. *She must be worried sick about me.* She wiped away tears that were fogging her eyes, took a deep breath and, stepping beyond the cover of the prickly branches, she shouted: "Who are you? What do you want?"

It was the younger voice that answered. "We want you to come over here and have a cup of tea—that's what we want," it said irritably. "Now hurry up."

With fists clenched, her whole body ready to deal with an attack, Salma moved steadily towards the oak, glancing from side to side as she went. Closer she moved, closer and closer until—

"Ah! There you are!" a younger voice exclaimed.

"Godric!" Salma shouted. She had learned taekwondo in order to defend herself, but all thoughts of defence flew out of her head as soon as she saw his face. Blinded by anger, she closed the distance between them in two steps and launched a punch with all her might.

Her fist was caught in mid-air by the hand of Byrhtnoth.

"Not so fast," he said, catching and holding her fist in his huge paw.

Salma stared at him, mouth-open, utterly astonished. He had been standing out of sight behind the tree but had shot out a hand and stopped her fist a centimetre from Godric's nose.

Byrhtnoth released her hand, and her arm flopped to her side.

"Good work," Godric said with a chuckle and sat beside the fire again.

Byrhtnoth, his penetrating blue eyes burrowing into Salma's, raised his eyebrows at her as if to ask, "Are you calm?"

After a hesitation, Salma nodded back.

"You're no doubt wondering who we really are," Godric said, passing her some tea which, weirdly, had first come from a beautiful teapot; then gone into a serving jug; then finally into the shallow bowl, she now held with both hands.

"Honey?" Byrhtnoth asked, offering her an opened jar.

Dumbly, she shook her head.

"Black rose tea," Byrhtnoth said, holding his cup and motioning for her to take a sip of hers.

Mechanically, Salma took a sip.

"Good?" Byrhtnoth asked. Salma just stared but the warmth trickling down her throat and into her stomach was soothing. Godric sipped noisily and declared it delicious. He smiled at Salma. Salma didn't return it. The fire gave a loud crackle. For a moment, they all watched the smoke as it curled upwards and away. It was Godric who eventually spoke.

"Have you ever heard of the Eight Immortals?" he asked. Still stunned by everything that had happened in the last ten minutes, Salma shook her head slowly.

Byrhtnoth and Godric looked at one another, and Byrhtnoth cleared his throat.

"Well, we are two of them," he said as a wolfish grin spread on his face making him suddenly look very different to the Byrhtnoth she had known. Before Salma's eyes, the man's white beard and hair disappeared, replaced by a clean-shaven chin and a wild, black thicket on his head. The clothes that Byrhtnoth had worn also changed. In the blink of an eye, a silken robe took the place of Byrhtnoth's rough tunic and a bare chest appeared, its skin covered with inky-black tattoos of animals that seemed to writhe like living beasts.

Her eyes fell on the face of the man she had known as Godric. The change was startling. Gone was the glumness and suspicion; in its place, a young man's impish face appeared, eyes full of mischief, cheeks plump and soft. Gone too was the stinking tattered tunic Godric had worn and, in its place, a robe as yellow as a buttercup shimmered.

"My name is Zhongli Quan and this," indicating Godric, "is Lan Caihe."

"Are you angels?" Even Salma was surprised by her question! Nonetheless, it sort of made sense. They weren't jinns—they hadn't tried to take over her body and they didn't seem evil; not like the one that had appeared in the Tube—so they might be angels.

Lan Caihe placed his bowl carefully on the ground. "Er…no, we aren't," he said.

Zhongli Quan took another sip and put his tea down too. "Actually, we were men and women once, a long time ago in China. But now, we are immortal and live between worlds. We can't visit yours. All we can do is bring you three to this one to…" he shrugged, "to see how you perform."

"Are you trying to tell me you engineered all of this to…to test me? Why? Why would you do that?"

"You'll see—when the time is right," Zhongli Quan said, his tough-looking face looking even tougher. "And by the way, resisting the urge to punch Wistan and steal his spear when you two were sitting outside the barn? Very commendable."

"No, no, no! I loved the fact you lost your confidence," Lan Caihe cried.

"I lost my confidence?" Salma repeated through clenched teeth.

Lan Caihe coughed. "Sorry, I meant you weren't over-confident—like you were in the dojang. Shows…greater maturity."

"Greater maturity?" Salma repeated, her voice rising.

Lan Caihe's eyes bounced off Salma, darted to Zhongli Quan, and returned to Salma.

"Is this some kind of sick—?" Salma asked in quiet anger and suddenly stopped. "Wait!" She turned to Zhongli Quan. "You… said 'you three.' 'All we can do is bring you three to this one.' Which three?"

Lan Caihe's smile was a knowing one. "You're about to find out," before Salma could reply, he dug into his pocket. "Oh, by the way, this," he said, stretching out a hand that held a shiny, triangular piece of metal towards Salma, "is what you must—"

"Don't forget the map," Zhongli Quan said.

Lan Caihe's eyebrows shot up. "I almost did! How silly of me!" He spun around and pulled the map, which was still as small as it had been in Salma's pouch, from a glistening gold box behind him. "Here," he said, handing over both items. "Take them."

Salma stared at the objects in her hand as her mind raced back to what had happened on the underground and that…thing's warning: "you must not leave your adventure with the triskelion in your possession. Follow my wishes and I shall not harm you—or your mother." *Was this what that thing had foreseen? Was this silvery object he did not want me to take…?*

"Is this a piece of a triskelion?" she asked.

Lan Caihe gave her a congratulatory nod. "Someone's been delving into the dictionary!"

"Just answer my question."

Lan Caihe reached up and smoothed his sleek dark hair—even though there was not a single hair out of place. "Yes, it is. How very clever of you."

Salma, ignoring the condescension, brought the piece of triskelion closer to her face. It was beautiful: the animal—a hare—was so real: every hair and every muscle seemed as though it might ripple at any second. Shan Wu had said she would get a piece of a triskelion; that was exactly what she was holding right now. Did that somehow prove she was in a different sort of reality rather than just dreaming? Maybe. Just maybe. Or was it like one stupid dream predicting another stupid dream. Did that even make sense? It was all so confusing, all so crazy ridiculous. Shan Wu! Immortals! Vikings! Triskelions! Her head was spinning. She looked up and stared into the blue sky beyond the treetops. *Calm*, she told herself. *Be calm…*

She took a deep breath and let it out slowly. She'd never heard of Chinese Immortals called Zhongli Quan and Lan Caihe. In truth, she had practically no knowledge of China or Chinese mythology. The idea that these…beings wanted her for some unexplained reason seemed fantastical to her. And yet…and yet here she was—in what seemed like an alternate universe where for the past eight hours, she had been chased through woods, nearly drowned, worn smelly clothes, been imprisoned in a barn, watched a horrific battle, and been given practically nothing to eat. It was impossible to believe it was a dream. And it was impossible to believe it wasn't!

Lan Caihe's voice suddenly interrupted her thoughts. "Cat got your tongue? Say something."

Salma gave them a tight smile. "OK—how about this: if this is really happening, I don't like it. I don't like playing your stupid little games."

Zhongli Quan's hairy eyebrows furrowed angrily and he opened his mouth. But before he could speak, Salma continued.

"What?" she scoffed, "Did you seriously expect me to be delighted? Oh, thank you so much for bringing me here, Oh Immortals. I'm so happy to be a part of your game, Oh Immortals. It was so good of you to kidnap me, Oh Immortals."

Lan Caihe, face darkening too, tutted loudly and started to speak, but Salma's raised hand silenced him as well.

"But I'll tell you what I really, really hate," she said. "What I really hate is being threatened. Shan Wu—" Salma could see by Lan Caihe and Zhongli Quan's reaction that they knew who he was, "threatened my mother and me. I don't know what's going on. I don't even know if this is a dream or not. But what I do know is I can't…I won't allow someone to threaten us. So, if this is real, if I'm not going crazy, then…then I'll fight. I'll fight whoever this Shan Wu is tooth and nail."

Lan Caihe and Zhongli Quan looked at one another and then at Salma. The last thing Salma saw before the blackness descended was the beaming smile on their faces.

PART 3

BRITISH MUSEUM,
LONDON,
UNITED KINGDOM
THE PRESENT DAY

CHAPTER 21

—

Groggily, Salma raised her head. A boy and a girl—*were they the ones she had seen before?* —were staring down at her. Salma felt like she'd just taken a roundhouse kick to the head. "Where am I?" she whispered.

"Are you OK?" the girl with long, dark hair asked. Salma felt the girl take her gently by the arm, cradling her head with her other hand.

"Take a deep breath. It'll wear off in a bit," the boy said, his deep brown eyes watching her kindly.

"What's your name?" the girl asked.

She hesitated just a second. "Salma."

A small crowd had gathered around her. Their worried face hovered behind the shoulders of the boy and girl.

"It's OK," the girl told them. "She's just a bit dehydrated."

"Can you stand?" the boy asked as members of the crowd began to disperse, reassured enough to continue their museum visit.

Salma grunted. "I think so." She glanced at her hand. What was she holding? Frowning, she unfurled her fingers. Her jaw dropped. She looked at her other hand. It was clutching something too. She opened it.

"Interesting," said the boy and looked at the girl.

"The third piece of the triskelion and…a map," the girl said.

"What…?" Salma whispered while the words *Not a dream!* boomed in her head.

"Let's find a place where we can talk, OK?" the girl said.

"Keep a hold of those," the boy said, meaning the map and the other shiny thing.

Salma gasped as two pairs of hands took her by the elbows and helped her to her feet.

When she was standing and was sure she wouldn't fall over, she politely but firmly pulled her arms away from the boy and girl. "Who are you two?" she asked suspiciously.

"I'm Sanjeev," the boy said, extending a hand which she did not shake. He retracted it, looking a little crushed.

"And I'm Sara," the girl said.

"I saw you two…earlier. Why were you looking at me?"

"We saw the things circling your head," the boy said.

"And I think you saw them around our heads too," the girl added.

Salma couldn't deny it.

"And why are you here?"

"I came to meet Sara," Sanjeev said.

"And I came to meet the Second Hare, him," Sara said, meaning Sanjeev, which made Sanjeev grin.

The Second Hare? The conversation she'd seen on her computer.

"The Second Hare?" Salma asked. "And just how many of these Hares are there?"

"We're not positive," Sara said, brushing a stray hair from her face, "but we think just three."

"So, who's the third?" As if she didn't already know.

"That…would seem to be you," Sanjeev said.

Salma breathed out slowly; what they were saying fitted the facts…so far. She eyed the two of them. Sara and Sanjeev gazed back at her.

"Listen," Sanjeev said, "I think we've all been through something similar."

"Really? You were at the Battle of Maldon?"

Sara and Sanjeev furrowed their brows. "The what?" Sara asked.

"The Saxons? The Vikings?" Salma said.

Sanjeev shook his head. "I was in Constantinople during the reign of Emperor Justinian."

"And I was in ancient China during the Northern Song dynasty," Sara said.

"This is crazy!" Salma muttered.

"Absolutely!" Sanjeev said.

"Let's get a seat," Sara said. "Then we can talk more."

*

Back at the coffee shop, they took the same table Sara and Sanjeev had been at before.

"You want anything special to drink?" Sanjeev asked.

"No. Just some water please," Salma answered, still feeling like her head was floating above her shoulders.

"Water for me too," Sara said.

As they waited for Sanjeev to return with the drinks, Sara said: "You said something about Saxons?"

At the mention of the word, a rush of images filled Salma's head: Byrhtnoth, Olaf, Wistan, the fleet of dragon-headed Viking ships, the causeway, the battle, clashing swords, the screams of injured and dying men. She closed her eyes and clasped her hands over her ears.

"It's OK," Sara said soothingly. "It's over now."

Salma opened her eyes again. Sanjeev, who had brought the drinks and was standing watching her smiled awkwardly and sat.

"I know it sounds crazy," Sara said, "it doesn't even make sense to me. But we've all travelled into the past."

"For me, it was a mosaic," Sanjeev said. "As I said, it sent me to Constantinople in the 6th Century."

"And I got pulled back hundreds of years into the Northern Song dynasty by a Chinese scroll. The Qingming Scroll."

Salma thought about the gold hare she had been looking at in the museum case before she had been transported to Maldon. Whatever was going on, it seemed the other two were as baffled as she was. Deciding to trust them for the moment, she released the map and the silvery thing with the rabbit running in a circle. Both Sara and Sanjeev's eyes locked onto it. A nice, normal day with a nice lunch with her mother? Where had that gone?

"I was in Maldon in 991," she said, seeing Wistan's face in her mind's eye as clearly as the faces of the two people nodding at her, "at a war between the Saxons and Vikings."

"Wow," Sanjeev said. "That sounds intense."

"It was."

"Been there," Sara said.

"Yeah, me too." Sanjeev said. He paused before he spoke again. "Now, here's a question for you. Did you meet any…er, Immortals?"

Salma's eyes opened wide. Was she ready to admit something as crazy as that? Finally, he decided there was no point hiding it. "Zhongli Quan was one of them."

Sara, completely familiar with the legends thanks to Granny Tang, nodded. "Yep," she said. "Zhongli Quan is one of them. I haven't met him yet."

"He was the Captain of the guards in the desert when I met him," Sanjeev said.

"And these?" Salma said, gesturing to the map and the silvery thing.

"We got objects too," Sara said. "I got a piece of silk that turns into a dagger. If you do it right." She pulled out a piece of brightly coloured silk from her pocket and laid it next to the map.

"A silk dagger? Really? Come on!"

Sara nodded. "It's supposed to be able to cut through anything."

"And I got a key," Sanjeev said, sounding deflated. He dropped it next to the silk dagger and map. "With a monkey on it."

"OK. And…what are we supposed to do with these things?" Salma asked.

Sara and Sanjeev shrugged their shoulders.

"No idea," Sara said.

"Me neither," Sanjeev said. He looked at the map. "What's that?"

"It's a Viking map," Salma told him, "of Yggdrasil and the Nine Worlds. But it isn't any old map—I could see myself on it, you know like the maps that say, 'You Are Here'? Except the map changed according to where I moved."

"You know," Sanjeev said, "we've all passed tests to get these things—the map, the key, the silk dagger—so they must be important somehow."

"Yeah, a test," Salma said thoughtfully. "What was that all about?"

Sanjeev shrugged. So did Sara.

"And the silvery piece of metal?" Salma asked.

Grinning, Sara and Sanjeev dropped their pieces next to Salma's on the table. "Pieces of a triskelion. They fit together to make one—"

Suddenly, Salma was on her feet: "What time is it?" and snatched away her metal shard. "I've got to meet my mother." Her eyes fell on the clock on the wall. What? Only five minutes had passed since she had gone into the other room? How was that possible?

Sara gave a quiet chuckle. "Yeah, time seems to stop when you have an adventure."

Salma sat down heavily. "We've got to tell someone." She looked at the other two. "This is too weird."

"You can try, but my best friend didn't believe me. She couldn't see my piece of the triskelion and the silk refused to become a dagger."

"I didn't tell my mom or dad. My dad would probably say a Nebulist had eaten my brain," Sanjeev said, taking his shard and handing Sara hers.

"My mother," Salma said. "I should talk to my mother."

"Why?" Sara asked.

"Because she's a curator in the Middle Eastern gallery here. She knows all sorts of stuff—maybe she knows something about this. We don't have to tell her about what happened, not exactly, but maybe we can get some info that we can use. I don't know." She pointed towards the back of the museum. "We can go to her office."

"OK…" Sara said. "I told my father I'd meet him in the Great Court at 3:00. We have time."

"I need you to confirm my story—so my mum doesn't think I'm nuts," Salma replied.

Sanjeev pushed his glasses to the top of his nose. "She'll probably think we all are."

"By the way," Salma said, mouth open, gazing above their heads, "what are these?" She pointed to the things still floating around their heads.

Sanjeev's dark eyes crinkled with mirth. "No idea, but if you find out, tell us!"

CHAPTER 22

—

Together, they walked through the museum, passing hundreds of display cases and visitors chatting, taking photos, marvelling at the ancient objects from all over the world. They entered a room for special exhibitions—long, with high, ornate ceilings, and a wooden floor.

"Hey, what era is this?" Sanjeev asked.

Sara knew immediately. "Ancient China. The reign of Qin Shi Huang."

"Who was he?"

Sara was surprised. "The first Emperor of China. Haven't you heard anything about him?"

"Only a little," Sanjeev said sheepishly. "The only thing I remember is that China is named after his dynasty."

"That's it?" Sara asked.

"I don't know. I guess I should have listened better."

"I'm not feeling too well," Salma said. Her head felt like it was in a doorway and someone was trying to jam the door shut. "Mind if we sit down for a couple of minutes?" and going to one of the benches, she sat and rested her back against the wall. Sara and Sanjeev sat, too.

Facing them were two terracotta warriors, reproductions of those found in the grave in the Chinese city of Xi'an. Next to the warriors was a life-size terracotta horse, its saddle and bridle repainted, its eyes wide. But for its unblinking eyes, it seemed ready to leap over the barrier between it and the crowds and gallop out of the room.

"We can take it easy here until you feel better," Sanjeev said.

Salma breathed deeply. "I was feeling OK a few minutes ago."

Sanjeev wandered over to a map on the wall beside the warriors and read the information there. "Says he brought an end to the Warring States period by defeating six other states. That he was a fierce warrior himself."

"True," Sara said, "but he did more than unify China through military power. I had to do a research project on him for school. As First Emperor, he standardised the Chinese script and the currency. He even standardised the length of the axles on carts so they could travel on the roads in different states easier."

Sanjeev frowned. "Huh? I don't get it."

"Well, back then, the roads weren't paved, so when it rained, the carts that crossed over them dug deep ruts in the earth. Different size axles on the carts, different size ruts. When he made one size standard, it became easier for the carts to cross state borders and trade improved."

Salma sat up, listening, glad her head was clearing, though her eye still throbbed a bit.

Sanjeev was impressed with Sara's knowledge. "Interesting."

Sara smiled. "I like history."

"Anything else?" he asked.

"According to the great historian Sima Qian, Qin Shi Huang wanted to live forever and ordered his physicians to make him immortal." She grinned. "So, some of them told him to eat mercury."

"Mercury? As in highly toxic, atomic number 80, quicksilver mercury?"

"Yup. In the end, years of eating mercury drove him mad and caused his early death."

"Yeah," Sanjeev said. "I'm not surprised."

"Qin Shi Huang was convinced he would live forever, but just in case he died, he had an entire city built to rule over in the afterlife." Sara pointed to the warriors. "That's where all this stuff comes from."

Sanjeev eyed the mad looking horse; the fierce faces of the warriors. "Imagine them charging at you!"

"Scary," Sara agreed. "And there are thousands of them."

Salma, feeling much better, said: "His tomb must be huge—to have all those things in it."

"Yes!" Sara said, excited now. "Sima Qian wrote about a massive tomb surrounded by rivers of mercury, but no-one knows for sure because his book was written a century after Qin Shi Huang's tomb was closed. Even today, we still don't know what's in it because archaeologists haven't opened all of it."

"Why not?" Sanjeev asked.

"See the statues? They were painted when they were buried but when they were dug up, the paint flaked off because they were exposed to air again."

"Oh, OK: so being underground protects them. I get it." Sanjeev looked at Salma. "Can you stand?" he asked.

"Yeah, I think so," Salma replied and planting her feet, rose unsteadily.

"Don't forget that," Sanjeev said, pointing to the shiny piece of metal still lying on the bench.

"Oops!" Salma said, reaching down; she picked it up.

Sanjeev tossed his shard lightly into the air. But just as he was reaching up to catch it, it swerved away from him as though it were a fish on the end of a fishing line with a hook in its mouth and dropped into Sara's hand.

"What the heck…?" Sanjeev cried.

"What's happening?" Sara said, eyes bulging.

The three of them stared at Sara's palm as Sanjeev's shard crawled like a metallic insect towards Sara's. A deep thrumming sound filled the air. The two shards made contact. The thrumming sound ceased and seamlessly, the ragged edges of the shards dissolved and two became one.

Sanjeev turned to Salma. "Where's yours?" he cried.

Salma raised her hand. The shard was pulsating, twitching from side to side. Gingerly, she leaned forward. The shard sprung from her hand and landed on Sara's. A flash of bright light blinded the three teens. When they were able to see again, what they saw drew their breaths away: the triskelion, now complete, had risen into the air and was spinning in front of them, its faces showing the three hares, their feet running around the edge of the circle, their heads pointed towards the centre. But instead of six ears, there were only three, each of the hares sharing one of theirs with the hare on either side.

Hovering at eye level, it began to glow, emitting a pale silver light.

This time the dizziness that swept over the three teens didn't come as a surprise. Sara held out her right hand, which Sanjeev took, and her left hand, which Salma grasped.

"Here we go again," Salma muttered as she watched Sara's, Sanjeev's and her own feet, ankles, knees, legs fade and disappear.

PART 4

THE JADE PALACE
THE PRESENT DAY

Chapter 23

⸺

As if she had been in an elevator whose cable had snapped, Sara's stomach had leapt into her mouth, and everything swam before her eyes. Unsteadily, she got to her feet and through the misty haze, she gazed down at the other two who were still lying on the ground in front of her, their eyes tight shut, faces pinched. Judging from their expressions, they were feeling as rough as she was.

Where on earth were they this time?

Just as she was pondering this, a gust of wind rose. Like a hand pushing aside a curtain, it shoved the haze away to reveal what lay around her.

Her stomach lurched again. "Oh!"

She and the other two were on top of a column of rock whose flat surface was no bigger than a bedroom. And she was standing centimetres from the brink!

Quickly shuffling backwards, she stared into the emptiness below. The sheer-sided column of rock seemed to plunge down for a thousand kilometres and even then, she couldn't be sure how far it went because she could not see the bottom. With her foot, she flicked a small, white pebble off the edge and watched it plummet to a speck and disappear.

She wasn't terrified of heights, but she didn't love this either. Moving two further steps away from the precipitous drop, she turned.

"Well, at least there's a way off," she muttered.

A wooden bridge, fifty or sixty steps long, stretched across the void, its near-end anchored to stone pillars on the column; its far-end bound to two giant trees on the other side. The bridge—its walkway and railings—sloped gently down to a mid-point and then rose towards the land on the other side. The walkway was made of wooden slats strung together with thick, cabled rope, but still—just rope, as were the railings to hold on to.

Beyond the far-end of the bridge, through the mist, Sara caught glimpses of a wide plaza whose stones shone with minty green lustre, the outline of a glistening yellow gate, and far in the distance, a forest green dome supported by pillars of the same colour: a pavilion, perhaps.

"Wow!" a shaky voice exclaimed. She turned. Sanjeev, who was standing beside her, was staring at the bridge's walkway, a nervous look in his eyes. Behind him, Salma had also stood up and was also staring the edge of the column and the bridge warily.

"Anyone scared of heights?" Sara asked.

Two hands went up.

Eyes returning to the bridge, Sara said, "Better if we go in single file."

When no-one disagreed or volunteered to go first, she reached up and took hold of the rope railings. She tried not to look down, but her eyes refused to obey.

"Is it safe?" Sanjeev asked.

"We're about to find out," Sara said and reaching out with her right foot, she placed it on first wooden slat. Gingerly, she allowed the slat to take her weight. As soon as she did, the whole bridge bobbed and swayed like a giant agitated jelly.

"Yikes!" Sara cried, clasping the rope railings tightly.

"Is this such a good idea?" Sanjeev asked, wringing his hands.

"Do we have any options?" Salma said.

Sanjeev grimaced.

Sara, blocking out Salma and Sanjeev, slid her left foot past her right and felt where the next slat was. Once again, the bridge shook like crazy. She glanced over her shoulder. "Anyone got a parachute?"

"You're doing great," Salma reassured her.

She was about to take another step when the bridge bucked and buckled. Turning, she saw that Sanjeev had also stepped onto the bridge and was moving uncertainly towards her, eyes tight shut.

"Let me get nearer the end before you come any closer," Sara said.

Sanjeev, not opening his eyes, nodded and froze.

Behind him, Sara saw that Salma was preparing to take her first step.

"Salma, don't—" she cried.

Too late. The bridge lurched to the right and swung crazily to the left, weaving back and forth like a rope pendulum, sending their hearts into their mouths.

"No!" Sanjeev cried.

"Just hang on," Sara said.

Crouching low, fingers like hooks, the three of them clung on, fighting against the bridge which seemed determined to tip them upside down and cast them into the depths below. "Lower your centre of gravity," Salma yelled.

"I'm lowering it, believe me!" Sanjeev yelled, which almost made Sara grin.

They hung on grimly, the sky swinging above their heads one second, the depths the next.

But eventually, the swaying calmed down. When it was finally just a gentle swing, Sara was able to straighten. "You guys OK?" she asked.

"Great! Loving every minute of it so far," Salma called, her tone suggesting she meant exactly the opposite.

Sanjeev, looking too shell-shocked to say anything, just nodded.

"Don't move. Let me get across, OK?" Sara told Sanjeev and Salma. "After I'm off the bridge, come along one at a time."

When all three had their feet on the plaza's smooth, green stones, Sara said: "I guess it helps if you live in a skyscraper: dealing with heights, I mean."

"I live in a block of flats, too," Salma said, tightening her yellow hairband, "but we have lifts, not crazy rope bridges."

"Are we supposed to go to that thing?" Sanjeev asked, meaning the yellow gate, which had once again emerged from the mist.

"I've been in the Forbidden City, but it's nothing compared to this," Sara said, awestruck by the monumental scale of the buildings in the distance.

They all peered through the mist at the yellow gate and the pavilion far beyond which, to Sanjeev at least, seemed to have become a deep green spaceship hovering above the ground.

"It's going to take ages," he groaned.

Sara slapped him on the back. "A journey of a thousand miles—"

"Begins with a single step," Salma said.

"Can we call for an Uber instead?" Sanjeev joked. His face grew serious. "I wonder if…"

All three immediately searched themselves, half-knowing it was pointless.

"No mobile," Sara said, patting her pockets. "You?" she asked Sanjeev. He shook his head. She looked at Salma, who also shook her head.

Sanjeev's shoulders slumped. "I sure could use an Uber and a margherita pizza."

Sara sighed. "Don't mention food. I'm starving."

"Maybe there'll be food in the pavilion," Salma said.

Sara stood between Salma and Sanjeev. "There's only one way to find out," she said and snaked her arms around both their waists. "Ready?" she asked.

Salma and Sanjeev nodded solemnly and took their first, single step together.

*

It got even bigger as they approached, so that by the time they arrived at the gate they had to tilt their heads all the way back to see the top of it. Even then, it was difficult to see the very top because of the swirling mist.

"Cool finials," Sanjeev said, squinting through the mist. He caught Salma's questioning look. "The things at the top of the spears that form the gate."

"Are those...finials golden heads?" Salma asked, glimpsing faces before they disappeared in the haze.

Sanjeev nodded. The heads were amazing, but his eyes had moved to the columns on either side of the gate. Though not as tall as the gate's spears, they were still the size of sequoias, which was fine...They weren't the problem. It was the creatures perched on top of them that were worrying him: dragons. Big, scary, very realistic-looking dragons with viciously sharp teeth, goggling eyes, and mouths that seemed capable of swallowing a small herd of fully-grown sheep and perhaps a cow or two as well.

"Er...those things are made of wood, right?" he said, blinking furiously up at the statues.

"Of course, they are," Sara laughed.

"At least the gate is open," Sanjeev said making a joke as there were no walls either side of the huge gate and its columns.

"Do we go through the gate? Or do we go around?" Salma asked. "Either way will take us to the pavilion," which she noticed was covered in mist and cloud again.

Sara looked at the gate and its eight gold spears. "Mmmm... why have a gate if we aren't meant to go through it?"

"Is it big enough to squeeze through?" Sanjeev asked, meaning the gap between the gate and the column.

Salma tightened her hair tie. "Only one way to find out," she announced, and watched by the others, she squeezed herself into the space, grunted, and passed through. On the other side, she grinned. "Come on. There's nothing to it."

Sara squeezed through next, high-fiving Salma when she reached her. "Your turn, Sanjeev."

Sanjeev, eyes pinned to the dragons, raised his foot. As soon as he did, a sound—like a giant clearing its throat—shook the air. One of the dragons had moved its neck and was looking right at him. Another horrible, grating sound. The other dragon had hunched its back and stretched its neck so that its cold, wooden eyes were also fixed on Sanjeev.

"Run!" Salma told him. "Run to us!"

Sanjeev ran, squeezing through the gap and tearing past Sara and Salma who had also taken to their heels. As the three of them sprinted away, Sanjeev turned and was relieved to see that neither of the dragons had left its plinth; they weren't even watching them.

"I think…it's OK now…" Sanjeev panted, coming to a ragged stop in front of the pavilion whose towering pillars and dome were once again shrouded in mist. With his back to the pavilion's shaded interior, he sat down heavily on the pavilion's lowest step.

In front of him, Sara and Salma had also halted and were doubled over, trying to catch their breaths.

"That…was crazy," Sanjeev puffed, head back, leaning against the other steps behind him.

"You can say…that…again," Sara replied.

"Didn't you… put on… your anti-dragon… cream?" Salma asked.

Sara snorted with laughter.

"Funny," Sanjeev said, trying not to laugh as well.

Getting her breath back, Sara stood up straight. Her face immediately changed. "Oh, oh," she said. "Now what?" Salma asked, also straightening.

"Look," Sara told them, pointing into the mist.

Salma and Sanjeev looked, but too late: the immense building had slipped away behind a veil of cloud.

"I know where we are," Sara said. Two expectant faces looked at her. "We're in the Jade Palace!"

"The Jade Palace?" Salma repeated, looking at the green pavilion, the green courtyard, and its myriad shades of green: as dark as deep forest; as bright as lime; as pale and translucent as…green jade. "Not a bad name," she said. "You want to fill me in?"

"The Jade Palace is…" Sara began but stopped: Salma had put a finger up to her lips and held up a hand.

"Do you hear that?" Salma asked. They listened.

"What?" Sanjeev asked. But now he could hear it as well—a rhythmic tapping, quiet, but louder now. Whatever was causing it was coming closer.

Sanjeev looked around. Run back to the gate? No way! There really was no place to go. He turned in the direction the sounds were coming from and took another deep breath.

More tapping.

"Don't let it be a dragon," he thought.

From the darkness at the centre of the pavilion, the tip of a crutch appeared, making a tapping sound as it struck the ground, and an old man hobbled into view, a filthy, torn robe barely covering his body and a large gourd hanging on a piece of rope around his waist. Around his balding head, a gold hoop shone, clean and bright: not like the dirty, haggard face that stared at them or the rough, unkempt beard that sprouted from his jowls. "Oh!" he grunted. "About time, too."

"Is it?" Salma asked sharply.

If the old man caught her voice's irritation, he showed no sign. "Welcome to the Jade Palace, the home of the Eight Immortals," he said.

"Are they expecting us?" Sanjeev asked.

"Yes, we are."

"We?" Salma asked.

"You are looking at one of them now," the old man said with a scowl. "I am Li Tieguai." He paused as if waiting for the three of them to say something. When none of them did, he folded his brows. "Right! Well, don't just stand there: follow me," he cried, hopping down the steps and limping towards a dark building that suddenly emerged from the clouds as tall and imposing as a mountain.

"Where did that come from?" Sanjeev said, gazing in wonder at the building, its courtyard, the gushing rivers that flowed around it, and the bridge spanning the rivers and leading to the door of the palace, a colossal wooden edifice as tall as tall sequoias.

"The Jade Palace is…wooden?" he said.

Sara shrugged.

He gestured towards Li Tieguai. "I don't remember meeting him, do you?" he whispered.

"Me neither," Sara said. "Did you meet him?" she asked Salma as they walked slowly behind Li Tieguai, in awe of the immensity of the scene before her.

Before Salma could answer, Li Tieguai spun around on his crutch and, making no effort to hide his displeasure, said, "I no longer do much astral travel. The last time I tried, I was gone long enough that the man who I had asked to guard over my body decided to cremate me instead. When I returned, my spirit had nobody to enter—this was the only one available."

He looked down at the body he now called his own. "You can say I don't get around as much anymore." He laughed, but when he looked back at them, his features were harsh again. "Now hurry up!" he cried. "We don't have all day."

Salma made a sour face. "I don't like being ordered around," she muttered.

Sara sighed. "Me neither, but what else can we do?"

"Not again," Sanjeev said, his neck craned back, his eyes on the top of the doorway where a dragon stretched, one clawed paw frozen in the air, its head turned towards those who would approached the palace, its eyes as big and fiery red as the magma oozing from a volcano's caldera. Suddenly, all he wanted to do was to put his arms around his dog Jigsaw and pretend none of this was happening.

Seeing his hesitation, Sara said: "Come on. They don't bite."

"I hope you're right," Sanjeev said. "I hope you're right."

CHAPTER 24

—

Leaving the courtyard, the unmoving dragon, the immobile lions, the glowing red lanterns the size of barrels decorating the doorframe of the Palace, the three teens entered a surprisingly small room where two people, seated on embroidered cushions at a low wooden table set with a teapot and cups, were sipping tea. Both stopped and turned.

Sanjeev flinched and took a quick step backwards. "You again!" he said pointing at the man nearest them. "Lieutenant Han!"

The man, dressed in a flowing blue robe, stood up smartly and pushed the sword that hung at his waist to the side. "Lu Dongbin at your service," he said.

His friend, slim, dressed in a brown wheat robe, his dark hair pulled tightly into a knot tied with a ribbon of red silk on the crown of his head, stood and bowed as well. "And I am Han Xiang Zi." He looked at Sanjeev. "You may remember I was—"

"The messenger," Sanjeev said.

Han Xiang Zi gave the nod.

Sanjeev opened his mouth to ask where the other one was—the captain. What was his name? Zhongli Quan? —but Li Tieguai was too fast.

"Enough of this time wasting," Li Tieguai cried. "Han Xiang Zi, these three seem…stressed. Heal them—we will need them in top form for the pains they may yet endure."

"Eh?" Salma said. "What is that supposed to mean?"

Ignoring her, Han Xiang Zi removed a small flute from inside the sleeve of his robe and began playing, and the pure, low tones that arose began to resonate in the middle of Sara, Sanjeev, and Salma's heads, pulsing in time with the beating of their hearts. As Han Xiang Zi's fingers fluttered on the flute, the notes rose and fell in long, gentle trills until they faded to nothing. When he took the flute from his lips, he smiled. "You feel better, I hope."

"Where can I get a flute like that?" Sara asked, astonished. It was as if every one of her worries had melted like snow in warm water.

Salma had enjoyed the flute playing too, but she wasn't grinning like Sanjeev and Sara. Instead, her eyes were wary. "What did you mean by 'pains we may yet endure'?"

"We will get to that," Lu Dongbin said.

"Let's get moving," Li Tieguai said, stomping away on his crutch. "Follow me!"

"Please," Han Xiang Zi said, looking a bit embarrassed and indicating the door Li Tieguai had just gone through. "If you wouldn't mind following him."

Salma bit her tongue. Sanjeev shrugged. Sara frowned. All three shuffled out into a long corridor whose walls, though they appeared to be made of stone, shimmered such that Sara wondered if she reached out to touch them would her hand pass straight through them.

After walking in front of them in silence for a while, Li Tieguai suddenly stopped and turned. "Almost forgot. I must go and find Zhang Guolao and Cao Guojiu," he said, and before Sara could ask where Zhang Guolao—the old man she had met in her adventure— was, Li Tieguai had gone through a door and vanished.

"Let us continue," Han Xiang Zi said politely, slipping both his hands into the wide sleeves of his robe and Sara, Sanjeev, and Salma had no option but to follow, continuing down the same, long corridor behind the two remaining Immortals. As they walked, the sound of a horrible rattling, choking noise, distant at first, grew louder and louder with each step.

Lu Dongbin and Han Xiang Zi shook their heads. With a look of irritation on his face, Lu Dongbin pushed open the door they had reached and ushered Sara, Sanjeev, and Salma into the room.

There, a bearded man with a huge bare belly and chest was lolling on a couch, eyes closed, head back, his snores gurgling and spluttering like a blocked drain. A small fan of gold and white feathers lay on the floor next to him, presumably having slipped from his fingers.

On a chair opposite, also fast asleep, was another person. Younger, with no beard, a lusher head of hair, and wearing a blue, tattered gown, he was breathing quietly, a contented look on his face. Next to him, a basket of wildflowers sat. The flowers' brilliantly coloured faces open, blooms splendid, their heady, intoxicating scent filled the room.

As the three teens breathed it in, they began to feel light-headed, giddy, and a wave of sleepiness approached, threatening to overcome them until—

"Lan Caihe!" Lu Dongbin cried at the younger one. "Zhongli Quan! Wake up, both of you! We have guests."

Lan Caihe's head snapped up, and eyes wide, he regarded the three teens. "Oh, hello," he said in a voice as smooth as treacle, deep as a bass drum, and standing, brushed a hand down his tattered blue gown, snatched up the basket of fresh flowers, and smiled politely.

Salma noticed he only had one shoe on but didn't seem to care.

Zongli Quan, still prone, huge belly and chest rising and falling, continued to snore, blissfully unaware that all their eyes were on him.

Lan Caihe reached over and shook Zongli Quan's shoulder.

"Hmm?" he said, opening his eyes. Lan Caihe nodded at the others. Zongli Quan's eyes widened and in a blustering panic, he scrambled off the couch, but not before his hand had touched its fabric, and gold coins, appearing from nowhere, had spilled onto the floor. "Oops," he said, looking embarrassed. Straightening and swaying slightly: "I do beg your pardon. I am Zhongli Quan. I do not think I have had the pleasure of meeting you," he said to Sara.

"But you two," he said to Sanjeev and Salma, pointing the gold fan at them, "I know already."

"I recognise that voice," thought Sanjeev and Salma, gazing at the being in front of them, though Sanjeev was the first to make the connection.

"Captain!" he cried.

"Byrhtnoth!" Salma cried.

They both turned and looked at one another and Zhongli Quan chuckled politely. "The look on your faces," he said, fluttering his fan.

"I believe you know He Xiangu," Han Xiang Zi said to Sara and pointed.

Sara followed the direction of Han Xiang Zi's finger. A beautiful woman, seated against the far wall and dressed in a bright yellow, red, and white robe, appeared as if from nowhere. "Is that you, Princess Li Mei?"

"Hello, my dear," He Xiangu said, twirling a lotus blossom in one hand and waving the fingers of her other hand at Sara.

Sara waved back.

Salma, who had turned her attention to Lan Caihe, suddenly realised who she was looking at. "Wistan!" she exclaimed.

Lan Caihe smiled and with a flourish, transformed into the Viking boy Salma had met, before clicking his fingers and swapping Wistan's rough tunic for the blue, tattered gown once more. "But still minus a shoe," Salma noted, and she was about to ask what had happened to it when a door behind Lan Caihe opened and Li Tieguai stomped in, the end of his crutch banging on the ground, his grumpy, dirty face so different to the soft, dreamy expression of the man in the white robe directly behind him.

"Zang Guolao!" Sara exclaimed, surprised at how old and frail he now looked compared to the person she had met in her adventure.

"Sara!" Zang Guolao said, his white silk robe gently swishing, his voice rasping, "how nice to see you again."

"You, too," Sara replied as a third man, also old, carrying a jade tablet and dressed in a red scholar's uniform with a tall hat emerged from the doorway. His eyes briefly held those of Sara, Salma, and Sanjeev before they shyly turned away.

"Cao Guojiu. Won't you say hello?" Han Xiang Zi asked softly.

Cao Guojiu seemed to shrink into his clothes and with his neck retracting like a turtle's, his tiny, dark eyes flew back and forth like flies being swiped away by invisible hands. "Hello," he finally whispered.

Sara, Sanjeev, and Salma returned the greeting and Lu Dongbin cleared his throat loudly. "We have summoned you here to discuss your, er, involvement with Shan Wu," he said.

"The wraith who threatened each of you," Lu Dongbin added.

The image of the boy's face came back to each of them. It was during her time at the edge of a cliff on Ben Nevis for Sara. For Sanjeev, he was a boy he'd encountered underwater. To Salma, he was the scary weirdo on the Tube, a meeting that seemed mere minutes ago.

"He was a very powerful shaman," Lu Dongbin continued as Zang Guolao and Cao Guojiu seated themselves on cushions, "who got to the Jade Palace all by himself. Quite a feat. If only he'd used his powers for good…" his voice trailed off for a moment before he continued. "And now he has risen again and must be stopped."

"And how are we supposed to do that, exactly?" Salma asked.

"We suspect that he will be weakened from his time in the Jade Dragonball. It has been a thousand years since he has seen the sun and—"

"Wait a second," Salma said. "Dragonball?"

"Yes. That's what I said. Dragonball."

"And a dragonball is…?"

"What's a dragonball!? Dear me!" Lu Dongbin exclaimed. "What else can a dragonball be but a dragonball!"

Not appreciating Lu Dongbin's evasive non-answer, Salma said: "I mean, what does it *do*?"

"I had a dragonball in my adventure," Sara said, brandishing the piece of silk and pointing to the patterning. "It's like the ones on my dagger."

"Be careful with that!" Lu Dongbin cried. "That weapon can cut through anything!" Lowering his voice, "But you're right—the Jade Dragonball looks similar to those embellishments. We entrusted Shan Wu's education to a monk we hoped would be able to show Shan Wu the path to righteousness and teach him ren, benevolence. It didn't work out that way. Shan Wu tried to steal the Elixir of Immortality and was imprisoned in the Jade Dragonball. For all time. Or so we thought."

Han Xiang Zi shook his head sadly. "We were wrong."

"So how come it didn't work?" asked Sanjeev. "The imprisonment, I mean."

Zhongli Quan answered the quickest: "Because we'd never tried to imprison anyone in a Jade Dragonball before."

Sanjeev made a "sorry-just-asking face" and before he could ask what his key was for, Salma said: "OK, so why don't you take care of him? Why do we have to do it? I mean, we're just three kids. Why would we be able to stop this guy when you can't?"

Cao Guojiu, clutching his jade tablet close to his chest, said in a small voice: "We can't appear in your time and space, which is why we always manifest through the medium of art. Shan Wu, however, is at this very moment a material being in your universe."

Salma looked at Sara and then Sanjeev. "You understand what he's talking about? because I don't have a clue what he means."

Before either could reply, Lu Dongbin said: "All will become a little clearer after we consult the Book of Immutable Deeds."

"The what?" all three teens said.

"The Book. It records all fates and cannot be changed," Cao Guojiu said in a hushed voice.

"Talk, talk, talk: it won't solve any of our problems, you know. Let's get on with it!" Li Tieguai shouted and exiting through the room's third door, called over his shoulder: "Follow me!"

Han Xiang Zi made an apologetic face at the three teens, and in Sanjeev's ear, Lan Caihe, still holding his basket of flowers, whispered: "Don't mind him: he gets short-tempered when he's stressed."

Sanjeev wondered what he was supposed to say to that and tried to summon a sympathetic expression, which was difficult because if anyone deserved to be stressed, it was him, Salma and Sara; after all, they were the ones who knew least about what was going on.

Zang Guolao coughed and straightened his back. In a croaking voice, he said: "I apologise for Li Tieguai's manners, but he is not wrong. Time is against us: we must move quickly."

"Same old story," Salma grumbled. "We ask a question and you lot avoid answering it."

Lu Dongbin gave her a sharp look but said nothing. But Han Xiang Zi, standing next to him, raised his flute, played a short, sharp tune, and said: "Our enemy, Shan Wu, waits for no one."

As she stood staring past Han Xiang Zi at Zhongli Quan, Salma felt Sara's hand on one shoulder: then Sanjeev's on the other. "I'm just sick of it," she muttered.

"Well, whether we like it or not, we're here. And unless we do what they want, we're not going to get back home any time soon." Sara said.

Salma, though still upset, had to acknowledge the truth of that.

"We need you," Sanjeev said.

"So, you've made up your mind?" Salma asked him.

Sanjeev shrugged. "It's like Sara says. We don't get home until we do whatever it is we've been brought here to do. And…and I guess Shan Wu isn't such a good guy. He threatened my dog, Jigsaw. And Sara," he added quickly.

Salma couldn't deny that Shan Wu seemed dangerous or that the Immortals had plans for them, plans that they were unlikely to give up on. All the same, she wasn't about to jump blindly into the unknown. "I want to know *exactly* what I'm getting myself into before I sign up for anything," she said.

Zang Guolao, addressing Salma, said: "And if we explain everything? Would that persuade you?"

"Well, I'm not guaranteeing anything," Salma said, seeking the faces of Sara and Sanjeev. "But it might."

CHAPTER 25

—

Zang Guolao's small eyes shifted beneath his bushy, grey eyebrows to peer at Salma, then Sanjeev, then Sara. "If you are ready to know more, follow me," he said and swept past the three teens, his white robe a blur of motion. Twisting her head, eyes struggling to follow other fuzzy images, Salma gasped, imagining what an invincible martial artist she would be if she could move half as fast.

To her astonishment and that of Sara and Sanjeev's, she saw that the other seven Immortals, including Li Tieguai, still using his crutch, had joined Zang Guolao and were now distant figures standing at a doorway to another room, impatience written on all of their faces.

"Please do keep up," Han Xiang Zi cried and played a run of ascending notes on his flute.

"Come on!" Sara cried as she and Sanjeev dashed towards the doorway where the Immortals stood.

"Hold your horses," Salma mumbled. Nonetheless, following on their heels, she ran, too, quickly catching up.

As they neared the doorway, the Immortals stood aside, swishing their hands and ushering the three teens forward.

"Whoa!" Sara, still in front, suddenly cried, and hitting the brakes, she scrambled backwards away from what lay on the other side of the door, practically knocking Salma and Sanjeev out of the way.

The three teens, gathering themselves, stared through the doorway. Beyond, an enormously long corridor, walls lined with shimmering, gleaming mirrors as bright as polished diamonds, its floor formed of gently bobbing, white clouds, stretched on and on.

"It's safe," Lan Caihe assured them in a deep voice. And putting the foot that was bare first and following it with the one with the shoe, he stepped onto the clouds. Whisps instantly rose up and gathered into swirling vortexes; they climbed Lan Caihe's ankles and calves until reaching above the hem of his blue gown, they began to dissipate, sinking and eventually disappearing into the clouds from which they had arisen.

Lan Caihe, swinging his basket of flowers happily to and fro, grinned. "See? Perfectly safe!"

"Even for lesser beings such as you," Zhongli Quan added, fanning himself as he grinned.

Salma, not really appreciating the quip, barely managed a smile.

"What is that place?" Sara asked from the doorway, still not wholly convinced that following Lan Caihe onto the clouds was a great idea.

"That," Lu Dongbin said in a rather severe, militaristic voice, "is the Grand Hall!" And with his right hand clasped on his sheathed sword, he swept his left hand out and held it there, palm open, an invitation, it seemed to Sara, awestruck by the majesty of what lay before them.

"Er…didn't we agree on *Great* Hall?" piped a small voice from somewhere.

They all turned to see Cao Guojiu practically disappear into his red uniform and hat.

"Great? Grand? What difference does it make?" Lu Dongbin said, his left hand dropping to his side

"He's correct," He Xiangu said quietly but firmly, the tiny white bloom in her delicate hand suddenly swelling and turning to crimson. "We did agree to call it the Great Hall."

"Fine," Lu Dongbin muttered, looked abashed.

"So, shall we?" Zang Guolao said, gesturing that the three teens should step onto the clouds and into the Great Hall. "Lan Caihe is right. It is perfectly safe."

After a pause during which Sanjeev looked at Sara, who looked at Lan Caihe, Salma said, "May as well." In one quick step, she was on the clouds next to Lan Caihe, her face and body reflected in the Great Hall's mirrors.

With her feet and legs up to her knees hidden in swirling, white cloud, she glanced back at Sanjeev and Sara. "I'm still here. Come on."

Sanjeev was next to step through the doorway. "We're walking on air," he cried when Sara joined him. But Salma, ignoring the grins of the other two, pointed ahead.

"What's that?" she asked, meaning a towering object at the end of the corridor.

"That!" cried Lu Dongbin, his voice once again reaching parade-ground volume, "is The Book of Immutable Deeds!"

"Seriously? That's a book?" Salma asked, peering into the distance at what she had assumed was the side of a small house.

"It's big," Lu Dongbin said.

"You don't say?" Salma replied dryly.

Sanjeev smirked.

"Er...Is it moving?" Sara asked.

"Oh-oh! She's right!" Lan Caihe cried, suddenly clutching hold of Sara's arm. "Hold on!" The words had barely left his mouth when a great gust of wind struck like a hurricane, tearing at their clothes, pushing them backwards, threatening to send them tumbling all the way back to the room they had just left.

"What's happening?" Sanjeev cried, and—cheeks flapping, glasses threatening to fly off his face—he grabbed hold of the thick arms of Zhongli Quan who unlike everyone else, had stood tall, planted his feet, and pushed his face into the howling gale.

"Don't worry, it's turning a page," Lu Dongbin shouted. "It'll be over in a—"

And before he could finish his sentence, the torrent of air became rippling puffs which became gentle trickles and finally whispering breaths.

The Hares got to their feet having crouched behind the huddled figures of the other seven Immortals.

"Come on!" Lu Dongbin cried, springing to the front and urging them forward.

"I'm getting too old for this," Zang Guolao grumbled.

Sara took the old man's arm, linking it with hers. "We'll walk together," she said, returning the old man's smile.

"Seven years, seven months, and seven days," Cao Guojiu said quietly, adding, "before it turns a page again," when he saw Salma's puzzled face.

Soon, with only a brief but polite disagreement between Lan Caihe and He Xiangu over whether the mirrors in the Great Hall needed polishing or not, they were all standing in front of it: the Book of Immutable Deeds.

Sitting on a huge, jade pedestal, The Book lay open, its gargantuan pages being filled with Chinese characters smaller than the smallest ants. No hands were visible, but the characters tumbled down the huge pages like running water.

"What's it writing?" Sara asked.

"The Book and its characters," Zang Guolao replied, "are recording the stories of everyone who is living. In the full pages lie the stories of those who lived before; and in the pages beyond, the stories of those who have yet to live."

"May I take a closer look?" Sara asked Zhang Guolao.

"Certainly," she said and still arm-in-arm, he accompanied her as she stepped forward and peered closely at the writing.

"It's too small, I can't—," Sara said, but felt a tap on her shoulder.

"Try this," Cao Guojiu said, holding out a magnifying glass.

Even with the aid of the magnifying glass, the characters were minuscule, the tiny writing reminding her of a street artist in Beijing who had written her name on a grain of rice. As she watched, she realised there were also fainter characters which, well beyond the darker ones, swarmed in a disordered mass and constant state of flux.

"The present," Zhang Guolao said, indicating the darker characters that were being formed as they watched, "and the future," he said, pointing to the ever-shifting, ever-changing lighter characters.

"Is it dragon script?" Sara asked.

"Something like that," Zhang Guolao said.

"What's dragon script?" Sanjeev asked.

"The first Chinese characters were written on bones and turtle shells," Sara said. "They were used in divination—the priests thought that when they wrote a question on the bone or shell and then put the shell in the fire, they could read the answer in the cracks. The priests believed the oracle bones came from long dead dragons, so they called the writing on them dragon script."

"Cool," Sanjeev said.

"I wish I could understand it," Salma said, "The stuff in The Book, I mean."

"Let me show you instead," Cao Guojiu said and began looking around for something.

"Is this what you're looking for?" Lan Caihe said, holding up what looked like a videogame's controller. Cao Guojiu reached over to take it, but Lan Caihe stepped back keeping it out of Cao Guojiu's reach. "I'd like to show our friends…if you don't mind?"

Cao Guojiu bowed graciously, and Lan Caihe returned the bow. Straightening and hooking the basket of flowers onto his arm, he pressed the controller.

The three teens stared in amazement as the pages of The Book turned from paper into a silvery liquid and a scene appeared. But instead of the people in it moving at normal speed, they were walking and talking at a gallop… as if an impatient person was fast forwarding everything, which was exactly what Lan Caihe was doing.

"Slow down, please!" He Xiangu said.

Crutch raised; Li Tieguai took a swipe at Lan Caihe. "Idiot!" he hissed as Lan Caihe, clutching his basket and the controller, ducked, his expression suggesting this was not unusual behaviour on Li Tieguai's part.

"Please be more dignified," Han Xiang Zi said softly, flute in hand.

Li Tenguai stomped his crutch and muttered but otherwise seemed to take the reproach to heart. Lan Caihe, also looking mindful of the rebuke, pressed the button again and the picture slowed to show a boy, in normal speed, dressed in tattered clothes, being roughly shoved into a room by a large man whose hair, instead of the traditional topknot, hung down, long and unkempt. The boy fell at the feet of a grey-haired man whose face was dry and wrinkled.

The man looked down at the boy. "You would be wise not to waste my time. Who are you and what do you want?"

"I am Gong Wei, son of Gong Liu," the boy said looking up. The man looked the boy in the face, saw the twisted tooth, and experienced a painful jolt as name and face joined in his memory.

"Gong Wei," he said.

"Help him up, Zhang."

Zhang set the boy on his feet.

"I see the years since we last met have been harsh to you." He gestured for the boy to take a seat. "Tea for both of us," he told Zhang. "Now," the man said, turning again to Gong Wei, "what brings you here?"

Gong Wei bowed. "I have important news for you, Shan Tuo. I have seen your brother."

Shan Tuo jerked upright. "Shan Wu? Where? When?"

'Four months ago. In Khotan,' Gong Wei answered. "He was looking for you."

Shan Tuo was silent as Zhang brought in the tea. "Drink, Gong Wei." He took a pouch from his waist, untied it, and removed two gold coins. "You deserve more. And will get more if you will help me find Shan Wu."

Gong Wei stood and bowed deeply. "It would be my honour."

The image in the silvery liquid grew scrambled for a few seconds. When it cleared, it showed a man who was unmistakably

Shan Tuo but whose age had become impossible to determine, lying in a bed. The room was enormous, its walls covered with tapestries and silk hangings. Gong Wei, now many years older, came and stood by the bedside. No longer was he dressed in rags but in leather and steel.

Gong Wei bowed deeply. "Boss?"

Opening his eyes and drawing out a dagger from under the blanket, Shan Tuo held it up. "I warn you."

Gong Wei stepped back. "It's me, Boss. Gong Wei."

"Ah, Gong Wei. Forgive me; I thought you were one of Baojun's men," Shan Tuo said, shaking his head. "I must have been dreaming."

Gong Wei stood at attention without saying anything.

"I wonder, Gong Wei, have we tried looking for Shan Wu in Loyang?"

"Yes, Boss."

"Try Chengdu then."

"Yes, Boss."

As Gong Wei turned to leave, Shan Tuo called him again. "One more thing, Gong. Before you go—bring me my son."

"Yes, Boss."

Gong Wei, leading the child, returned a minute later. Shan Tuo had raised himself up in bed. "I wanted to tell you this Gong Wei, with both you and Shan Ming present. Should anything happen to me, you, and all of our men, are to regard Shan Ming as your new Boss. Is that understood?"

Gong Wei stood at attention and clasping his right fist in his left hand in front of him, bowed deeply. "All will be done according to your wishes."

Shan Tuo waved Gong Wei away with the back of his hand and smiled at the ten-year old boy in front of him.

"When the time comes, you will lead a great many men, Shan Ming. Ensure they are loyal—at any cost."

The shy boy's eyes burned bright in his wrinkled face, his aged features at odds with his high voice. "Yes, Father. I understand."

The scene dimmed and went blank.

"The person we imprisoned in the Jade Dragonball a millennium ago was Shan Wu, Shan Tuo's brother," said Lu Dongbin.

"And Chan got the condition from Shan Tuo," Sara said, remembering what her research had uncovered. Salma watched her, puzzled.

"Yes, it afflicted Shan Tuo's entire lineage. Shan Tuo is Chan's ancestor, the man who built the foundation for Chan's empire," replied Lu Dongbin.

Sara nodded eagerly. "Shan Tuo was thrown out of the Imperial Palace bureaucracy—"

"Correct," Lu Dongbin said, "And afterwards, he became a wealthy overlord, head of the Gang of the White Fawn, as ruthless as those who had pillaged his village when he was a boy. He died completely unaware of the fate that had befallen his older brother: of his transformation into the shaman Shan Wu and of this," Lu Dongbin said.

The silvery liquid once again showed a scene. This time, the three teens saw a boy simply dressed in the robes of a monk but with dark eyes so powerful they seemed to emit an electrical charge. They watched as the boy received a map from a plump, sly-looking merchant accompanied by a guard towering over them.

"Shan Wu," Zang Guolao whispered to Sara.

As they continued to watch, Shan Wu made his successful astral travel to the Jade Palace, drank the Elixir of Immortality, and confronted the Immortals. Fighting with them, Shan Wu fired a bolt of energy at Li Tieguai. The bolt struck the silver amulet around Li Tieguai's neck and broke into three pieces...

"The triskelion!" Sara and Sanjeev said at once.

Cao Guojiu said: "Yes, it was he who, straying from the Way and upsetting the proper order of the universe, destroyed the triskelion which is—"

"I still don't get it," Salma cut in. "Why us?"

"Let me explain," Lu Dongbin offered. "The wheel of time turns and that turn takes one thousand years. Shan Wu's banishment was one thousand years ago. You were born exactly one thousand years later, so you have the thousand-year power."

"That's it, in a nutshell," croaked Zang Guolao.

"Riiiight…" Salma said. "But what exactly is the thousand-year power? What does it do?"

He Xiangu rolled her eyes. "It doesn't do anything!" she said. "It just means that Shan Wu's fate and the fate of the children born at exactly the same time a thousand years after he was imprisoned in the Jade Dragonball are connected. The wheel of time is a wheel!" Her index finger traced the shape of a circle in the air.

"Yeah, great! Like drawing a circle in the air explains it all!" muttered Salma.

"What don't you understand?" asked Lu Dongbin.

"Er…lots of things," Sanjeev said.

"Be specific," Lu Dongbin shot back.

"OK. This thousand-year thing! Does it mean that every event that has ever happened is connected somehow to every child born a thousand years later?" asked Sara.

All of the Immortals answered at once: "Yes!"

Li Tieguai leaned over on his crutch and whispered in Han Xiang Zi's ear loud enough so everyone could hear. "I thought you said the Three Hares were smart?"

Han Xiang Zi hung his head in embarrassment.

Salma gave Li Tieguai a look.

"And the triskelion?" Sanjeev asked, "is like…a kind of transporter? To materialise and dematerialise us?"

Lu Dongbin frowned. "It's what stands between us and disaster, a disaster that Chan's actions have brought all of us closer to."

Sanjeev's eyebrows shot up. "Um… What?"

"You'll find out," He Xiangu said.

Salma threw her hands up. "Would someone tell me who this Chan person is!"

In response, Zhongli Quan slapped his great belly with one hand as though he found the idea that someone didn't know who

Chan was impossible to digest. "Chan," he replied, fanning his face, "is the greatest of all dangers to every human alive because he has succeeded where countless others have failed!"

"Succeeded ... how?" Salma asked.

"Chan has created what humankind has long sought," Zhongli Quan answered.

"I see," Salma said and when Zhongli Quan's dramatic and somewhat irritating pause had gone on long enough: "Which is?"

Zhongli Quan blinked in surprise. "Why," he replied in a tone that suggested it hardly needed explaining, "he has the Elixir of Immortality!"

CHAPTER 26

—

"Has created?" Salma said, narrowing her eyes and pausing to let her brain fully work out the implications of this revelation. "You mean this Chan person has already made it?"

Zhongli Quan nodded. "Indeed, he has."

"Soooo," Salma said, starting to grimace, "a future in which Chan uses the Elixir has been written in the Book of Immutable deeds?"

Zhongli Quan nodded again.

"And if it's in the Book of Immutable deeds, that means it can't be undone, right?"

"Chan has created the Elixir," Zhongli Quan agreed. "And yes, a future with Chan succeeding in his plans has been written."

"Right! Exactly! So that means there's *nothing* we can do about it. The future's been written, and we can't change the future because the Book of Immutable Deeds cannot be changed. All of which means," Salma cried triumphantly, "we're off the hook!"

It was Cao Guojiu who broke the silence. "Er…" he said, "I'm afraid…" From under his red hat, his eyes darted left and right in his almost perfectly round face. "I'm afraid that's not quite true."

"How come?" Salma asked, her smile dissolving.

"Because," answered Lan Caihe, plucking a flower from his basket, tossing it in the air, and watching it dissolve in a shower of petals, "you can tear the page out of the Book of Immutable Deeds and reset the future!"

"Rip out a page? From that thing? Are you serious?" Salma said, her eyes slowly climbing to the top of the Book's mountainous pages.

"Hold on," said Sanjeev. "If we can rip the pages out of the Book of Immutable Deeds and change the future, why can't we rip out the part where Chan creates the Elixir?"

"Yeah! Great idea Sanjeev!" Salma agreed. "Let's rip out those pages; then we can all go home!"

"Unfortunately," Han Xiang Zi said, looking as if he wanted to play something happy on his flute to mitigate the unhappiness he knew he was about to inflict, "it's more complicated than that."

"Surprise, surprise," Salma muttered. "And how's that?"

Cao Guojiu, clutching his tablet tightly to his chest as though it were a child, said: "The past is the past; it cannot be changed. But the future is mere potential: it is a river with many channels. The Book's words about the future Chan wants to create are a channel along which the river will run if and only if tomorrow becomes today."

Salma stared at him. "Seriously?" she said. "So, we only have the power to change the future if we act now."

Zang Guolao, chuckling at Sara's side, gave Salma an admiring look. "Precisely, young woman."

"Shall we show them?" Lan Caihe asked, his voice deep again.

"Yes, let's show them," Zang Guolao said.

"Show us what—?" Salma began, but before she could finish her question, the clouds below the feet of the three teens cleared and they found themselves looking down on a dimly lit room in which three men were gathered around a small cage.

"Where is this?" Sanjeev asked.

"You are looking at a room in Chan's underground complex in Xi'an," Lu Dongbin informed him.

"Live from Las Vegas…" Sanjeev said in a silly voice and looked around. When no one laughed, he cleared his throat and pushed his glasses to the bridge of his nose. "Tough audience," he said under his breath.

"Quiet!" Lu Dongbin told him.

Sanjeev shushed and returned his eyes to the scene below where one of the men had put on surgical gloves and was reaching into the cage. To the surprise of the three teens, he pulled out a dead rat, its eyes closed, its small paws clenched, mouth hanging open so that its yellow teeth were visible. Lifting it by the tail, the man raised it up, showing it to another man.

"The one looking at the rat is Chan," Zang Guolao said.

"That…that's not Chan!" Sara cried, remembering the withered old man's face she had seen in the newspaper and on the Internet. This boy was far too young, far too healthy-looking, and yet… there was something about the boy's expression: an obnoxious mixture of slyness and amusement. "It can't be!" she gasped.

"It is," Lu Dongbin replied.

"But how?"

Lu Dongbin pointed to the tall man holding up the rat. "His name is Lin Dan and he is the world's foremost bio-engineer. Chan used him to accomplish one of the phases in his Tian Shan Project."

"To cure his degenerative disease?" Sanjeev said, putting two and two together.

"Precisely," Zang Guolao said, smiling appreciatively.

"One of the phases?" Salma asked.

"There were a number: finding the Jade Dragonball, stealing the jade suit, building an underground complex in Xi'an, extracting Shan Wu from the Jade Dragonball, creating, with the help of Lin Dan, an Elixir of Immortality from Shan Wu's blood…many."

"So, thanks to him and his Tian Shan Project, we're floating on clouds," Salma muttered.

"I suppose so," Zang Guolao agreed.

"So, is he a bad guy?" Sanjeev asked, meaning Lin Dan.

"He was kidnapped, threatened, and forced to work for Chan," Zang Guolao said. "No blame attaches to him."

"Who's the other one?" Salma asked.

"The square-shouldered one is An Ho," Lu Dongbin replied, and as they all continued to watch, Chan grinned.

"Dead enough," Chan said, prodding the rat.

Lin Dan nodded, and placing the rat back in its cage, he picked up a small beaker containing a bright blue fluid, took a syringe, inserted it into the liquid and filled it partway. He held it up to the light, needle point up, measured the contents, and squeezed the plunger so that a little fluid squirted out. "After the improvements, synthesising and isolating the active ingredients in the fingerite, I adjusted my calculations. As a result, an animal this size should only require 1.5 cc," he said, and injecting the contents of the syringe into the rat's neck, he stood back.

"How long?" Chan asked, his eyes riveted on the dead animal.

"A few minutes," Lin Dan answered.

Chan continued staring at the rat, so hard he did not appear to be blinking. Lin Dan looked at his watch and at the rat. With the back of his forearm, he wiped the sweat droplets gathering at his brow.

Chan's brows furrowed. "When—"

He stopped. One of the rat's whiskers quivered. Leaning down, his nose almost touching the animal, he stared intently at the little corpse in front of him.

A tiny paw twitched. A leg shook. An ear curled. An eyelid flickered. And suddenly, the rat's whole body was convulsing, leaping, and flapping around like a fish out of water.

Startled, Chan shuffled a few steps back but quickly came forward again, watching while the rat continued its jolting dance until the movements slowed and finally ceased.

Chan's eyes narrowed. He raised his head and glared at Lin Dan.

"There!" Lin Dan said, pointing at the rat which was lying on its side.

Chan looked down. A grin spread across his face as he stared at the rise and fall of the rat's chest. As he watched its tiny lungs busy filling and emptying with air, the rat opened its eyes and, as if waking from a long sleep, it blinked rapidly. Lifting its head, it emitted a high-pitched squeak, and with its tiny nails scuffing against the tabletop, it flipped itself onto its front and stood on all four legs, stationary except for its small, dark eyes which scanned its surroundings, its tail flicking back and forth, and its darting nose which sniffed cautiously at the air.

"Excellent!" cried Chan, watching as the rat was captured by Lin Dan and stuffed back into its cage. "And now we are ready for further testing, are we not?"

Eyes down, Lin Dan closed the cage and nodded

Chan turned to An Ho. "Bring him in."

Chan gave a curt bow and moments later returned with a narrow-shouldered man half his size. From below bushy eyebrows, the man's eyes scanned the room before he bowed low to Chan.

"Sit," Chan told him.

The man obeyed immediately, sitting on the only chair in the room.

"Fang," Chan said, "as a reward for your many years of service…you have been selected to lead a program that will give our conglomerate world-wide power. It will require some small sacrifice on your part, but it will bring you and your family great honour. Can I rely on you?"

"Sure thing, Boss. What've I got to do?"

"You will be receiving two injections, Fang. You will feel unwell, but you are not to worry."

"Yes, Boss," Fang said.

"Roll up your sleeve," Chan said.

Without hesitation, Fang rolled up his left sleeve, revealing the tattoo of a large phoenix, its long red feathers encircling his forearm. He beamed at Chan. "Thank you for this honour, Boss."

Chan nodded at An Ho who circled Fang's wrists with leather straps, fixing them to the arms of the chair. After checking to make sure both were secure, An Ho nodded at Chan who ushered Lin Dan forward. Taking a syringe, Lin Dan filled it with pale yellow fluid. As he approached Fang, An Ho tied a rubber tube around Fang's upper arm, which made the veins on his arm bulge.

Leaning down, Lin Dan found the largest of the veins and using one finger to mark the spot, he stuck the needle in, depressed the plunger, and emptied the contents into Fang.

As Fang watched with delight, Lin Dan removed the needle and spoke to Chan. "I injected 50 mg. of tetrodotoxin obtained from the Japanese blowfish. This is twice as much as is regarded lethal for a 75 kg human. The toxin blocks the patient's sodium channels, leading to a loss of sensation, muscular paralysis and, within 5 minutes, death."

Fang's mouth fell open. "Wha—?" he said, his eyes shooting from Lin Dan's face to Chan's. "Did...did he say death?"

Chan's voice was gentle. "Relax, Fang, relax."

"Boss..." Fang began, but stopped. His eyes rolled mouth suddenly sagged, and drool ran from its corner.

Three minutes later, Lin Dan pronounced him dead. Turning and filling another syringe with a blue fluid, Lin Dan said: "As instructed, I will now administer 1.5 cc. of the Elixir."

The injection was straight into Fang's neck. Once the syringe was empty, Lin Dan put it back on the table and took a couple of steps away.

The room was so quiet, Chan could hear An Ho's watch ticking. Each second seemed to take longer than the last until Fang's shoulders twitched without warning, and a spasm moved through his body as though he were being electrocuted: his legs quivered; his back arched; his head thrashed from side to side.

A deep-throated scream tore from Fang's lungs, startling Chan.

But a second later, Fang's shoulders slumped. His face slackened, his eyelids flickered, and his eyes blinked opened. "Boss?" he said weakly.

Chan patted his arm and smiled. "How are you feeling?"

"Like I've gone one too many rounds with a pro-boxer, Boss." He shifted his weight in the chair. "But better every second."

Lin Dan measured Fang's vitals. "At present, the patient is exhibiting a slower heart rate and lower temperature than before the first injection, but both are within the normal range and stabilising. We have witnessed complete recovery."

"Did I do well, Boss?" Fang asked.

"Very well," Chan assured him.

Fang grinned at Lin Dan. "So, when you gonna let me outta these?" he asked, pulling at the straps that were still wrapped around his wrists.

There was no reply.

The smile that had spread on Fang's face disappeared. "Hey!" he said again, fear creeping into his voice, "let me out of these." And trying desperately to rise, he yanked at one of the straps holding his arm to the chair.

"Be patient," Chan snapped at him.

"Yes, Boss," Fang replied obediently.

Time ticked by: five minutes, ten, fifteen, and it was a minute before the expected twenty that Fang's face, watched carefully by Chan, suddenly contorted into a grimace and Chan saw it—a dull, stone-coloured patch spreading from the spot where the first injection had been administered. As he watched, the grey patch race Fang's arm, covering the skin in what looked like quick-drying cement. A second later, Fang's face was covered in greyness and his body, no longer moving, was frozen like a statue.

Only his eyes remained mobile. Panic-stricken, pleading, they sought out Chan.

Chan seemed lost in delight for a long moment, looking at the eyes that silently begged for help. When he finally spoke, his voice was rapturous.

"You have served us well, Fang. Thanks to you, we know we have succeeded. We raised you from the dead and made you immortal, but the dose we gave you was too small. Those who want to become immortal—billions and billions of people—will need to inject a sufficient quantity of our Elixir every day of their lives unless they want to spend the rest of eternity as Stones like you!"

He did not see Fang's eyes widen in horror as he turned and spoke to An Ho.

"We begin bottling immediately," he told him.

CHAPTER 27

—

Calmly, thoughtfully, Salma said: "OK, so Chan's a bad guy: he plans to make everyone addicted to and reliant on his Elixir of Immortality. Got it. But how are we supposed to defeat him? And Shan Wu? I suppose we've got to deal with him too?"

"That is correct, my dear," Zang Guolao said. "Though Shan Wu is in the same complex, he is not yet fully reanimated."

"OK. So, to repeat: my question is how? How are we supposed to deal with Shan Wu when not even you could deal with him?"

"You have everything you need," Lu Dongbin said. "In addition to the triskelion, you were each given objects of great power: the Hands of Fate. These will aid you in your efforts to—"

"You mean my Monkey key?" Sanjeev said. "If he comes close, I should poke him in the ribs with it?"

Lu Dongbin's scornful expression wiped off Sanjeev's smile. "These are no ordinary objects," he said gravely. "Used correctly, they will help you to win this battle."

Sara tried prompting him. "And they'll help because…"

A silence fell until Zang Guolao, still beside her, finally spoke. "The key is also a lock; the silk a knife; the map a desire."

"Great," Sara muttered in sarcastic tone. "That certainly made everything so much clearer."

"What I will say—" Zang Guolao said.

"Yes?" Salma said, eager to hear more.

"Is that the Hands of Fate and the triskelion can only be wielded by the good."

"Oh," Salma said, trying to hide her disappointment.

"The good?" Salma asked.

"The good," Zang Guolao repeated.

Salma sighed. But Sanjeev said: "If we're really the only ones who can stop Chan, we have to do it, right?" He looked at Sara who looked at Salma, who looked unconvinced.

"You said we'd have to rip out a page in the Book of Immutable Deeds to reset the future?" Sara said to Zang Guolao.

Zang Guolao smiled sweetly and patted her hand. "Indeed, I did. But don't worry: it's easier than it looks."

"Anyone got a ladder?" Sanjeev smirked. A stony silence met his joke. "Er, just trying to…you know."

"He's got a point," Salma said. "How are we supposed to rip anything from that thing?"

"Reach up," Cao Guojiu said, his voice so faint, it was barely audible.

Salma, gazing at the pages towering above them, snorted. "Did you say 'reach up'?"

Eyes down, the jowls on his round face quivering, Cao Guojiu nodded five times in quick succession.

Salma raised her eyebrows so high, they threatened to fly off her forehead.

"Try it," Zang Guolao said, and coming forward, he gently took Salma by the arm and guided her to where Sara and Sanjeev were standing.

Watched curiously by Salma, he said: "Now please join hands with one another."

Salma grimaced. "If you want us to line-dance, you'll need to put on some music," she grumbled but did what the old man wanted and clasped Sara's hand.

Now that they were in a line—Sara in the middle, her left hand held by Salma; her right, held by Sanjeev—Zang Guolao said: "Reach up to the nearest page, Salma." He motioned towards her free hand.

He turned to Sanjeev. "Reach up to nearest page, Sanjeev," he repeated, gesturing towards Sanjeev's free hand.

Eyes on one another, Salma and Sanjeev tried not to laugh.

"Be serious," commanded Zang Guolao. "On that page lies a future," he told them.

Straightening their faces, Salma and Sanjeev slowly raised their hands.

"Now grasp it at the top," Zang Guolao continued. "Good. Good, that's it," he whispered as the tip of the page twitched.

"Do you…?" Sanjeev asked, amazed.

"Yeah!" Salma said, equally astonished.

"Good! Now hold tight and pull!" Zang Guolao said. "Pull as hard as you can!"

Sanjeev and Salma's eyes riveted to the page, finger and thumbs pressed tightly together, heaved, watching in amazement as the page began separating from its spine.

"Keep going," Lan Caihe whispered, his voice suddenly softer than He Xiangu's.

"It's coming away," Salma cried as the page curled over and like a racing wave, started tumbling down the face of the book.

"Er…" Sanjeev said, eyes on the roaring sea of paper rushing towards them. "We should—"

"Have faith!" Lu Dongbin yelled. "Keep going."

Like a mountainous wave, the page loomed above them, its crest casting the darkest of shadows, its weight threatening to squash them like bugs.

"Don't stop!" Zhongli Quan bellowed, belly wobbling, fan flapping furiously.

"It's going to crush us!" Sanjeev yelled.

But just as the paper tsunami threatened to land on all three of the teens, it began to dissolve, the paper turning into a billion tiny flickers of light, the sparkling drops falling harmlessly on them like brilliantly-lit snow and instantly disappearing.

"C-coool," Sanjeev said, feeling relieved.

"Well done, all of you," Zang Guolao said, patting each of the Hares on the back in turn as the other Immortals joined in the praise.

"So," Lu Dongbin said when the congratulations had ended, "if there are no more questions, we'll push on and you can go and stop Chan selling the Elixir of Immortality…"

"Er…I've got a question," Salma said, looking at the faces of the Immortals which wore mixed expressions: interest, amusement, puzzlement, and irritation.

"When did you find out Chan was making the Elixir of Immortality?"

He Xiangu, wafting her lotus blossom, said in a sweet voice: "how clever of you."

"During Sanjeev's adventure," Lu Dongbin muttered, not meeting Salma's eyes. "We saw Chan find the Jade Dragonball, kidnap Lin Dan, make his plans."

"So, let me get this straight: you had already chosen Sara before you saw Chan making the Elixir, right?"

Zhongli Quan harrumphed and slapped his belly, readying to interrupt.

"Let her speak," Zang Guolao said with a knowing look. "Yes, my dear. That is correct."

"So," Salma said, eyes narrowed, "the reason for choosing Sara couldn't have been to stop Chan from making the Elixir because Chan made it *after* Sara's adventure!"

Sara and Sanjeev stared at Salma.

"She's right!" Sara told Sanjeev.

"You're right!" Sanjeev told Salma.

"I knew she was smart," Li Tieguai said, pointing his crutch at Salma. Lan Caihe gave him a disbelieving glance.

"Well?" Salma asked. "Are you going to explain or not?"

Zang Guolao, white robe rustling, stepped forward and gently placed a hand on Salma's shoulder. His ancient eyes looked into hers. "We saw the future: Chan's *plans* were also written in the Book of Immutable Deeds. Those *plans* told us that Chan wanted to make humans slaves to his potion. And we," he gestured to the other Immortals, "initiated a course of action to stop them coming to fruition."

"And of course," he continued, having given Salma time to digest what he had said, "we sensed Shan Wu's power inside the Jade Dragonball was growing; that he was reaching out and we would need the help of the Three Hares. That was *before* we approached Sara."

"OK, but can't we just tear out Shan Wu's role in history from the Book of Immutable Deeds? Make him disappear?" Salma asked, trying to sound hopeful but suspecting she knew the answer already.

Zang Guolao shook his head slowly. "The past cannot be undone. We can only do something about the future."

After that, a silence fell, eventually broken by Sara, who addressed Salma. "If we don't stop Chan and people take his elixir?" She puffed out her cheeks and shook her head.

"How do we know they're telling the truth?" Salma asked.

"Well, we kinda have to assume they are," Sanjeev said. "Because the consequences of not believing them and doing nothing are worse." Registering the puzzled faces of Salma and Sara, he stumbled on. "If the intended consequences are good, it's better to do something rather than nothing even if the reasons for doing it aren't—"

"We're their puppets," Salma said, silencing Sanjeev. "Not very heroic, is it?"

"I'd say it is," Sara replied. "We're not doing any of this for some kind of personal reward."

"Heroes," Zang Guolao said before Salma could reply to Sara, "are called forth to do great work."

The three teens gazed into one another's faces. Wordlessly, the same thought was being exchanged: Chan and Shan Wu had to be stopped, and they would have to do it, for the sake of everyone.

And with that decision, the tension in the air eased and faded away.

"So," Lu Dongbin said, "if there are no additional questions?"

Salma shrugged, which was good enough for Lu Dongbin.

"Excellent," he said. "Please join hands and make a circle."

Reluctantly, Salma retook Sara and Sanjeev's hands.

"The future," he cried, "is shared by those who trust one another!"

"Yeah. I think I read that on a fortune cookie once," Salma said, her tone acid.

"But you haven't told us how to use the Hands!" Sara said.

Too late, Sara realised as everything around her warped and twisted and her stomach turned to jelly. Salma uttered the last words she heard before the darkness fell.

"Oh, goodie," she heard her say grumpily.

It made her smile.

PART 5

XI'AN, CHINA
THE PRESENT DAY

CHAPTER 28

—

When the spinning and dizziness ended and their heads cleared, they stared at one another and at themselves. Each carried their own piece of the triskelion and what the Immortals called their Hand of Fate. They were standing inside some sort of compound whose tall fence, topped with barbed wire, surrounded them on all sides. Barely an arm's length away, one on top of the other, hundreds of black barrels stood, each carrying the a painted mark of white skulls and crossbones.

"Poison," Sanjeev whispered as all three edged as far away as they could, which wasn't far at all.

"What a great place to land," Salma sighed.

But it was what lay in front of them that really shook them. Beyond the compound fence, rising into the night like the world's biggest chemistry experiment and lit by glaring spotlights, a huge factory sat: its bulbous chambers, colossal funnels, towering chimneys, massive storage tanks all connected by a thousand steel pipes that snaked and branched like the veins of a giant, metal monster.

Sanjeev pointed. "Look!"

High above the ground, on the tallest of the chambers for all the world to see, a sign shone in neon lights:

CHAN CHEMICALS
Establish The Hegemon

A shiver ran down Sara's back as she remembered Shan Wu's haunting eyes and the tattoo with the same words on his arm.

"I could be wrong," Sanjeev said, "but I'd say this is Chan's bottling plant."

"What would we ever do without you?" Salma grinned.

The sound of voices.

All three hunkered down behind the nearest barrel, careful not to touch it.

As they watched, two men passed by, each carrying guns. When they were sure the men had gone, they rose.

Salma whispered: "Now what?"

Sanjeev eyed the sturdy-looking padlock and thick chains wrapped around the compound's gate. "I guess I could try unlocking it with this." He waved his key.

"Or Sara could use the dagger," Salma said. "Does it really cut through anything?"

Sara shrugged. "So, we get out of here; then what? I mean, we need to know where we're going, right?"

The three gazed at the massive factory in front of them.

Sanjeev puffed his cheeks. "Anyone see a sign for 'Bad Guy This Way'?"

Salma reached into her pocket. "Who needs a sign when you've got a map?"

"Does it…?" Sara asked.

"Let's find out," Salma said and opened the map.

Sara and Sanjeev goggled at the small, wispy objects that had risen.

"The Viking cosmos: the nine worlds and the sacred tree, Yggdrasil," Salma told them, enjoying the fantastic looks on their faces.

But as she watched along with Sara and Sanjeev, the cosmos began to sink slowly into the skin of the map until it had disappeared entirely. In its place, like fast-growing plants, tiny three-dimensional factory buildings were sprouting up to reveal rooftops, walls, and alleyways between them. This jungle of tiny buildings quickly covered most of the map, but a small house sat by itself in one corner next to a smooth, dark mound the size of a large, flat pebble.

A spider's web of lines ran below it, extending out towards the mound and off the edge of the map.

"Are those…?" Sanjeev asked, pointing to three tiny, neon-green icons next to the factory.

Salma held the map closer to her face. "Rabbits…" She shrugged. "Or hares."

"That," said Sanjeev, stabbing a finger at a small building with dark lines under it running to the far corners of the map, "could be the start of Chan's underground complex."

"Could be," Sara agreed and paused. "That hill and those lines…" she said indicating the mound towards the middle of the map.

Sanjeev saw an odd look in her eyes. "What?" he asked.

"I recognise this now. We had to study these layouts in our history class."

"You studied Chan's lair?" Sanjeev said.

"No," Sara said, rolling her eyes. "The tomb of the First Emperor. See, we're not just close to the excavation grounds in Xi'an; we're practically on top of them."

"What do you mean?" Salma asked.

"Well, here's where we are," Sara said, pointing to the icons glowing next to the Post-it sized sign. "And here," she said, pointing farther up the map to a mound that rose out of the map like a small paper volcano, "is Qin Shi Huang's mausoleum."

"Where he's buried?" Sanjeev asked, even though he was pretty sure he knew the answer.

"Oh, not just where he's buried," Sara said. "In preparation for the afterlife, he buried hundreds of people with him. It's more of…" It took her a second to find the right word. "A necropolis."

"A city of the dead?" Sanjeev asked, his eyes wide.

"Exactly," Sara replied.

A shiver ran down Sanjeev's spine, and someone began whistling tunelessly from some unseen place nearby.

"If there are guards here," Sanjeev whispered, "there are probably guards everywhere. I wish the Immortals had put us closer to Chan…"

His voice trailed off. Sara and Salma were giving him funny looks. "What?" he asked. Quickly, he replayed what he had just said in his head. "Oh…" he said, "I got it. But how does it work?"

"Your wish is to go to Chan's underground complex, right?" Salma asked.

"I guess so," Sanjeev said, a little warily.

"And Zang Guolao said the map is a desire, right?" Sara asked.

Sanjeev nodded his head. He wasn't sure he liked where this was going…

Sara and Salma took a few steps backwards.

"Er…what are you two—" he began, but before he could finish his sentence, Salma put her finger on the icon that was slightly separate from the others, dragged it across the map and released it.

"Cool," Sara said, laughing at the empty space where Sanjeev had been standing a second ago. "But we should bring him back."

"If you insist," Salma chuckled, and placing her finger on Sanjeev's icon, she dragged it back to where they were.

"Hey!" Sanjeev cried, appearing as suddenly as he had disappeared, "that was unauthorised! I ended up in a cupboard!"

"I guess it works," Sara said, biting her lip and trying not to laugh at Sanjeev's irritation.

"Now," Salma said, "no whining or…" She motioned with her finger towards what looked like a distant hilltop.

"Great," Sanjeev said. "You've got a teleporter. Sara's got a knife, according to Lu Dongbin, that cuts through anything. And I get a key to poke the bad guy in the ribs."

Sara said, her voice full of mock sympathy, "There, there."

"You are so mean," Sanjeev said, trying not to smile.

"Hey," Sara said, pointing to two men striding towards them, guns off their shoulders, barrels pointing, "I think it's time we got out of here."

"Fasten your seatbelts," Salma cried and with three fingers on the icons, she swiped them across the map.

CHAPTER 29

—

As though they had fallen down a hole, they landed with a thump on their backs and groaned.

As soon as Salma had swiped, lights had sparkled, air had rushed over them, and a noise like someone talking a thousand times faster than normal had filled their heads. Now, as they lay on the ground, it felt like they had left their stomachs behind and needed to wait for them to catch up.

"That was worse than when you swiped me the first time," Sanjeev croaked, struggling to get to knees.

"Not fun," Salma agreed, clasping her stomach, and standing next to Sara who was doing likewise.

They were in a dark passageway whose low height, narrow width and rough stone walls made Sanjeev think of a subway tunnel. A bead of sweat, then another and another formed on his brow. Ahead of him, the tunnel broadened, opening out into a bigger, more brightly lit cavern.

"We can read it better over there," he said, his throat tightening, a part of his brain insisting that the tunnel's walls were narrowing, the air thinning, the temperature rising.

"Are you OK?" Salma asked, looking concerned.

Before Sanjeev could answer, someone hissed.

"*Psst!*"

The three turned.

A pair of hands were wrapped around the bars in a grille set in a heavy wooden door. Behind the bars, staring, bloodshot eyes, deep-set in a thin face, regarded them. "What are you doing here?"

The three immediately recognised the man who had administered the poison and the Elixir to Fang: Lin Dan.

"We're here to save the world," Salma said breezily. "You?"

For a second, Lin Dan looked dumbfounded. Gathering his thoughts, he eyed them suspiciously. "Who are you?"

"I'm Salma. This is Sanjeev and this is Sara. And you are Lin Dan, the man who helped Chan develop the Elixir of Immortality."

Lin Dan's jaw dropped.

"We saw everything," Sara said, answering his unvoiced question.

"From the Jade Palace," Sanjeev added.

For a moment, it was clear from Lin Dan's face that he didn't know whether to laugh or scoff. "How did you get in here?"

"The Eight Immortals transported us," Salma said, kind of enjoying how ridiculous it sounded.

Lin Dan fell silent for a moment. Quietly, he said: "Get me out here?" The tone of his question suggested it was a test to see what the three teens would say or do.

"No problem," Sara replied, pulling out a rectangle of soft, highly patterned material. "My silk dagger can cut through anything."

Salma's eyebrows shot up as she regarded Sara's hands and the floppy, brilliantly coloured silk there.

"Wait," Sanjeev said as Sara pinched a corner of the silk, preparing to flick it three times, "I wanna see…" And taking out the gold monkey key, he slipped it into the cell's locked door. But no matter which way he twisted and turned the key, the door stayed locked. With as much dignity as he could muster, he pushed his glasses to the top of his nose and slipped the key into his pocket. "I'll be waiting for you over there," he said, indicating the end of the tunnel.

"OK," Salma said distractedly, still wondering how on earth a piece of fabric was going to cut through the massively heavy looking door in front of them. Even a chainsaw—ten chainsaws—would struggle to do *that*!

"I'm going to try the silk dagger now," Sara said, raising her hand once again. To Lin Dan, "Stand back." But before she could flick the silk dagger even once, a door next to the cell opened and a man dressed in a black suit and a white, unbuttoned shirt came out.

"What the…" the man said, reaching for the gun strapped under his arm. It was all he managed to do. A moment later, he had crumpled, the flying kick from Salma having caught him under the chin and knocked him senseless.

Sara was almost as stunned as the man unconscious at her feet. "Whoa, how did you do that?"

Salma stifled a laugh. "It's not a superpower," she said. "I do taekwondo I'm, er, a red belt."

"You've gotta teach me when we have time. That was awesome!"

Salma smiled and pointed to the gun. "Should we take that?"

"Do you know how to fire one?" Sara asked.

"Nope," Salma said. "You?"

Sara shook her head. "Me, neither." She looked towards Sanjeev who was standing at the entrance to the tunnel, back turned.

"Sanjeev!" Sara breathed. "Do you know how to fire a gun?"

Turning, Sanjeev frowned. "Yeah, you point it and pull the trigger."

"But seriously…" Sara asked.

"There's no way I'm gonna use one," he said firmly.

Salma shrugged. "He's probably right." Suddenly her eyes lit up and reaching down, she extracted something from beneath the man and held it up.

"A mobile. Nice," Sara said. "Face recognition?"

"Yup," Salma said. Sara held the man's head straight, Sanjeev instinctively came over and opened the man's eyes, Salma held the phone over the unconscious man's face and the home screen instantly opened. Salma quickly went into security and changed the screen lock setting, making sure the phone wouldn't lock them out.

"OK?" Sara asked.

"Done," Salma told her.

"Back to where I was," Sara said, and stepping over the still unconscious guard, she flicked the silk three times. The next moment, the soft fabric was a glistening double-edged dagger, its hilt wrapped in Sara's fingers, its lethally sharp blade decorated with the same dragon-and-puzzle ball pattern.

Lin Dan was staring wide-eyed at her. "How...?"

"Stand back," she told him.

As soon as he had gone far enough away, Sara raised her arm and paused. A flicker of doubt crossed her mind. *Can it really cut through anything?* She brought the tip of the dagger to the wood and touched it. As though the wood were chocolate and the dagger a red-hot knife, the wood began to dissolve and with a start, she realised the dagger had cut through the door and she could see into Lin Dan's cell, which was filled with books and all sorts of chemistry and computing equipment. "OK. Guess it does," she said to herself and with dagger's tip barely touching the surface, she traced a circle all around the door, feeling no friction as the dagger sliced through iron hinges and dense wood. When she returned to her starting point, she stood back and with the satisfaction that came from a job well done, prodded the door with her finger and watched as it creaked and tipped backwards.

The door hit the ground with a heavy thud and a grimy cloud rose. Sara, coughing, flicked the silk dagger three times and returned it to a less deadly form.

Through the dust, Lin Dan's face peeked out.

"It's safe," Salma told him. "You can come out now."

"That...that was *amazing*," he said, eyes on the door, stepping his skinny legs over it like a crane over a stone.

"She's amazing," Salma said.

Sara grinned.

"You're all amazing," Lin Dan said, and grabbing Sara and Salma, he hugged them tight. "I've been that monster's prisoner for months. He made me—"

"We kinda know," Salma said, feeling awkward.

"You're not the bad guy," Sara assured him.

Lin Dan released them. "I had to do what he asked…" he said, wiping away the tears that had flooded his eyes. "My family? Are they safe?"

"I'm sure they are," Sara said.

"I've got to get out of here," Lin Dan said. "I've got to see my family!"

"Come on," Salma said, and as the three of them exited the tunnel, they found Sanjeev staring at a huge brightly coloured painting that reached from the dusty cavern floor to its lofty ceiling.

"Who's he?" Sanjeev asked, pointing to the huge canvas.

Sara recognised the man immediately. Sword at his side, wearing a yellow robe whose gold border was richly embroidered with intertwining dragons, two long curtains of beads fell from the tall cap on his head, reaching down to the man's sturdy shoulders and framing his solemn, black-bearded face and dark, penetrating eyes.

"Qin Shi Huang," Sara said, "the First Emperor."

Tearing her eyes away from the monumental face, Salma handed the mobile to Lin Dan. "Take it and call the police when you get out. We've got an appointment with Chan and a thousand-year-old shaman called Shan Wu that we need to keep."

Lin Dan snatched it from her. But instead of running to wherever the exit was, he stood very, very still, head bowed, gazing at the device that lay in his hands. In the silence, the three teens gave one another puzzled looks, and Sara was on the point of asking what the problem was when Lin Dan suddenly gave a tortured "Agh!", looked at them, squeezed his eyes shut, and opened them again. "I…I should help you," he said.

"Are you sure you want to do that?" Sara asked.

Lin Dan tightened his jaw and nodded. "I extracted blood from…" his face clouded at the memory, "an ancient body inside a jade suit, and I used its blood to develop the Elixir, so I should—"

"Ah, ha!" Sara and Sanjeev said together.

Lin Dan and Salma's faces were like two big question marks.

"When Sanjeev was at the Met in New York," Sara explained, "he told me someone stole an ancient jade suit."

Salma shook her head. "Still don't understand."

"The ancients," Sara continued, "believed a body encased in jade would be preserved for ever."

"Oh…now I get it: a Jade Suit to keep Shan Wu's thousand-year-old body fresh," Salma said.

"Zackly," replied Sanjeev.

"Hold on," Sara said, "instead of running through this place, we can use the map. All you need to do," she told Salma, "is swipe us there!"

Lin Dan looked bewildered.

"We'll explain later," Sara told him as Salma unfolded the map.

"Do you see Shan Wu?" Sanjeev asked, eyes scanning the map.

Salma shook her head; so did Sara. But suddenly Sara practically leapt on the spot. "Wait! The map's a desire!" she cried.

Salma understood immediately. "Map!" she said, "show us Shan Wu's, er, present location so I can swipe us there."

Breaths held all three scoured the map. But there was nothing to see: no flashing sign, no pointing finger, no jade suit icon. Nothing. Clearing her throat, Salma addressed the map again, her voice stern: "Show me Shan Wu." They waited. Still nothing. Salma glanced at Sara and Sanjeev and back at the map. "Er… Please?" she said. Still nothing. She was starting to get angry when she realised her mistake. She gave Sara and Sanjeev a knowing look. "Map, I wish to see where Shan Wu is."

They all waited. Slowly, the expectant smile on Salma's face disappeared. "I don't believe this!" she hissed. "Why isn't it working?"

A little hesitantly, Sanjeev said: "The Immortals called the dagger, the key, and the map the Hands of Fate, right?"

"And?"

"So maybe, using the map to get to Shan Wu isn't part of our fate."

Salma threw up her hands. "Not part of our fate? What's that supposed to mean?"

"I'm just trying to think of reasons why it didn't work. No point getting angry with me," Sanjeev told her.

Salma gazed at him. "Yeah. You're right. Sorry." She gave an apologetic smile.

Sara, glad to see they hadn't fallen out, said: "Whatever the reason the map didn't work, we still need to get to Chan and Shan Wu." She turned to Lin Dan. "Can you lead us to where the Jade Suit is?"

"I can try," he replied. "But he's got an army of henchmen."

"We'll just have to be careful. So…" Sara looked at the five tunnels that led out of the cavern. "Which one?"

"I think…" Lin Dan said, "it's…er…" He turned and turned again. "To be honest, I'm not sure."

"Best guess," Sara urged him. "If you're wrong, you're wrong. We don't have any other ideas."

"OK." He took a deep breath. "That one!" he said, pointing to the tunnel next to the huge portrait of Qin Shi Huang.

"Let's go!" Sara said.

As Salma folded away the map, she realised that, now she thought about it, there was something else about the map that didn't quite make sense: not only was there no sign of Shan Wu, the Jade Suit, or Chan, there had only been three pale-green icons huddled in a circle. Where was Lin Dan?

"This way," Lin Dan said, leading Salma and Sara into the tunnel.

As Sanjeev followed on behind, the poster of the First Emperor caught his attention once again and he had the horrible impression that its dark, watchful eyes were alert to his every step, his every breath; even, perhaps, his every thought.

Sanjeev had a very bad feeling about him.

CHAPTER 30

—

Creeping through passageways small and large, and with Lin Dan's warning that Chan had an army of thugs at the forefront of his mind, Sanjeev was feeling uneasy: half-expecting one of the many doors they were passing to fly open and a screaming horde of armed men to come rushing out and surround them. So far, that hadn't happened: each door had remained firmly closed, each corridor and tunnel eerily silent. The whole place was…dead. Not that he wanted a bunch of murderous villains to appear—but their absence was beginning to spook him. *Where were they all? Why hadn't they seen anyone?*

"Is it a thug holiday?" he whispered, following Sara, Salma, and Lin Dan, who was a couple of paces in front of everyone.

"Yeah," Sara said over her shoulder, "they got time off for bad behaviour."

Sanjeev grinned. "But don't you think it's weird we haven't seen a soul?"

"Kind of," Sara agreed.

As they approached another turn ahead with a large open door, Lin Dan suddenly stopped and put a finger to his lips. Motioning for them not to move, he stepped forward. Gripping the packed-dirt walls and a timber strut, he leaned past the turn. A moment later, he retracted his head and signalled for them to come closer. Gathering in a huddle, the three teens listened as he whispered about what he had seen. Now that they had been told, the faint sounds became clearer to them—distant roars of laughter, people singing, music playing, party poppers popping.

"A thugfest!" Sanjeev said. "But why?"

Lin Dan's eyes seemed to grow even more bloodshot. "If I had to guess, I'd say it's to celebrate what I helped Chan do."

"The Elixir?" Sara asked.

Lin Dan's expression was shamefaced. "Yes," he said quietly.

Salma felt like telling him not to beat himself up about it. Instead, she said: "Is there another way to get past them?"

Lin Dan shook his head. "This is the only way I—"

"Shhh!" Salma said, eyes widening. "Someone's—"

Before she could finish her sentence, the person she had heard coming towards them had turned the corner and crashed into Lin Dan. The man bounced off Lin Dan but in an instant, he had recovered and like an attack dog, he lunged at Lin Dan's throat, knocking Lin Dan to the ground. Lin Dan fought back, and as the two men grappled with each other, feet and arms flying, rolling, and twisting in the dust like snakes, Lin Dan forced an arm around the man's neck and trapped the man's head. Grunting, the man's face went red and swung his fists, trying to land punches on Lin Dan. Lin Dan avoided them, but the man wrenched his head away and, though one of his wrists was held by Lin Dan, with his free hand, delved into the black jacket he was wearing. Lin Dan, sensing the danger, grabbed the other wrist but the hand had found the revolver. In a tangle of limbs, the two men fought on, each desperate to get control of the weapon waving in the air. "Help!" Lin Dan cried, but before the three teens could do anything, the man tore the gun away from Lin Dan and, gasping for air, pointed the barrel at Lin Dan's face. "Enough," the man panted, and chest heaving, he began to get off his knees. "I don't know who you are but—"

Before he could finish his sentence, a blur of movement interrupted him. Half a second later, the man's mouth had dropped open. The gun's grip was still wrapped in his palm and his finger was still on the trigger, but the barrel and the front sight were lying on the ground in front of him, sliced cleanly away. He stared up at the girl who had stepped forward and touched the gun with something and now he saw she was holding some sort of knife. In an instant, he was upright.

"Intruders!" he screamed at the top of his lungs, turning, and running away as fast as he could back through the doorway. "Intruders!"

"The door!" Salma cried, rushing towards it. "Help me!"

All four heaved it shut and piled against it.

"Push!" Lin Dan cried as fists behind the heavy wooden door beat against it and the door began to edge slowly open.

"We can't hold it any longer," Salma said, the dirt oiling up behind her heels, the gap between the door and its frame widening centimetre by centimetre.

"The key!" Sara yelled. "The key!"

Sanjeev's mind raced. He fumbled in his pocket with his shoulder still hard against the door.

"Any time you're ready!" Salma cried, smashing a fist down on a hand that had pushed through the gap.

Sanjeev dropped the key.

"Come on!" Salma yelled, kicking at a thug's foot.

Snatching up the key, he plunged it into the door's lock and turned it: once, twice, three times…And with every turn, he and the others were pushed back as one door, then another, and another, and another—ornate and gilded; iron and rusted; teak and brass; slatted and folding; bronze and massive—came out of nowhere and landed behind the original door until more than twenty were between it and the goons inside the room.

"Huh!" Sanjeev exclaimed, gazing admiringly at the doors barring the thugs' escape. "Neat." Feeling the eyes of the others on his back, he nonchalantly extracted the key…

"Not a silk dagger," Sara said, inhaling deeply and letting her breath escape slowly, "but not bad."

"Yeah, not a teleporter either, but not bad," agreed Salma.

Both smiled with relief. Even Lin Dan was smirking.

"Just kidding," Sara admitted, "your key's cool."

"It is, right?" Sanjeev said, holding the key by the stem and eyeing the monkey's gold face. "Totally cool." The monkey's glowing eyes stared back at him, grinning. Sanjeev's face lit up. "It's—" he was about to say, "smiling" but jumped when another voice spoke instead...

"Enough," it said.

They all turned.

In the shadows of the tunnel to their right, a broad, powerful-looking figure stood partly hidden in darkness.

Sara raised the hand carrying the piece of silk; Salma brought up her clenched fists.

"Do not," the figure warned, and illuminated by the light dangling from the tunnel's ceiling, first a gun, then a thick arm, a meaty face, and finally a pair of cold eyes appeared out of the gloom.

"An Ho," all four muttered.

"Move," he grunted, and shifting his bulky body so that his back was against the tunnel wall, he flicked the gun to his left. "Let's see what the Boss wants to do with you."

CHAPTER 31

The four of them were forced through a doorway into a small chamber dimly lit by torches set in the walls. When their eyes had adjusted to the light, they found themselves in a circular room decorated with paintings at the four cardinal points on the walls. Torches in sconces flickered, the light from them illuminating a figure, who, back turned, was standing in the middle of the room on a short platform, leaning over what looked like an Egyptian mummy. But instead of being wrapped in cloth, the body was swathed in a mosaic of small, greenish stones. The same colour as the ball sitting on a pedestal next to it.

Shan Wu, the Jade Suit, and the Jade Dragonball.

As the three teens watched, the figure twisted around, and his dark, surprised-then- amused eyes fell on them. A sneering grin spread across his face. "Children?" Chan said.

"And how old are you?" Salma asked. "Thirteen? Fourteen?"

Sara smirked, knowing Salma was saying that to make him mad.

Chan smiled though his eyes were icy. "I presume they sent you?"

"They? You mean your mummy and daddy?"

Chan nodded to An Ho and a heavy hand struck Salma across the ear and back of the head, hard enough to be painful but not hard enough to knock her out. She'd been hit harder in the dojang. All the same, she saw stars.

"That was brave of you," Sara hissed at Chan, putting a comforting arm around Salma's shoulder. "Getting your ape to hit someone for you."

"Would you like me to repeat the order?" Chan threatened.

Sara opened her mouth, but Salma said: "I'm fine." She gave An Ho a backwards glance. "He hits like a five-year-old."

An Ho stared at her blankly.

Chan, stepping off the platform and standing beside the pedestal upon which the Jade Dragonball sat, the faces of its resplendent, fierce dragons shining vividly, he touched the nearest of the carved figures. "His prison," he said. "Can you imagine? Entombed alone for aeons in darkness. And for what? For having the most natural desire there is? For wanting to defeat death and be immortal? The sentence was barbaric. Cruel. Utterly inhumane. But that's what the Eight Immortals are. They have the power to bestow immortality on all of us, and yet they do not. Shan Wu? He is a hero, not a criminal. He wanted to bring us immortality. For that, he should be praised, not condemned. We should be worshiping at his feet."

"And should we worship at your feet, too?" Sara scoffed.

Chan, still gazing at the Dragonball, absent-mindedly traced a line top to bottom, his finger bumping over snarling snouts, jagged teeth, curling claws, and sinewy limbs. He looked up and locked eyes with Sara. A genuine smile spread across his face. "Billions soon will."

"Not if we can help it," Sanjeev said in his most determined voice.

Chan guffawed. "Is that so?"

"Why are you doing this? Is it the money?" Sanjeev asked.

Chan gave a curt laugh. "I'm an entrepreneur. I'm meeting people's wants. I'm not going to force them to do anything—they'll come begging."

"It's unnatural."

Chan seemed to consider that. "Is it? The elixir amplifies the life force, what we call qi in China. It is like charging a battery. Human bodies are, after all, mostly water, minerals, and a variety of chemical compounds...And where does one find 'life' in this?

The answer is in our qi. The elixir merely charges our existing life force…What's unnatural about that?"

"But then they run out of power," Sanjeev interrupted. "Which means more doses of the elixir become necessary. We saw what happened. When people who don't have enough of the elixir in their bodies, they turn to Stones."

"The Immortals showed you?"

Sanjeev nodded.

"They become immortality junkies," Sara said.

Chan's eyes glowed. "I suppose they do."

"And if people take the elixir and can't afford to buy more? What happens to them?" Salma asked.

Chan shook his head. "I have no plans to make my elixir unaffordable. Quite the opposite. I want everyone to have it. I want everyone to enjoy the gift the Eight Immortals have denied us."

"Don't you have a conscience?" Sanjeev asked.

Chan rounded on Sanjeev furiously, raising a hand to strike. But the hand wavered, and when it finally dropped to his side, he said: "You are young. You've never experienced the loss of a loved one. You never had a condition that meant death, night and day, breathing down the back of your neck. You can't understand." He opened his hand. "Give them to me."

"Give you what?" Sara asked innocently.

"The Hands of Fate," Chan replied. "And the triskelion."

The three teens looked at one another.

"Do you know what he's talking about?" Sara asked Salma.

Salma shrugged. "Not a clue. How about you?" she asked Sanjeev.

Sanjeev grinned. "What do you Brits say? Must be off his trolley?"

Chan sighed. "Well, I'm sorry to hear that. Truly, I am." He nodded at An Ho and a choking sound behind the three teens made them swivel their heads. What they saw appalled them. With his arm fixed around Lin Dan's neck, grunting and leaning backwards,

An Ho had levered Lin Dan off the ground and was slowly crushing his windpipe.

"Stop!" Sara cried as Lin Dan, his face turning from red to a deeper crimson, desperately clawed at the arm holding him. "Stop!" Sara cried again.

Chan nodded and An Ho released Lin Dan whose feet touching the ground once again, fell to his knees in a coughing heap.

Chan extended his open palm at them. When the three teens hesitated, he said in a bored voice: "I know you are the Three Hares. I know you were chosen because you have the thousand-year power. I know the Three Hares are always given the Hands of Fate." He stopped, seeing the surprised look on the teens' faces. "Oh! You thought you were the first! Oh, no, no, no," he chuckled, "there were others in the past. After I failed to bring back my master the first time, I did further research. Now I know that the triskelion is needed to bring him fully to life. And you have the triskelion." The fingers on his hand curled. "Give them to me."

The eyes of Sara, Sanjeev, and Salma met. Each face said the same thing: they were cornered, and though they hated the solution, they knew there was only one way out.

"Quickly," Chan urged as Lin Dan began to lose consciousness. "He'll die if you don't."

"Argh!" yelled Salma. "Take them!" And eyes blazing, she launched her piece of the triskelion at Chan. It bounced off his chest as did the map and Chan had to scramble to keep them from falling.

"Here!" Sara said, slapping her piece of triskelion and silk dagger onto Chan's hand.

Wordlessly but with disgust, Sanjeev gave up the gold monkey key and his piece of the triskelion.

"Sensible children," Chan said with a victorious grin. He caught An Ho's eye and nodded. Immediately, An Ho unlocked the arm around Lin Dan's throat and Lin Dan fell to his knees in a coughing heap.

"Today," Chan said, shuffling towards a low table where a flagon and bowl sat, "I will make history," and taking his time, he laid the pieces of the triskelion and the Hands of Fate on the table's dark wooden surface.

"Today, you'll make a big mistake if you try to use the triskelion to resurrect Shan Wu," Sara said in a matter-of-fact voice.

"Is that so?" Chan sneered. He turned to the three teens again.

"It is," replied Sanjeev.

"And why's that?" Chan asked, smirking.

"The triskelion can only be used by those who are good. The Eight Immortals said so," replied Sara. She looked at Sanjeev and Salma, who nodded.

"Pfff!" Chan exclaimed.

"You don't believe us?" Sara asked.

"I believe you'd say anything to stop me using the Hands of Fate," Chan replied. "*That's* what I believe."

Salma sneered back at him. "Well, go on then. Don't say we didn't warn you."

CHAPTER 32

⚊

Chan, standing at the low table, his back to the three teens, raised the flagon and poured. A dark, gloopy liquid tumbled into the bowl. It took the teens a moment to realise it was blood. Sanjeev felt very squeamish. Nevertheless, he kept his eyes on Chan who, having gathered the pieces of the triskelion and climbed the steps of the platform, had taken a deep breath. Lungs inflated, chest out, he looked to Sanjeev like he was about to sing a song. Instead, he bellowed: "To neither the 33 realms of Heaven nor the 153 jails of Hell shall I go! Suit! I command thee to serve! I command thee to bring him forth! I command thee to be the eternal saviour, defeating all that ages and diminishes!" With those words, he tipped the contents of the bowl onto the suit, tracing a weaving path over it, head to toe. Having emptied the bowl, he placed it at his feet and bent over, inserted the first shard into the chest of the suit. As it slid into place with a click, the suit seemed to grow brighter, the green stones taking on an inner glow.

The green light illuminated Chan's face, which broke into a huge grin. Fumbling, almost dropping the second shard in his excitement, he slipped it into the suit next to the first one. This time, the suit glowed even more brightly, disappearing every shadow in the room. The three teens and Lin Dan shielded their eyes.

Chan picked up the third shard.

"Don't do it!" shouted Sara.

His body silhouetted by the suit's blazing light, Chan turned, holding up the third piece for all to see. "Watch as the Master returns!" he cried and reaching over, guided the shard into the last remaining space.

At once, green flames rose, dancing in the air above the whole length of the suit. Chan stumbled backwards grinning wildly as the flames burned incandescent and soared, reaching up towards the roof, their light unbearable to look at. And yet Chan stared at them.

"Look!" he cried to the others who had shielded their eyes. "Look at them!" he insisted, awestruck, pointing to the flames above his head which had converged into a single cord of energy... But as the words left his mouth, so his expression changed: the three pieces of the triskelion exploded from the chest of the suit, with the broken pieces flying across the room and landing on the floor near the Hares. A twisting cord of green light was snaking towards him in slow motion, the air crackling as it descended.

"No!" Chan cried, throwing up his hands as the ribbon of green weaved towards him. "No, please."

But just as a boa constrictor circles the body of its prey, so the green lightning circled Chan until he was wrapped in its coils, head to toe. It squeezed with a sizzling sound and a burning smell filled the air. As it squeezed, so the dimensions of the body in its embrace shrank until Chan's screams were no more and the brightness of the light diminished. In horror, the three teens watched as the lightning bolt loosened its grip on Chan and his body—as thin as paper—floated to the ground. Like newspaper exposed to flame, the desiccated sheet began to turn up at the edges, and shrivelling, crumpling, and darkening, it turned to grey and then to pale ash.

As though its job was done, the green bolt of lightning split itself into three parts, each flowing into the three pieces of triskelion, disappeared.

A door opened behind them.

When the three turned, An Ho had already gone.

"Don't blame him," Salma muttered.

"What just happened?" Sara asked, shocked at what the green lightning had done to Chan. "I mean, why did the triskelion attack him?"

"Verification failure," Sanjeev said. Salma and Sara waited. "It's like in computing," he continued. "Fingerprint scanning or iris recognition to get into a system. When the verification fails...you get rejected."

Sara eyed the ash. "That's a rejection I could do without."

"You did try to warn him," Lin Dan said, rubbing his neck.

Sara nodded. "I tried."

Eyes also on the ash, Sanjeev said: "I guess he didn't do enough research on the triskelion. If he had, he would have believed you." They were silent for a moment until Sanjeev spoke again. "So... er...now what? We all go home?"

Salma shook her head. He looked at Sara who also shook her head.

"OK...Why not?" he asked, and reaching down, picked up the pieces of the triskelion and handed Salma and Sara theirs.

"Shan Wu tried to kill me," Sara said, swapping Salma's shard for her own. "I almost died on Ben Nevis."

"And he threatened my mother," Salma said. "But besides that, the Immortals are never going to leave us alone unless we deal with him."

Salma picked up the map again, and Sanjeev the key. Without another word, Sara snatched up the silk dagger and flicked it three times. Dagger gleaming, her eyes met Salma and Sanjeev's.

"I gotta be honest," Sanjeev said. "I don't like this."

"It's the only way," Salma urged.

"But...he's just lying there. Are we really going to kill a defenceless—"

"Don't say man, human or person. Because he isn't any of those things," Sara said.

"It isn't right." Sanjeev said, shaking his head. "If he were attacking us and we had to defend ourselves, that would be different."

"He's already attacked Sara," Salma said, her voice rising, "And he almost made me jump in front of a tube train…and you want to give him another chance?"

"You don't know for sure he will attack us again," Sanjeev replied. "Maybe he's changed!"

Salma scoffed. "Leopards don't change their spots."

Sanjeev took a deep breath, trying to regain his composure. "OK…why don't we—"

But before he could finish his sentence, Sara, dagger in hand, watched by the other two and Lin Dan, had rushed to the platform and climbed its steps. "I've had enough of this," she said, and raising the dagger, both hands on its hilt, she plunged it down.

CHAPTER 33

Suddenly, Sara's world went black.

For a moment, she was too stunned to think. Swivelling, she looked up, down, and around, seeing nothing but darkness.

"Wha—?"

She told herself to blink and felt her eyes blink. She touched her face, ordered her arms, legs, and fingers to move which they did. It didn't seem like she was asleep. If not asleep, then what? Thrown into a deep dark pit? But there was no air rushing past her, no wind rustling her clothes. She tilted her head back. Which way was up? Which way down? There was nothing to tell her: no weight on her limbs, no earth or sky. Was she falling? Rising? Was she upside down? It didn't feel like she was. She was about to call out, ask for help, but, like the stage in a theatre when the play begins and the actors, already standing in the darkness are lit by spotlights, a world appeared: sky, land, a village, huts, fields, crops.

A grunt behind her.

She snapped her head around as a man, hands tied, eyes lowered, stumbled and fell towards her. In astonishment, she gasped as first the man's hands and then the rest of his body passed straight though hers. Spinning, she saw him land on the dirt, scramble to his feet, and face another man coming towards him—heavier, swaggering, a ragged scar across his face. The man raised his sword. "No!" Sara screamed. The body hit the dusty ground with a thud.

A whispered word, everywhere and nowhere at the same time, filled the air: "Father."

The scene suddenly changed. Now she was standing in a hut, its walls poorly pieced together, snow blowing in through the cracks. A meagre fire was glowing a few feet away, where a young boy, watched by an even younger one, was trying to shake life back into a woman.

"Mother. Shan Tuo," the voice said softly.

That voice. She recognised it. Shan Wu's.

Yet another scene. This time, she was high above a valley, standing at the entrance to a cave, as a gentle-looking man with concerned eyes and berries in his hand passed her by. As she watched, he entered the cave, gently woke a boy lying below blankets, and fed him.

"Tian Lan."

The mountains and valleys disappeared. Other people and places whirled into view and flitted past her like swallowtails. The images slowed and she saw a fat man with a loud laugh and eyes that were filled with greed, his muscular guard standing behind, arms across his chest.

"Ochlik," said Shan Wu, sounding angrier.

More people and places whizzed past, everyone and everything blurred with movement. But the images were slowing: fuzzy shapes were becoming people, buzzing insect sounds, their voices.

She was in a vast, misty space with a bridge that spanned a gushing river and led to a towering wooden door.

"The courtyard of the Jade Palace," she whispered.

She was wondering if she might see herself come into the courtyard along with Salma and Sanjeev when she realised she wasn't alone. A dark-haired boy had suddenly appeared from nowhere. Ten paces in front of her, his back turned, he was drinking at the courtyard's fountain, scooping the water greedily into his mouth and chuckling. After a moment, he reached for the gourd at his side and filled it. That done, he poured a last handful of water into his mouth, wiped his face with the back of his hand, gave a satisfied "Aaah!", and turned. When he turned, and his dark eyes looked in her direction, her heart stopped and her breathing caught in her throat: Shan Wu was staring at her, his eyes seeing yet not seeing. She held her breath. A frown creased Shan Wu's brow. But just when she thought he had seen her, his attention slid away and he looked towards the palace, a determined look on his face.

In the blink of an eye, once again the scene changed. She and Shan Wu were in the Palace, and Shan Wu, surrounded by the Immortals, was yelling, his face defiant, firing a bolt of energy that struck the talisman Li Tieguai wore on his chest, shattering it and sending Li Tieguai flying. The Jade Dragonball was in front of her. Looming large, its carved dragons writhed on the ball's surface one minute; the next, they had disappeared, and she was plunged into darkness again. As she stood, arms at her side, wondering what was going to happen next, a sense of despair hit her, crashing into her body like a breaking wave and leaving her hollow and gasping.

Ha, ha, ha.

The laughter echoed all around her. And as it echoed, she felt the bitterness in it, felt it as if she were being burned by it. The burning got worse, a searing pain that burrowed deep into her head.

"Now you understand the torture I endured? The revenge I am entitled to?" Shan Wu screamed. "This is what they did to me, your friends the Immortals."

Sara wanted to cry out that the Immortals weren't her friends, that she, Salma, and Sanjeev had been given no choice. But she knew it would be pointless. The anger Shan Wu felt towards them blinded him: the Immortals were his enemies, and whether it was fair or not, so was she, Salma, and Sanjeev.

Out of the darkness, a greyish, slithering smoke was creeping towards her, low to the ground, and Sara had the sensation that the air had chilled. Eyes locked on the smoke, she backed away. But there was no escape. It curled around her feet and like a python, rose up, circled her, and slowly tightened every coil, locking her arms to her sides, her legs to one another. She struggled to loosen its grip. It was impossible. A swirling mass was rising in front of her face. She gasped as she stared at it. A skull was forming out of the grey smoke: dark orbs first, white bone and bared teeth next. Terrified, she closed her eyes but reopened them a heartbeat later. No, she told herself. I'll look him in the eye. Summoning all her willpower as pink flesh and pale skin adhered to Shan Wu's cheekbone, chin, and forehead, she stared at him, remembering who she was, how she had succeeded in the task the Eight Immortals had set her, how she had climbed Ben Nevis, how she had triumphed in the interview with the editor of her school's newspaper. She was *not* going to be terrorised by Shan Wu again.

Not now; not ever.

Clang!

Suddenly, he was gone and she was looking down on her own hand, feeling juddering vibrations rise up her fingers and hands. In astonishment, she stared at the silk dagger.

It had struck the Suit's topmost layer and gone not a millimetre further.

"Are you OK?" Salma asked, laying a hand on Sara's shoulder. "You kind of just froze."

Sara blinked. "I…I went places in Shan Wu's life," she replied and lifted the silk dagger's blade away from the Jade Suit, glared at the shrivelled body wrapped in the Jade Suit's armour like a pupa in its cocoon.

"Stay at any good hotels?" Salma asked with a sympathetic smile.

Sara shook her head. To herself, she wondered what it would take to be rid of Shan Wu.

As if reading her thoughts, Salma said: "If your dagger can't kill him…" Her voice trailed off.

Sara nodded and rubbed her shoulder. The force of the reverberations had made it feel like she'd struck an anvil with a sword. "If my dagger can't kill him, what can?"

When his attention was drawn away, Sanjeev was about to make a suggestion, or at least pose a question. He had spied something out of the corner of his eye: movement? Something on the Jade Dragonball? He turned but saw nothing unusual.

"I was wondering," he said, returning his attention to Sara and Salma, "if there's a lock on the suit? Cause if there is, I might have the answer." He grinned as he brandished the golden key.

"Good thinking," Sara said and immediately set about examining every centimetre of the chest and arms while Salma checked the legs.

Five minutes later, after they had finished scouring every nook and cranny of the Suit, they looked up and shook their heads.

Sanjeev sighed. What was the point of having this Monkey Key? "What next?" he said, his voice betraying his disappointment at the uselessness of his Hand of Fate.

Salma's answer was immediate: "So now we use our pieces of the triskelion to reanimate him. That's what."

CHAPTER 34

—

"Are you nuts?" Sanjeev cried. "Why would we do that?"

"I told you about my adventure, remember?"

"Yeah, about the Saxons and the Vikings. I remember."

"OK, so the Vikings landed on Northey Island and came across the causeway—" Seeing Sanjeev's puzzlement, Salma explained. "It's like a long, narrow strip of land. The one in my adventure connected Northey Island to the mainland."

"OK," Sanjeev said.

"The Vikings were on the causeway and the Saxon army was on the mainland. The Vikings couldn't get off the causeway because it only needed a handful of Saxon men to block their way."

"Like loads of people in a packed cinema trying to leave through one door. If someone blocks it, no one can get out," Sanjeev said.

"Right! Anyway, the Saxon leader, Byrhtnoth, told his men to stand back and let the Vikings come onto the mainland."

"Why did he do that?" Sara asked.

"Because he was worried that if the Vikings didn't get off the causeway, they would sail away and attack a different village or town. He wanted the chance to defeat the Vikings once and for all…"

Their eyes on the Jade Suit, Sanjeev and Sara nodded slowly.

"We bring Shan Wu back to life," Sara said. "Bring him out of the suit, reanimate just like Chan wanted."

"Like Byrhtnoth bringing the Vikings onto the mainland," Sanjeev breathed.

"And we can defeat him once and for all," finished Sara, brandishing the silk dagger once again.

Salma raised her piece of the triskelion and slipped it into the chest of the Jade Suit. "Once and for all," she whispered.

Sara met Salma's eyes, nodded, and reaching over, slipped her shard into the chest of the Jade Suit next to Salma. They turned to Sanjeev, who pushed his glasses to the bridge of his nose.

"It makes sense," Sara said.

"I…I guess it does," Sanjeev said, his eyes finding Lin Dan whose shrug suggested he had no advice to offer. "I hope it thinks we're good. The triskelion, I mean," he said.

Salma tutted. "Are you kind to animals? Do you help old people across the street? Of course, it thinks we're good!" she cried.

Sanjeev held up his hands. "OK, OK," he said and reaching over, he pushed his shard into the remaining space.

As soon as he had, all four edged away. Once again, green flames rose along its length, and once again, they danced, flickering and reaching for the ceiling.

"Look!" Sanjeev gasped, finger outstretched, pointing.

They gaped.

Amidst the flames, particles, like a billion gooey pieces of dough, were oozing out of the spaces between the suit's tiles, joining with one another, forming conglomerations and recognisable shapes. A hand, not yet connected to a wrist appeared. It stretched out to grasp the air, clenching and unclenching its fingers. An elbow with no forearm or upper arm, bent and straightened itself. A neck, its muscles and tendons visible, twisted. A chest, its ribs yet to circle its heart, breathed. A jaw, its white bones shining, opened and closed a toothless mouth. A head, its nose, an ear, two eyes missing, turned. A bottom lip and half a top lip curled.

"Fools!" a booming voice cried.

The three teens and Lin Dan clutched their ears. And as the word echoed away, so the particles began to disassemble, furiously separating themselves and pouring back into the suit through the gaps.

"No!" Sanjeev cried, realising their error as the flames died away to nothing. "He knows!"

It was too late.

The nearest arm of the Jade Suit gave a sudden jerk, twitching as though it were a cat's tail. The opposite leg did the same. In horror, the four watched as the suit's torso surged upwards, one foot then the other touched the ground, arms pushed, and legs straightened.

Shan Wu, his body safely ensconced in the Jade Suit like a knight in armour, his head and neck poking out from the suit's tiles like a turtle's from its shell, swayed, his cobra-dark eyes locked on the stunned faces before him.

"Boo!" he suddenly cried, throwing up his hands and watching as the four of them scattered like terrified rabbits.

"You can run," he called, enjoying the sound of his own manic laughter as it followed them out of the room and deep into the tunnels, "but you can't hide," and clomping very slowly and gingerly down the steps of the platform, he looked at the pedestal next to him. His snorting laughter died in his throat.

Someone had snatched the Jade Dragonball.

CHAPTER 35

—

"I…can't…run…any…further," panted Sanjeev, and knees buckling, he half-slid onto the ground, the Jade Dragonball on his lap.

Chests heaving, lungs on fire, Lin Dan and Sara did the same while Salma, doubled-over and panting, stood next to the only light—an open-flame torch hanging on the wall.

"Is…he…following…us?" Sara gasped.

All four turned to peer along the tunnel in the direction they had come.

The dimly lit walls receded into a dead-as-night darkness forty or fifty steps away that seemed to swirl and shift. With stifled breaths, they waited, muscles tensed ready to run again if need be. But no sound reached them, no figure broke from the shadows, and slowly, very slowly, their panic ebbed.

"Does anyone know…where we are?" wheezed Salma, getting slowly to her feet. "Lin Dan?"

Lin Dan, rising, mouth open, shook his head.

Salma, still gulping air, pulled out the map and unfurled it.

Sucking in air, Sara said: "You grabbed the Jade Dragonball?" and stood as Sanjeev got shakily to his feet.

"Yeah," he said, his eyes staying on the stone artefact in his hands and its surface which was glowing a darker, more mysterious green.

It seemed to Sara that Sanjeev was searching the Jade Dragonball for something. "What—?" she began but was interrupted by Salma. "That's weird."

They all turned. Salma was frowning at the map.

"What is?" Sara asked.

Salma turned the map towards them.

Sara and Sanjeev saw what Salma meant: three glowing icons that had moved towards the outer edge of the mound and were stationary.

"Lin Dan's not there." Sanjeev said. "I saw it earlier."

They looked at Lin Dan.

"Er…should I be?" he asked.

"If you're not on it, it means—" Salma began but stopped.

The others had heard it too: a very faint, very distant booming sound.

"What is that?" Salma asked in a hushed voice.

"Whatever it is, it's getting louder," Sara said.

"I've got a bad feeling about this," Sanjeev muttered, hugging the Jade Dragonball to his chest.

They strained their ears, trying to make sense of the sound.

"What is it?" Sara breathed.

The sound was changing, becoming clearer, more differentiated. And simultaneously, they knew what they were hearing. Not one sound: but many smaller, similar sounds that were combining to make one big sound.

"Feet!" the three teens yelled a moment before a torch, its burning light carried aloft, brightened the darkness into which they were staring.

"Boss!" a voice yelled. "Boss!"

The low rumble that had previously filled the air became a sound like stampeding horses. More torches appeared behind the first torch, and An Ho, a grimace on his face, breathing hard, rushed out of the dimness, his thick legs motoring like pistons.

"Run!" Salma cried.

Turning on their heels, the four ran for their lives, desperately pumping their arms and legs, forcing the exhausted limbs to work again and ignoring the burning agony in their lungs and muscles. On they ran turning this way and that, into tunnels that grew narrower and narrower, colder and colder. Until they could go no further. Because there was nowhere else to go. They stopped and fell to their knees, desperately filling and emptying their lungs. In front of them, lit by the glow of the last torch they had passed twenty steps before, a wall of earth stared back.

They had run into a dead end.

Lurching towards the torch, Lin Dan pulled it from its holder. "We have to…retrace…our steps," he panted.

But the words had barely left his mouth when all four heard the same sound again. Helplessly, they listened as the pounding footsteps of the henchmen grew louder.

"Need…to use…the map," Salma gasped, unfolding it.

"No," Sara said, which was all she could manage to say.

"We have to," Salma told her. "We're on the map. It'll transport us." She looked at Lin Dan.

He understood immediately. "Do it," he said. "Get out of here. Save yourselves."

"We can't leave him," Sanjeev cried.

"We have to," Salma said, her fingers dropping onto the map as the face of a henchmen emerged from an adjoining tunnel and Lin Dan, still holding the torch, swung his fist and knocked the man onto his backside.

"Go!" Lin Dan cried as the man scrambled to his feet and ran off, yelling, "Boss!" at the top of his lungs.

"Don't—" Sanjeev told Salma.

Too late. With her fingers on the icons, she swiped.

CHAPTER 36

—

They were standing in the middle of a circle of torches, each on a short pole that had been stuck into the ground at roughly equal intervals. Beyond the poles and the torch light, lay a silent deep darkness. Sara had the sensation that the illuminated area that they were standing in was a tiny island surrounded by an ocean of emptiness.

Taking a torch from one of the poles, she held it up as Sanjeev stood beside her, both of them gazing into the void beyond. "Where are we?" she breathed…

Smoothing the map open, Salma said, "I've got some good news and bad news."

"That almost always means things are bad," Sanjeev said, sniffing at the dampness in the air…and something else he couldn't put his finger on.

"First, the good news: the map very clearly shows where we are."

"OK, that is good," said Sara. "So, where are we?"

"That's the bad news. According to the map, we're standing in the middle of Qin Shi Huang's tomb."

Sara gave a low whistle. "Qin Shi Huang ordered thousands of artisans to make life-size replicas of people to serve him in the afterlife: terracotta warriors, musicians, acrobats, government workers, even horses and chariots. Hardly any of them have been dug up." Lifting the torch high above her head, she peered into the gloom. "So where are they all?"

"Is this where you meant to take us?" asked Sanjeev, turning to address Salma.

Salma shrugged. "Didn't have time to choose: just swiped."

A silence fell, which was soon broken by Sanjeev: "I still think we shouldn't have left Lin Dan."

Salma sighed. "There were too many! We couldn't have fought all of them even with Sara's knife. They would have captured the Hands of Fate and us. And then where would we have been?"

Sanjeev said nothing, just shook his head.

"So, what do we do now?" Salma's eyes met Sara's and Sanjeev's, as they all searched one another's faces for ideas.

When it was clear no one had a clue, Sara walked hesitantly to the edge of the circle and peered into the blackness. "It feels like we are on a tiny island," she breathed.

Still holding the torch aloft, Sanjeev followed Salma as she joined Sara.

"Yeah," Salma agreed, reaching for the torch which Sanjeev gave her, "and we're all alone, floating on an ocean of emptiness."

Sara, her toes at the very edge of the circle of light, said: "There has to be a reason the map brought us here."

Sanjeev tucked the Jade Dragonball more tightly under his arm. "Any idea where we should go?" he asked her.

"Weird. That wasn't there a minute ago," Salma said.

Sara and Sanjeev looked to where she was pointing and saw a faint, white line that seemed to be some distance from where they were. The pencil-thin line was falling vertically, coming down from somewhere high above them, slowly drawing itself towards the ground. Astonished, the three watched as the line extended further and further until it finally met the horizontal plane and illuminated the area it touched, a small rocky, hillock.

"I'd say that's a sign," Sanjeev said but the words had barely left his mouth when a voice from behind him called his name.

"Sanjeev?"

The Hares jumped at the voice which had come from behind them. Spinning around, they stared out at the darkness beyond the torches.

"Sanjeev?"

The voice had moved. It was behind them again. They twisted around.

"It's me," the voice said.

The Hares, shoulders touching, stared into the darkness in front of them. And like a pale spectre from a crib, Lin Dan, eyes lowered, his face and body half-lit by the torchlight, ambled forward and stopped an arm's length from the invisible line that marked the boundary between the inside and the outside of the circle. "It's me," he said his eyes rising to meet the stares of the three teens. "Don't be afraid."

Sanjeev gaped. "How did you…?"

Lin Dan smiled. "They let me go. I don't know why."

"They let you go?" Sara asked.

Lin Dan kept his eyes on Sanjeev. "I can help you," he said, reaching out both hands. "I can take you all to safety."

"You can?" Sanjeev said eagerly.

"How did you get here?" Salma asked.

Lin Dan's voice was low and soft. "The Dragonball is heavy, Sanjeev. It's a great weight, and your arms are tired. Very, very tired. I can carry it. Give it to me, Sanjeev. Let me help you."

With every word from Lin Dan, Sanjeev felt his body relax.

"That's it, Sanjeev," Lin Dan whispered. "Raise up your hands. Pass it to me."

As if in a dream, Sanjeev saw his arms extend.

"No!" Sara cried and grasping Sanjeev's arms, she pushed the Jade Dragonball away from the edge. "Look at his feet. They aren't touching the ground. It isn't him. It isn't Lin Dan."

As though he had been awakened from a sleep, Sanjeev shook his head and stumbled backwards.

"It's you," Sara hissed at the figure in front of them. "Isn't it?"

The figure gave a hideous smile. "How are you, Sara?" it asked softly.

As if two enormous hands had gripped her temples, Sara felt her head squeeze. In horror, she stared at her own hands as they rose and reached towards Sanjeev and the Jade Dragonball. "No!" she cried as Sanjeev, eyes wide, backed away. She turned to Salma. "Help!"

Salma leapt forward, grabbed Sara's hand, wrapping it tightly in her own and fighting the efforts it was making to shake her off, reached out to Sanjeev. "Take my hand," she cried as Sara's other hand clawed at her throat. "Take it!"

Sanjeev grasped Salma's hand, and as soon as he did, Sara stopped fighting with Salma, her breathing calmed, the pressure squeezing against her head disappeared, and her body relaxed.

The figure pretending to be Lin Dan vanished.

"What just happened?" Sanjeev asked, heaving a sigh of relief, still holding on tightly to Sara and Salma's hands.

Her voice shaking, Sara said: "Mind control. He did it to me when I was at the top of Ben Nevis. I almost stepped off a cliff."

From nowhere yet everywhere a voice whispered: "Give up. Give up now."

"Or else what?" Salma said defiantly, casting her question into the blackness above their heads.

A wheezing laughter chilled the three teens to the marrow. "Or else, this…" the voice said.

CHAPTER 37

—

The darkness was changing.

Like the very first moments of a sunrise, a line was being drawn across the horizon now, its blood-red light slicing through the fleshy darkness and extending as far as could be seen.

The next instant, the crimson light had drawn back. Retreating at a phenomenal pace, it swept towards its origin and almost died to nothing, but not quite. Faint yellows and oranges remained and now these rose and began flickering. As the three stared, the flames surged and swelled and having grown huge, they writhed like giant snakes.

The three shielded their eyes from the intense light.

But as quickly as they had appeared, the flames began to shrink and die away, and in their place a great, curved shape was rising, its icy light dousing the flames completely. The disc continued to rise, and as it did, it revealed more of itself until finally it was complete.

"A supermoon," Sanjeev whispered, head tilted back, gazing at the gargantuan moon, twenty, fifty, a hundred times the size of a normal one as its ivory face bathed the teens in its bone-white light.

Sara, who had almost dropped the torch, closed her gaping mouth. The supermoon was like nothing she had ever seen before, but what had appeared in the distance was even more astonishing. Beyond a stretch of featureless land, a river, and bridge, a massive building perched on a rammed-earth platform had sprung out of the darkness and revealed itself.

"Wow!" Sanjeev breathed.

"You can say that again," Salma said.

The building was a squat, mean-looking fortress. Broader than it was tall, its jagged towers, swooping roofs, narrow, barred windows, and slanting ramparts shouted out one thing: stay back, or else. At its centre, perhaps two hundred steps or more, a staircase rose from ground level to the gateway whose double doors, guarded by two towers on either side, were firmly, resolutely closed. Everything, including the earthen platform on which the whole edifice sat, was one colour: red. Red earth. Red walls. Red roofs. Red towers. Red door.

A shiver ran through all three. Though shrouded in silence, the building felt as menacing as its dark, blood-spilt appearance, as though the stillness in the humid, charged air might be torn apart at any second by a tortured scream.

But it wasn't just that.

Despite the supermoon's radiance, everything in front of them—the expanse of flat land, the river and the curving wooden bridge that crossed it, the red fortress beyond—all had a strange, shimmering appearance, as though they were slowly pulsing in and out of existence: as though they were there and not there at the same time.

"Like they've been draped in spiderwebs," Sanjeev said. "What is that place?"

"The Epang Palace," Sara said.

Salma, who had just noticed that a tiny building along with a minuscule bridge crossing a crescent-shaped river had suddenly and inexplicably appeared on the map, lifted her head. "Eh?"

"It's Qin Shi Huang's imperial palace."

Sanjeev's mouth made an "O" shape and his eyes grew big behind his glasses. Salma, frowning, muttered: "Now what?"

Her question was answered immediately by the voice that had spoken before. "They have lain in the dark for nearly twenty-three centuries, buried in the earth, awaiting the moment when they would be able to serve their lord," the voice cried.

Looking at her feet, Sara said: "Did you feel that? I thought the ground …"

"Yeah, I felt it," Sanjeev replied.

"Me, too," Salma said, quickly folding away the map.

The vibrations got stronger and the air was filled with a strange rumbling. Instinctively, the three moved to the centre of the circle, eyes scanning left and right, Salma and Sanjeev holding up their extinguished torches like cudgels.

"Is it an earthquake?" Sara asked.

Before anyone could answer, the air was torn by a colossal roar behind them.

The three turned. The sound was growing in enormity, a thunderous noise like a jet plane taking off.

The three stared in horror.

Things were coming out of the ground. Not plants: fingers. Thousands of them: wriggling like thick worms, pushing back the soil, scraping it to the side. Hands emerged. Then wrists. Suddenly, as though obeying a silent command, everything stopped moving.

The three teens pressed together, shoulder to shoulder.

An instant later, a rumbling noise echoed across the great space, the soil erupted, and clay heads pushed through its surface, the skulls sprouting up like terrifying plants and locking their clay eyes on the teens.

As the three teens backed away, staring at the frozen expressions of the warriors, the figures leaned over, clawed at the ground, and heaving with all their might, dragged their bodies centimetre by centimetre from the hole in which they had been buried to emerge like cicadas from their long sleep. Once out of the hole, they rose to their full height and standing in perfectly straight lines, shook off the clumps of earth from their clay armour, hundreds, and hundreds of them.

As though a signal had been given, each simultaneously raised one leg and stamped it down, the movement sending a violent tremor through the stunned earth. Each raised the other foot and still in the same spot, stamped it down. This they repeated over and over: *Boom! Boom! Book! Book!*

"Attack!" the voice from nowhere cried.

The first rank immediately jolted forward in perfect unison, followed by the rank behind them and the rank behind them until slowly, interminably, the entire army was in motion, headed straight towards the trio.

CHAPTER 38

—

Through a cloud of dust, Sara watched the army coming at them; watched them moving their clay limbs with short, uneven jerks, watched as one soldier stumbled and fell, watched as those behind came on, trampling the fallen figure to pieces. She was rooted to the spot and only became aware that Sanjeev had been yelling her name when he grabbed her by the elbow.

"Come on!" he cried, pulling her. "Let's get out of here!"

Snapping out of her daze, she took off, running with Sanjeev and Salma as fast as her legs could carry her while behind her the warriors pounded the ground, their march not fast, but steady, moving forward one identical, measured stride at a time after another, on and on and on.

"The bridge," Salma cried, running at the front and pointing to the wooden structure 500 metres ahead.

"Use…the map!" Sara shouted at her back. "Swipe us!"

Of course! Still running, Salma unfolded it. She turned a panicked face to Sara and Sanjeev. "Not there!"

"What?" yelled Sanjeev, running awkwardly with the Jade Dragonball tucked under his arm and the key clenched in his fist. "What's not there?"

"We're not there! We aren't on the map!" Salma stopped and replied; she waited for Sanjeev and Sara to catch up. "Look!" she held the map up.

Sanjeev and Sara's eyes scoured every millimetre of the map: there was the Epang Palace; there was the white pole sticking up;

there was the mass of tiny heads of the terracotta army shuffling towards them; there was the bridge; there was the river. But where were they? Where were the glowing icons?

"I don't believe this!" Salma cried; for a moment, no one spoke, their eyes fixed on the real-life terracotta warriors marching grimly, unwaveringly towards them.

As Sanjeev stood horror-struck, the word "inexorable" echoed in his head, in the part of his mind not wrecked with fear. Yeah, that's the word, inexorable. That part of his mind started thinking harder. Shouldn't the Immortals have given us something better to fight with than a map, a key, and a dagger? Wait…maybe the Immortals thought these were enough…maybe they are enough…

It hit him.

"Keys open doors, they create empty spaces, right?" he yelled at Salma and Sara. "Well, how about if we try to put a hole in the map?"

"A what?" Salma said.

"A hole in the map!" he shouted at the top of his voice, shoving the map back into Salma's hands.

Salma looked at him like he was crazy. "How?"

"With the key!" he cried, waving it like it was a flag.

"But what if…"

"Yeah, I know," he said. "If it works and I make the hole too big, we're going down with them," he said, nodding towards the terracotta warriors.

Salma drew a breath; looked into his eyes. "Do it," she said.

He turned to Sara. She nodded.

"Make it taut," he told them.

They took hold of the map's edges and pulled gently, smoothing out the map's crinkles.

"Ready?" he asked, placing the Jade Dragonball at his feet and holding the key above where he estimated their location on the map was.

Both signalled they were. "Here goes…everything," he said, and wishing his hands were steadier, he began pressing the point of the key into the map, hoping the three of them wouldn't be cast into a deep, dark hole. *Which is exactly what's going to happen*, he thought, *if I press too hard.*

Breath held; he watched the map buckle a little. Shifting his grip on the key, he pushed just a little more. The space under the tip of the key began to yield and a shudder went through his hand and arm. Below their feet, the whole necropolis heaved.

"Keep going!" Salma yelled.

He pressed harder still. Suddenly the tip of the key punctured the map, and all at once, an area under the terracotta warriors fell away. A great rush of air flew up and with it, a deafening crashing sound: the sound of pottery smashed to smithereens. A gust of wind hit them, filling the air with dust, making them gag. For a moment, they coughed and rubbed their eyes, unable to see.

Sanjeev, still coughing, stared. Where moments earlier a sea of clay automatons had marched, there was now an immense hole: a pit, he assumed, filled with pottery shards. But the relief he felt was momentary: only half the army had gone. The hole was at the rear of the warriors: those at the front marched on, their steps quickening, the distance between them and the three teens diminishing by the second and all three knew that if Sanjeev tried to make another hole, they risked being dragged into it along with the remaining warriors. There was only one thing to do.

Run.

"Running…again!" Sanjeev panted; the Jade Dragonball tucked under his arm once more.

At the front and urging them on, Salma was the first to enter the shadow cast by the tallest of the Epang Palace's towers.

"We can use…the key…if it's locked," Sanjeev panted, meaning the palace's door. He was moving his arms and legs as fast as he could, but he knew his body had had enough and that with every step, he was getting slower. Next to him, he could see that Sara was exhausted too.

"Keep going," Salma said, noticing the strain on Sanjeev and Sara's faces. "We're almost at the bridge."

Somehow, Sanjeev and Sara kept going: plodding, stumbling, staggering.

"I have to…rest," Sanjeev cried, and short of the bridge, he collapsed onto the dry earth knees first. Sara did the same: flat on her back, desperately trying to fill her lungs.

"Is…it…your taekwondo training…that makes you…so fit?" Sara panted at Salma.

"I guess so," Salma said, hands on hips, breathing hard but still upright.

"I'm going…to take up…taekwondo," Sara said, rolling onto her knees.

"Just a little further," Salma said, placing a foot on the arched wooden bridge, trying to sound positive but eyeing the hundreds of steep steps beyond the bridge's rounded apex that reached up towards the palace's red door.

"Just…a little…further," Sanjeev told himself, and with the Jade Dragonball in one hand and a searing pain in his lungs, he crawled onto the bridge and lay face-first on it, the cold wood rough against his cheek. He caught a glimpse of Sara who having managed to get to her feet, had staggered past him and fallen back against the bridge's handrail, her body as limp as a doll's.

Lying flat, his limbs refusing to move, Sanjeev peered through one of the gaps between the wooden planks that formed the decking. Below, a shiny river was flooding past, the liquid in it silver. Suddenly, he knew that what he was looking at was highly toxic, highly dangerous and that they shouldn't be breathing in its vapours. "Mercury," he wheezed, rolling onto his back. "There's mercury below us." The same metal that the First Emperor had taken in his attempt to become immortal, the same metal that had likely driven him insane before killing him.

"We have to get to the door," Salma said, eyes on the doorway high above them, not seeming to hear him. "We can use the key and—" She stopped.

"What is it?" Sara began, but then she saw it too.

Sanjeev's eyes followed theirs to the top of the palace steps, giving an exhausted, maddened wail. "Are you serious?"

CHAPTER 39

—

At the top of the steps, in front of the palace's double doors, a terracotta horse stood: its unblinking red eyes wide open, its nostrils flaring; its ears pointing like horns above its parted forelocks; its chest and leg muscles quivering as though made of flesh and blood.

On a curved saddle, reins in hand, as sturdy shouldered as his horse, the First Emperor sat motionless, dressed in yellow silk robes, a sword at his side, a tall, black cap on his head.

"Oh, oh!" Salma whispered.

The First Emperor lowered his chin. Eyes as red as the terracotta horse's, glared down at them and slowly, a grin lifted the ends of the small mouth and the thin lips parted to reveal… nothing—just darkness—as if the outer layer surrounded a hollow shell.

"That's all we need: terracotta warriors on one side, a mercury river beneath us, and a phantom on the other," Sanjeev said, not proud his voice had wobbled.

"You're a sci-fi guy! You should know all about this!" Sara replied.

Sanjeev threw her a questioning look.

"The crew of the intergalactic spaceship *Phindol* when the entire Taiji fleet surrounded them?" She shook the piece of silk three times.

"But they all died!" Sanjeev cried. "Mercilessly slaughtered by the…Oh!" His face dropped when he realised that was exactly what she meant.

"You guys are such geeks," Salma said, running to stand shoulder-to-shoulder with Sara as warriors at each end of the advancing army's nearest line peeled away, gathered in front of the main battle group, lifted their swords, and began running towards the bridge in single file.

"Here goes," Sara said grimly, raising a fist.

"Here goes," Salma echoed, fist-bumping. "At least all of them can't get on the bridge at the same time. Gives us a fighting chance."

"A fighting chance is all I want," Sara said quietly, her eyes on a looming warrior as she flicked her wrist three times.

Sanjeev, his back to Salma and Sara, standing at the other end of the bridge, stared up at the First Emperor who had spurred his horse forward. The horse's limbs moving jerkily came to the first step and paused. Its head rose and fell as it bowed uncertainly.

"Yes!" Sanjeev hissed. "There are no stairs in nature, which means horses can't climb down them. Ha, ha—"

The laughter died in his throat. The terracotta horse had laid a hoof on the first step.

"Seriously?" Sanjeev moaned.

The terracotta horse's red-ember eyes locked on to Sanjeev's. It stretched its neck, opened its mouth wide, and bellowed. It was a cry that sounded more like an enraged bull than any horse that had ever lived. That done, it lowered its ever-open eyes, dropped its head as much as it could and reached for the next step and the next, its massive hooves landing on each narrow earthen ledge and sending up a cloud of dust that spiralled into the air.

The bridge quaked.

Sanjeev, who had been transfixed by the effort the horse was making and the hoarseness of its breathing, spun around.

The first warrior was on the bridge, five metres away from Sara and Salma. Though his topknot, square-jawed face, patterned armour, and scarf wrapped around his neck made him seem totally human, his unblinking eyes and expression were as cold as stone.

"Yours!" Salma cried as the warrior suddenly quickened his pace and raised his sword.

Sara swept the silk dagger down and across the warrior's chest. Cut cleanly through and through, it tumbled onto the decking, rolled, fell into the river, and was immediately swallowed by the silent, shimmering greyness below them.

Sanjeev returned his attention to the First Emperor who, reins extended, had leaned backwards, putting his weight over the horse's hind quarters so that the terracotta horse was better balanced. It was working. Instead of one step, the terracotta horse, snorting and whinnying in excitement, was taking two at a time.

"They're almost at the bottom of the steps! What're we going to do?" Sanjeev cried, hating the fact his voice had wobbled again.

"Kinda busy right now!" Salma shouted over her shoulder as her foot connected with the face of a second warrior and knocked him over the bridge's rail.

Sanjeev dragged his own eyes away from the Emperor's fiery ones and gazed down at what he was holding. The Monkey key sat in his right hand; the Jade Dragonball in his left. *Why just a key? What good was it? What was it for?*

"They're coming over the railing!" Sara yelled.

Sanjeev swivelled around. Some of the warriors had split from the queue that had formed and having stretched over, had grasped onto the bridge's rails and were dragging themselves over it so that three, four, five warriors were now on the decking. While dodging their outstretched hands, delivering slicing cuts and punishing blows, Sara and Salma were fighting furiously. Even so, they were being forced back towards where he was standing.

We really are the crew members of The Cove surrounded by the entire Taiji fleet.

"We can't…give up," Sara cried, slashing left and right.

We're doomed. No sooner had Sanjeev said the words in his head than a triumphant whinny made him turn again.

The terracotta horse had navigated the last of the steps and was standing, head held majestically high, its barrel-shaped body swelling and contracting with each panting breath. Like the First Emperor, its red eyes were locked firmly on the bridge and the three of them.

The same grin spread across the First Emperor's face. He swung his legs, jabbed his heels into the terracotta horse's flank, and snapped the reins. The terracotta horse responded immediately. It raised a muscled leg but paused as if enjoying the sight of its own knee and fetlock suspended in the air and the terror on Sanjeev's face. It crashed its hoof down. It repeated this swaggering performance, arrogantly stamping one leg down after another, slowly coming closer, taking pleasure, it seemed to Sanjeev, in every last morsel of his fear.

Behind him, Salma's voice was urgent. "Pull back!" she yelled, and a moment later, Salma and Sara's backs bumped up against his.

"Any ideas, Sanjeev?" Salma called out as she kicked and punched furiously at the warriors still pouring towards them. "Because now's a good time to have one."

"I-I..." Sanjeev stammered. He stared at the Jade Dragonball. He stared at the key. He remembered what he had seen in the room where Shan Wu had materialised. But before he could say or do anything, he realised Salma and Sara were no longer fighting and everything had gone very quiet. He looked up and saw to his amazement that the First Emperor and the terracotta horse having descended the stairs were now motionless 20 metres in front of him, literally statues. He turned. Beyond the pile of broken pottery on the decking, all the intact warriors were standing in battle formation: some frozen in mid-step, some arms raised. Nothing moved except...

"I was wondering where he was," Salma said, her voice full of disgust, her eyes on the figure stomping its way through the columns of warriors, the jade and gold threads in the suit sparkling; the neck and face that protruded from it even paler, even more bloodless under the supermoon's giant eye.

"Having fun?" Shan Wu said, clearing the last line of warriors and stopping a few steps from the bridge's other end.

Salma did her best to grin. "Tremendous fun," she assured him. "But I'm really looking forward to knocking your head off."

A dry laugh gurgled from Shan Wu's mouth. "Such impudence."

"I prefer sassy," Sara looked at Salma. "Don't you prefer sassy?"

Salma, eyes on Shan Wu, nodded, "Much better."

Shan Wu slipped a little closer. "Do you play chess?" he asked, surprising the three teens. "It's an inferior game compared to Go, but nevertheless, it serves to illustrate an analogy in that—"

"Don't you just hate it when the bad guys give a big speech at the end?"

"Yeah," Sara replied. "Especially when it's cliched stuff like, oooh, I don't know…'You're checkmated!' or 'Your king is mine!'."

Salma grinned. "Yeah, anyone who would say that stuff needs a better script-writer."

Together, Salma and Sara fake laughed. Behind them, half-hidden, his eyes locked on the Jade Dragonball, Sanjeev felt his pulse quicken and his spirits lift.

"You are correct about one thing," Shan Wu said, a sly grin spreading.

"Oh, yes?" Sara said, tensing. Salma raised her fists.

"Oh, yes!" Shan Wu replied, placing a foot on the bridge. "This *is* the end."

Sanjeev, realising the transformation he was seeing was happening too slowly and making sure the hand holding the Jade Dragonball was out of sight, cried: "Wait! I have a question!"

Caught by surprise, Shan Wu paused.

"How come An Ho called you 'Boss'?"

"What?" Shan Wu spat.

"Earlier in the tunnels. How come An Ho called you 'Boss?' Chan was his boss, not you."

Sara and Salma were giving him sidelong glances like he was loopy.

Maybe he was. He glanced down at the Dragonball. Just a moment longer…

Shan Wu waved a hand dismissively. "Mind control. How else!" he cried and took another step.

And that was when Sanjeev did it.

CHAPTER 40

Later, after he had done it, it seemed crazy that he hadn't thought about doing it sooner. It seemed *so* obvious. But that was the problem with hindsight. Everything was crystal clear after the event. It was much harder to come up with ideas while crazy things were happening: like when a thousand-year-old corpse was attacking you on a massive, red-eyed horse and there are a zillion terracotta warriors all around you.

It had taken him a while—too long if he was being honest—but in the end he had understood. And man, it had felt good! He didn't just have a key, he had *the* key. The Hand of Fate that was the answer to all their problems. And it had been in his hand all along!

Still, once he had realised what the key was for, he had acted immediately: or at least, as fast as the Jade Dragonball had allowed him to move. The aperture had first appeared when Shan Wu materialised. He'd seen some pretty weird things but even so, he'd hardly believed his own eyes when it happened. Come on! Since when did Jade Dragons come to life and open their mouths? OK! He should have known better: it was no crazier than some of the things that had happened to him over the past year. All the same, he'd doubted himself. Who wouldn't?

That was his excuse, and he was sticking to it!

But when the Jade Dragon opened its mouth a second time, that was when he knew he hadn't been imagining things. He'd grasped, finally, what it meant. But he'd had to wait. That had been the worst part: waiting for the Jade Dragon to fully open its mouth again. Who knew they moved so slowly? Sheesh! That was why he'd asked that daft question about why An Ho had called Shan Wu "Boss". It was a ruse, a stratagem to gain some time. He'd tricked Shan Wu to give the Jade Dragon time to open its mouth, and as soon as its mouth was completely open, he'd thrust the key in and turned it. *What had the old man—Zang Guolao—said? The key is a lock.* A bit misleading, to say the least. It was true in as much as it was a lock.

But a door has to be opened before it can be closed and locked forever.

CHAPTER 41

—

"Stay away!" Sara cried.

Shan Wu gave a short, cruel laugh and took another step forward. "Everything was taken from me. My family, my home…I was taken from my village by a fool of a monk who thought I was worth saving." They could hear the hatred in his voice, centuries old. "I swore that I would never have anything taken from me again; that I would do the taking instead."

He let out a high cackle, a sound devoid of any humour. "I would have preferred to stay out of sight a few hundred years more, gaining strength, preparing. But thanks to Chan's meddling and your help," his hand dropped to the triskelion still embedded in the Jade Suit's chest, "I have been freed and you have sealed your fate." He took another step as Salma and Sara retreated. "Be sure to tell the Immortals how easily I defeated you."

"Not so fast!" Sanjeev cried, and pushing between Salma and Sara, he held up the Jade Dragonball. "I've got a better idea," and raising the key, he plunged it into the mouth of the Jade Dragon whose snout and head were most prominent, turned it, and pulled it out, a triumphant look on his face.

The three others stared at the Jade Dragonball as Sanjeev held it aloft like he'd just won the World Cup.

Shan Wu snickered. "And…?"

Sanjeev blinked rapidly five times as his mind whirred. He had done what the Jade Dragon seemed to be instructing him to do. Now nothing was happening. Maybe they were just kids. Kids against a mad shaman who knew incantations and spells and had been waiting a thousand years for this. What did they have? They had each other! That's what! Two images came to him, one that had grown familiar but was still as mysterious as when he first saw it. The Three Hares, a circle of running hares that shared the same ears, a symbol of the generative, life-giving energy of a universe that had existed for eternity. And the second: when Zang Guolao had asked them to join hands to turn the pages of the Book of Immutable Deeds. The answer had been staring them in the face the whole while. "To activate it," Sanjeev cried, putting the Jade Dragonball onto the decking in front of them. "We have to hold hands!"

Sara and Salma didn't stop to ask questions. The idea seemed so obvious they knew he was right as soon as he said it. Before Shan Wu could take another step, Sara shook the silk dagger three times, stuffed it away, and grasped hands with the others. Rearranging themselves, they formed a circle at the centre of which lay the Jade Dragonball.

As soon as the circle was complete, the Jade Dragonball began spinning, turning faster and faster until it suddenly stopped and a wave of white light flashed out, followed after a brief pause, by another and another, each pulse emanating at a regular interval, each as bright as the last.

"Like a lighthouse," Salma breathed.

"Or a super-dense neutron star," Sanjeev said.

The flashing white light had no effect on the three teens—it seemed no brighter than a torch's—but its effect on Shan Wu was dramatic.

"No," he groaned. And knees buckling, head lolling, he collapsed onto the decking. "No!"

With every pulse that struck him, his body seemed to weaken. Desperately, he tried to lift his hand and conjure, the three teens assumed, some spell, some incantation to countermand what was happening to him. But the effort defeated him, and like a flower left to stand without water in the burning sun, he wilted.

Tremors vibrated the air. The dragon unlocked by the key was swelling up: its snout growing, its neck rising, and its head towering high above the teens. Teeth flashing, green skin shimmering, fiery eyes, it gave a gargantuan roar as the white light continued to pulse. The dragon breathed in. And when it did—like they were specks of dust caught in a vacuum cleaner—its breath pulled at the teens' bodies lifting their heels off the decking, raising their hair from their scalps, tearing at the clothes.

"Hold tight!" Sara cried, squeezing Salma and Sanjeev's hands. "It's not us it wants. It's them. Look!"

Beyond the bridge, every terracotta warrior in the entire army had been pulled off its feet and was rising into the air. A moment later, they were all heading towards the three teens, flying through the air like hundreds of clay missiles

The three cowered low.

But as though they were passing through some kind of shrink-wrap, the figures began to change, growing smaller and smaller until, tinier than the most minuscule toy soldiers, they whizzed past the ears of the three teens and disappeared into the dragon's mouth.

A deafening screech from behind them made the three teens turn.

The terracotta horse was squatting on its hindquarters, desperately trying to back away from the force that had gripped it. But whinnying madly, nostrils flared, head thrashing side-to-side, it was being dragged forward, its hooves digging into the soft ground and ploughing deep furrows. Centimetre-by-centimetre, it was losing its battle to resist the dragon's pulling force while the First Emperor, lying horizontal, feet facing the dragon, desperately clung onto the edge of the saddle.

The dragon gave another roar.

The First Emperor's fingers were slipping. He turned and glared at the teens. His burning eyes flashed brighter in his strangely empty face, his top lip curled in a sneer, and he released his grip on the saddle. Silently, he hurtled past the teens, shrinking and shrinking until, like a golden shooting star, he entered the dragon and disappeared down its throat.

A moment later, the terracotta horse's hooves lost traction. Its hindquarters rose up, and it somersaulted into the air, shrank, and disappeared into the dragon's gaping mouth without a sound, following its master into the void.

"There's more!" Salma said, pointing over Sanjeev and Sara's shoulders.

Sanjeev thought she meant more terracotta warriors. She didn't. An Ho was tumbling towards them, arms and legs thrashing, and behind him, all the rest of Chan's goons, crying and begging, their voices turning to high-pitched squeaks as their bodies shrank and shrank until they too passed the dragon's lips and were effortlessly swallowed with everything else.

Still drawing in its breath, the dragon lowered its head. Its raging eyes locked on Shan Wu, who was refusing to let go of the bridge. His fingers were wrapped tightly around the bridge's wooden rail. He was snarling, cursing, and clinging on even though his legs were off the ground and his body was horizontal. The dragon continued to breathe in. The flashing white light from the Jade Dragonball pulsed faster and faster. With each passing second, Shan Wu was being pulled and stretched longer and thinner: his legs, arms, torso—everything—narrowing. Looking more like a grotesque green string, his face became the length of a leg, his body the length of a car. And yet he did not let go.

With a tremendous roar, the dragon doubled, trebled, quadrupled in size.

Shan Wu screamed, and the three teens flinched in pain as the noise climbed into their ears and clawed the insides of their skulls. The three pieces of the triskelion leapt from the chest of the Jade Suit and clattered onto the decking of the bridge in front of them. Shan Wu's body continued to elongate, so that the edges of his toes were touching the dragon's lips. One after the other, his fingers began to release their grip on the bridge's rail until a single pinky remained hooked there. It was the most bizarre sight the three teens had ever seen. As though it were made of dough, the pinky was being stretched and stretched, growing in size until it was the length of a leg. But its grip was loosening too, and with a shrill scream Shan Wu let go and was sucked into the dragon's mouth, slithering through the air and into the chasm like an enormously long strand of spaghetti.

With Shan Wu gone, the dragon roared and diminishing in size even faster than it had grown; it snarled, turned its head, opened its mouth, and pointed its gaping jaws at Sanjeev. Sanjeev understood immediately. Darting forward, he plunged his hand inside the dragon's mouth which was now no bigger than a dog's.

He turned the key.

CHAPTER 42

The supermoon disappeared like a light had been switched off and at their feet, giving no indication of the horror that had gone before, the Jade Dragonball glowed benignly, its pale green light as gentle as a toddler's nursery light, the dragon that had grown to gargantuan proportions once again just a small, intricately carved figure, one amongst many.

Sweaty palmed, the three teens reluctantly released one another's hands. It was Salma who eventually stooped to pick up the Jade Dragonball. Holding it up and using it like a lantern, she collected the three shards of the triskelion and returned Sanjeev's and Sara's.

Silently, the others took theirs.

"I think we should get off this bridge," Sanjeev said.

Without discussion, they shuffled off in single file. Sara in front, Sanjeev behind, the ball still in Salma's hand.

"I am exhausted," Sara said, the features of her face, like that of the others, softly lit by the light still emanating from the Jade Dragonball. "By the way, good thinking."

"Thanks," Sanjeev said as they gathered in a loose circle away from the river.

"Yeah," Salma said. "Nice one!"

Sanjeev grinned. "Now what?"

"Well, I hate to say it, but I'm thinking…" Salma pointed past Sanjeev's shoulder to the shaft of white light that had re-emerged or perhaps had been there all the time.

All three gazed at it silently for a moment. The thought of a long trek weighed heavily on all of them.

"Wait," Sara said. "Can you swipe us there?"

Salma handed the Dragonball to Sara and unfolded the map. "I can try," she replied. "Great," she said drily, seeing the three glowing icons next to the Epang Palace. "Now it works!"

"Thank goodness!" Sara said.

Sanjeev, feeling equally delighted, opened his mouth to agree but Salma had already swiped, and in the blink of an eye, they found themselves next to the shaft of light.

The image at their feet immediately caught their eyes. Like a projector throwing a picture onto a cinema screen, the shaft of light was shining a painting onto the ground. Hunkering down, Sanjeev reached out a hand and passed it through the light. The image of the painting disappeared and reappeared as his hand moved. "From Cave 407 in the Mogao cave complex," he whispered.

Sara answered Salma's unspoken question. "The Mogao cave complex—near the city of Dunhuang in Northwest China. A long time ago, it was an important stop on the Silk Road. Buddhist monks carved out four or five hundred caves there and decorated them for centuries. Seventeen have images of the Three Hares symbol, just like this one. Just like the triskelion."

"It's beautiful," Salma said, eyes on the delicate greens and pale yellows.

Sanjeev raised his head and followed the path of the shaft. "Oh, that's kinda interesting."

Salma and Sara leaned in and peered up too.

"How? How's that possible?" Salma stuttered.

The shaft of light rose straight up but near the top and swerved to the right. "Light waves can't bend!"

"Yes, they can!" Sara and Sanjeev said at once. They grinned and Sanjeev said: "In his General Theory of Relativity, Einstein predicted gravity would bend light."

"It's called gravitational lensing," Sara added.

"Oh, OK," Salma replied. "That's good. Because I'd hate anything to break the laws of physics."

For a moment, there was silence. Then all three burst out laughing, finally a release of tension.

Their laughter was interrupted by the disappearance of the Three Hares symbol at their feet. In its place, a circle of white light shone like a mini moon.

"Where did the symbol go?" Salma said and looked up. "Oh!" The direction of the cone of light had changed and instead of bending, it now climbed vertically, a barely visible white thread in the void above them.

A voice they all recognised suddenly spoke.

"Hello, everyone!" the deep voice boomed. "Can you hear me?"

"There!" Sara cried, pointing at where the Three Hares symbol had been. As though he were standing at the edge of a pond and peering into it, Lan Caihe's face appeared on the ground as he called out.

"Can you see me?" he asked, grin widening.

"Yes, we can," Sara said, unsure whether to address the image on the ground or the top of the light cone. Her arms were beginning to ache: the Jade Dragonball was heavier than it looked.

"They can see us!" Lan Caihe cried as Zhongli Quan's round face appeared. "Ha! There they are!" he said, fanning himself, and one after the other, other faces crowded in until all eight Immortals were in the circle of light.

"Oh, bravo!" Lu Dongbin cried, eyes flashing. "Great work."

"Fabulous!" echoed He Xiangu, waving a lotus flower in time to the cheerful tune Han Xiang Zi was playing on his flute next to her.

"I wasn't sure it would work," Cao Guojiu said nervously and flinched when Li Tieguai slapped him appreciatively on the back and told him to have more faith in himself.

Zang Guolao, bushy grey eyebrows furrowed, calmed the others. In a sober voice, he said: "You must be exhausted."

"You can say that again," muttered Salma.

"Well, this won't take long," Zang Guolao replied.

"What won't take long?" Sanjeev asked suspiciously. He gazed at the other two. Both looked equally dubious.

Zhongli Quan, grinning, said: "We just have to do a quick eradication. Then we'll be done."

"A what?" cried all three teens.

Lan Caihe, squeezed between He Xiangu and Han Xiang Zi, said in a voice that was now as soft as water trickling in a brook: "An eradication. You know, from the verb 'eradicate' meaning 'get rid of', 'remove any trace'."

"I know what eradication means," Sara said, "but what are you going to—"

Too late. The eradication had begun.

CHAPTER 43

—

As though the Hands of Fate were fish hooked out of the sea, the silk dagger and the map leapt from the hands of Sara and Salma, jumped into the shaft of light, and started floating upwards.

But Sanjeev had other ideas about the key. "Can't I keep it?" he cried, holding on to it with both hands as it tugged at his arms, heaving him into the air.

"You have to let go," Sara cried, pulling at his knees as his arms stretched above his head and his feet lifted further and further off the ground. "*Let go!*"

"Ugh!" Sanjeev grunted, landing heavily beside Salma. Jumping to his feet, he dusted himself off, watching the key longingly as it, along with the piece of silk and the map, climbed higher and higher until, in the circle of light, Lu Dongbin reached out and gathered in all three objects.

"Next comes the Jade Dragonball. If you would be so kind…" Zang Guolao said, motioning towards the ball which Sara was still holding.

Stepping forward into the light, Sara raised the weighty ball— *no wonder it is so heavy with all those little people and things inside it*—but paused. Shan Wu and his minions had threatened the world with a terrible fate, and Shan Wu had tried to kill her and Salma and Sanjeev. Criminals deserved to be punished. About that, she was certain. But the doubt she had concerned the nature of that punishment. Putting all of them in the ball for the rest of eternity? That sounded like torture to her. Was it necessary? Was it humane? Her hands gripped the Dragonball more tightly. Down at the circle of light, she saw each and every Immortal; their eyes fixed on her, frowning.

"What's she waiting for?" Zhongli Quan said, his fan a blur of motion.

"Let's have it!" Lu Dongbin cried, eyebrows meeting like clashing swords.

Zang Guolao, wrinkled face as unperturbed as ever, hushed both of them. "Sara," he said, "you are kind and thoughtful and these are wonderful qualities. But—"

"But what? Do I need to be nastier? I need to be tougher?"

"You need to be *realistic*," he replied patiently. "There is nothing else: the Dragonball will keep Shan Wu imprisoned. For all eternity, he will want to enslave the human race. What else can we do?"

"I don't know," Sara admitted, "but the punishment should fit the crime."

"It does!" Lu Dongbin yelled as Han Xiang Zi played five sharply discordant notes on his flute.

Sara looked at Sanjeev and Salma. "There must be another way," she said.

Salma grimaced and Sanjeev dropped his eyes to his feet and shuffled uncomfortably.

"I dunno," he muttered. Meeting Sara's eye, "I kinda think they deserve it." He glanced at Salma who shrugged apologetically at Sara.

"They asked for it," she said gently.

"It's a majority decision!" Lu Dongbin cried. "You're outvoted!"

Zang Guolao lifted a finger, indicating he wanted no more outbursts.

Sara closed her eyes. *Was it true? Was imprisonment in the Jade Dragonball the only way to protect the human race from Shan Wu? Should she believe the Immortals, or not? Should she do what Sanjeev and Salma wanted, or not? What was the *right* course of* action? It seemed like one thing, a general rule—be kind—told her *not* to give the Immortals the ball, and another thing—thinking about the consequences if Shan Wu escaped—told her to do the opposite.

When Sara finally opened her eyes again, she took a deep breath. A line from the Analects of Confucius had run through her mind— *In dealing with the world, the excellent person was not invariably for or against anything*—a reminder that all important decisions required careful thought. She had done that, and without another moment's hesitation, she brought her hands away from the cold, hard surface of the ball, content that she trusted herself; trusted her *Yi*; trusted her ability to craft a just answer.

The Jade Dragonball, bobbing in the air like a jewelled cork on an invisible plane of water, glowed deep green and its dragons, rising from its surface in seething waves, whispered her name before the ball, faster than a bullet, shot up to Zang Guolao's outstretched hands.

"Good girl!" Lu Dongbin cried, making a triumphant fist.

Salma placed a hand on Sara's shoulder and squeezed it gently.

"And now the final step," Zang Guolao said, passing the Jade Dragonball to Lu Dongbin. He snapped his fingers and the shards of the triskelion sprang from the three teens. Hovering in the light just as the Jade Dragonball had done, they gently rotated to align themselves. With their jagged edges positioned correctly, they smoothly slipped together, and with a loud metallic *thunk*, they became one.

It too zoomed upwards and a moment later, Li Tieguai was reaching out to snatch it. "Mine!" he said, almost dropping his crutch in his determination to get his hands on
it first.

Sanjeev's face suddenly clouded. "Er…"

"What is it?" Sara asked.

"I've just had a thought."

Salma grinned wickedly. "Of course, you have."

But Sanjeev wasn't smiling. "How do we get out of here?" he asked.

"Oh!" gasped, immediately realising what he meant: the shards of the triskelion had transported them and now they didn't have the means of getting back home.

In the circle of light, Zhongli Quan's flabby face leaned forward. "You are 100 metres below ground, inside a tomb with no exits."

As the words sank in, beads of sweat prickled Sanjeev's his forehead and he returned Sara and Salma's nervous glances.

"Enough!" Zang Guolao said as Zhongli Quan leaned back, his jowls and stomach jiggling with suppressed laughter.

"We need the shards!" Sanjeev said, chin tilted up at the heavens. "We need to get out of here."

Zang Guolao shook his grey-haired head. "Unfortunately," he said, "the Hands of Fate and the triskelion are the property of Heaven. They can be loaned; but they cannot be given away."

"So, loan the triskelion back to us and get us out of here!" Salma yelled.

"Yeah!" Sanjeev shouted, panicking at the thought of being trapped in the dark emptiness of the tomb.

"But the danger has passed, which means there is no mandate to lend the Hands of Fate or the triskelion," Cao Guojiu said, his usual meek and timid voice sounding as if he couldn't believe the need to explain such as a basic, well-known fact.

"So...what? You're going to entomb us?" Salma shouted. "After all the things we've done for you? Seriously?"

Zhongli Quan's podgy face turned serious again, and turning to Zang Guolao, he said: "I think you should tell them."

"Tell us what?" Sara said fiercely.

"Be calm," Zhang Guolao said in a soothing voice. "We have no intention of leaving you in that tomb."

"We aren't monsters," Zhongli Quan said brightly.

Salma snorted. "Yeah, right."

Zhongli Quan, sniffing and raising his fan, pretended not to hear.

"So, how do we get out of here?" Sanjeev said. "Click our heels three times and say, 'there's no place like home?' I mean, how?" He was practically yelling this.

"Look at your wrists," Lan Caihe said, pointing to a yellow flower plucked from his basket.

The three teens looked at their wrists. "Oh!" Salma exclaimed. "My mother's going to kill me."

Sara traced the edges of the shape with her fingertip, feeling the swelling where the design was inked. "Mine too," she said.

"That," Sanjeev said, "is totally cool." He shrugged at the other two who were gazing at him. "Come on!" he said. "It is!"

"So, what are we supposed to do with this?" Salma asked Zang Guolao.

"Each of you has a tattoo of your piece of the triskelion," Zang Guolao said. "When you put them together, you will be transported."

"As simple as that?" Salma asked doubtfully.

"As simple as that," he assured her.

A silence fell which was broken by Zang Guolao.

"Well," he said. "I believe that is all. So, on behalf of my fellow Immortals, I'd like to say thank you and—"

"Wait! One minute please," Sara said.

Zang Guolao's grey eyebrows rose.

"What do you mean 'That's it'? We passed your tests, fought an army of terracotta warriors, were chased by a madman in a Jade Suit, saved the world, and all you can say is 'thanks?'"

"Well, what else would you like us to say or do?" Zang Guolao asked calmly, holding up a hand to silence Zhongli Quan and Lu Dongbin, both of whom had leaned forward.

Sara looked at Salma and Sanjeev, who gazed back at her, saying nothing. "I…er…dunno," she muttered, suddenly feeling deflated.

"Actually, I have a question," Sanjeev said.

"Yes?" Zang Guolao said.

"What happened to Lin Dan?"

"Oh, he got shot," Zhongli Quan replied in a jolly voice.

"What!" all three Hares cried.

Zang Guolao sighed loudly, shook his head, and gave Zhongli Quan the kind of look a parent gives a very naughty, very disobedient child. "Lin Dan," he continued, "was captured and thrown into a cell. The henchmen did not bother to search him so they did not find the mobile phone you gave him. He called the police and they are on their way as we speak."

Salma, resisting the urge to give Zhongli Quan a piece of her mind, raised her wrist, exposing the dark, jagged lines of the tattoo. "So," she said, addressing Sara and Sanjeev, "I'm not a celebrity, but get me out of here!"

Sara grinned, raised her arm, and pressed her wrist next to Salma's. "Yeah, time to go."

Sanjeev, grinning and stepping forward, raised his wrist too. "Home sweet home, here we come!"

PART 6

BRITISH MUSEUM, LONDON, UNITED KINGDOM
THE PRESENT DAY

Chapter 44

The nausea subsided faster this time, but the sight of two terracotta warriors and the life-sized terracotta horse in the British Museum caught Sara so much by surprise she gave a loud shriek, which caused both Salma and Sanjeev to jump. A guard rushed in from the adjacent room.

"Anything wrong, Miss?" he said to Salma.

"No, thank you. We're fine now," Salma said, turning to face him. As they recognised one another, she said, "Oh, hello, Mr. Carter. Nice to see you."

"Hello, Salma," Mr. Carter said with a smile. "You sure you're OK?"

"We're fine, really. Thank you. Off to see my mother."

"Give her my regards," Mr. Carter said, touching the side of his cap and waving goodbye.

When he'd left the room, in unison, all three sighed with relief.

"Wow! Am I glad that adventure is over!" Sanjeev said.

Salma scoffed. "Adventure?"

"Er…episode?"

Sara and Salma shook their heads.

"Escapade?"

Head shakes again.

"Nightmare is a better word," Salma said.

"Or torment?" Sara suggested.

"Yeah, torment's good," Salma agreed.

Sanjeev titled his head. "OK. So, let me try again. Wow! Am I glad that torment's over!"

"Much better," Salma said.

Something chimed.

Delight spreading across her face, Sara reached into her pocket. "Hey, look what I have!" She waved her mobile...The others immediately pulled out theirs and began checking for messages.

Sanjeev's eyes boggled.

"What is it?" Sara said anxiously.

"A message from Shan Wu: loving the new house; pop in any time!"

"Ha! Ha! Very funny," Sara said, trying to keep a straight face.

"Why do you think the Immortals didn't let us take our mobiles to the Jade Palace or Xi'an?" Salma asked.

Sanjeev shrugged. "Dunno, but I'm glad they didn't."

Salma sighed. "OK, what's the punchline?"

Sanjeev grinned. "Can you imagine the roaming charges?"

Salma and Sara groaned simultaneously.

"I'm under-appreciated," Sanjeev complained, voice full of exaggerated woe...

"You know..." Sara said as they continued to walk through the crowds towards the office belonging to Salma's mother. "I do feel a little bad."

Salma gave her a puzzled look. "About saving the world?"

Sara laughed. "No! I feel bad about what happened to all the terracotta warriors. I mean, they were works of art."

"Works of art that were trying to kill us," Sanjeev reminded her.

Salma dodged a kid who was staring at the ground where his half-eaten sandwich lay. "I know what you mean. But it was Shan Wu's fault: he made them attack us."

Sara shrugged. "I guess so. All the same, I hate the idea that they were destroyed.""But..." Sanjeev said thoughtfully, "were they really?"

"You saw them in the pit all smashed up." Sara said.

"Yes...but they could have been all smashed up in the first place and Shan Wu put them together to attack us. And after the 'eradication' I'm sure they were left the way they had been before. In a way, they were returned to their natural state." Salma said.

"Mmmm…" Sara responded. "Unlikely."

"Or maybe the Immortals—put them back together again. They said they could interact with our world through artworks, so…" Sanjeev surmised.

"Yeah," Sara said, happier. "Yeah, that's possible, I guess."

"Forget about that," said Salma, "We'll never know for sure until the First Emperor's tomb is opened. What I'm way more worried about is this!" She turned her wrist to display the tattoo of her piece of the triskelion.

"I'm not," Sara said.

"I thought you said you were!"

Sara shook her head. "Nope. I'm just going to tell my mum that an Immortal did it and ran away."

All three laughed as Salma slowed and stopped outside a closed office door.

"Well, this is her office," she said.

The three looked at one another, suddenly embarrassed and unsure. Their lives had depended on being able to work together as a team, and now it was time for them to go their separate ways. No one quite knew what to say.

It was Sanjeev who finally ended the embarrassing silence. "I'll look you up the next time I'm in London," he said, trying not to squirm.

"Do that," Salma replied stiffly.

"You'll both have to come and visit me in Beijing," Sara added.

"Feel like I've been there already," Sanjeev mumbled.

"No, really," Sara said. "There's a lot of great stuff you want to check out. We could go to the Temple of Heaven or the Summer Palace." She smiled at them. "Or we can go on one of the tours to the Terracotta Warriors. You know, when you're ready for it."

Sanjeev was opening his mouth to reply when the office door suddenly swung open.

"Oh, hello everyone," a tall woman said and coming out of the doorway, she wrapped an arm around Salma's shoulders and hugged. "Who are your friends?"

"This is Sanjeev," Salma said.

Sanjeev waved a hand. "Hi! Nice to meet you."

"And this is Sara," Salma said, gesturing. Her heart stopped. Too late, she realised that the gesture had revealed her tattoo. There it was! On her wrist, as clear as day!

Sara's eyes were on it too. "Er…Hello…nice to er…meet you," Sara said, flicking her eyes from Salma's horrified face to the tattoo on Salma's wrist, to the face of Salma's mother.

The smile on Salma's mother face did not flicker. "So, have you three been hanging out in the museum?"

The three looked at one another, sharing the same thought: what just happened?

"Yeah…great!" Salma said. "We've been deeply immersed in ancient Chinese culture."

The others did their best to hide their smiles.

Her mother looked a little puzzled. "Well…that's good. It's a fascinating history."

"I've got an itchy wrist," Salma said, and stretching out her arm again, she slowly scratched the tattoo, gazing at her mother's face while she did it. When it was obvious her mother couldn't see the tattoo, her eyes met Sanjeev and Sara's. Sara looked relieved, Sanjeev a bit disappointed.

"So, we're heading for some lunch. Would you like to join us?" Salma's mother asked.

"Actually, I'd better watch my time. I'm supposed to be meeting my father in the Great Court at 3 p.m."

"And my parents," Sanjeev said, "are having a nap at our hotel: they don't even know I'm gone, so I'd better be getting back."

"Are you sure?" Salma's mother asked.

For a moment, no one said a word. Then, to the bemusement of Salma's mother, they all walked forward and smothered one another in each other's arms, holding on tightly until, when they finally parted, their eyes had somewhat dried.

"I'll miss you guys," Sanjeev said.

"Why? Are you planning never to speak to us again?" Salma asked her face mock serious.

"That depends," Sanjeev replied.

"On?" Sara asked.

Sanjeev grinned and pushed his glasses to the bridge of his nose. "On whether the world needs saving again…"

PART 7

BEIJING, CHINA
LONDON, UK
HOBOKEN, USA
ONLINE, PRESENT DAY

CHAPTER 45

—

A few weeks later, the Three Hares' chat-box having disappeared from their computers, Sara, Sanjeev, and Salma were texting one another in their own chat group, The Three Hare_s_s_s.

SanjeevR:	So…did it go well last night?
Sal_M:	Yup! Grandmaster Cho said my destruction was OUTSTANDING!
DeadStone:	Brilliant!
SanjeevR:	You've had plenty of practice.
Sal_M:	I know!
DeadStone:	And now you're a black belt?
Sal_M:	Red-black.
SanjeevR:	Niiiice. Well done.
DeadStone:	Yeah, congrats!
Sal_M:	Thx.
DeadStone:	BTW—the essay for Mrs Greene about the poem and the Battle of Maldon? Did you get the grade back?
Sal_M:	I forgot to tell you. Got it weeks ago.
DeadStone:	And?
Sal_M:	Killed it!
SanjeevR:	LOL
DeadStone:	I bet you did.
Sal_M:	How about you guys? What's been happening?

There was a pause as Sara thought about how much she was looking forward to chatting with Granny Tang after she finished her calligraphy practice tonight. They'd grown much closer, but there was a problem: it was so difficult not to mention anything about meeting the Immortals when Granny Tang started talking about them. Sanjeev was also thinking about how much fun it would be to talk about the stuff that had happened in Xi'an with Anton and the rest of his friends, though he knew if he did, they would never believe him.

Sal_M:	Hello?
SanjeevR:	Still here. Just thinking it's hard not telling anyone.
DeadStone:	Was thinking exact same thing.
Sal_M:	But we really can't, right?
SanjeevR:	Suppose not.
DeadStone:	I know what I'd like to do…
Sal_M:	What?
DeadStone:	Write about the whole thing.
Sal_M:	Like a story, you mean?
SanjeevR:	Put it in your school newspaper! Fiction, of course.
DeadStone:	Would be kinda fun.
Sal_M:	I'll help you.
SanjeevR:	Me too. But are you sure the story has finished?
Sal_M:	Plzzzzzzzzz!
SanjeevR:	No, seriously. How do we know there won't be another Shan Wu?
DeadStone:	'Cause the Immortals would have told us there was?
SanjeevR:	Did they ever tell us everything?
Sal_M:	@SanjeevR has got a point. The Immortals didn't exactly tell us everything, did they?
DeadStone:	No, I suppose not.
SanjeevR:	Although I guess if the Immortals needed help with something they wouldn't use us.
Sal_M:	OK…Why not?
SanjeevR:	The thousand-year power: we only had it because we were born a thousand years after Shan Wu.

DeadStone:	Right! And if another bad guy comes along, he or she will probably have a different birthday to us. Meaning we'd be of no use to the Immortals!
Sal_M:	Excellent! So, the next time the world needs saving, we're off the hook! Dunno about you, but I'm glad!
DeadStone:	Planet still needs saving though.
SanjeevR:	You're thinking about the environment?
DeadStone:	Yes.
SanjeevR:	Very true.

In his bedroom, Sanjeev petted Jigsaw who, eyes locked on him, was sitting next to the bed and panting noisily, tongue lolling. He'd gone bananas after they'd driven from the airport to the kennels and picked him up and even now, he wasn't letting Sanjeev out of his sight. Sanjeev whispered his name and Jigsaw, listening, leaned his head left and right.

Sitting in her kitchen, legs squeezed under the table and teaspoon in hand, Salma stirred her tea.

In her bedroom, Sara, staring at the blinking cursor on her computer and the unfinished article, realised she was procrastinating on today's word on the *Word of the Day* app.

DeadStone:	You know, if I did write about it for my school newspaper, I'd want to know the answer to one question first.
Sal_M:	Just one?
DeadStone:	It's been bugging me for a while.
Sal_M:	Is it what the Immortals are going to do with the Jade Dragonball?
DeadStone:	I think I know the answer to that one.
Sal_M:	Put it at the bottom of a cupboard and leave it there for all eternity?

DeadStone:	I don't think Shan Wu or any of the rest are going to see blue sky for a looooong time. But that's not what I've been wondering about.
SanjeevR:	So, what is it?
DeadStone:	It's our names: Sara, Sanjeev, and Salma. Why do they all begin with "S"?
Sal_M:	Funny you should ask 'cause I've been trying to figure it out too and doing online searches. I have an idea.
DeadStone:	Tell! Tell!
Sal_M:	OK, stay with me here. You'd agree the letter "S" is serpentine, yes?
DeadStone:	I guess it is a bit like a snake, yeah.
SanjeevR:	OK. So…?
Sal_M:	So, I think it's no coincidence that the oldest known allegorical symbol in alchemy is ouroboros. I think it originated in Egypt.
DeadStone:	The snake that eats itself: a symbol of eternity, of endless birth, death, and rebirth.
Sal_M:	Yes, Zackly!

Sanjeev grinned and pushed his glasses to the bridge of his nose.

SanjeevR:	It's not a *completely* watertight theory.
Sal_M:	Well, I'm thinking it's pretty leaky but…
DeadStone:	Well, it sort-of makes sense. We *did* go back in time and return.
SanjeevR:	Like a loop!
DeadStone:	Put it this way—do we have any better ideas?
Sal_M:	I guess not…
DeadStone:	We'll never know for sure unless we ask the Immortals.
Sal_M:	Please! I've had enough of them to last a lifetime.

242 ~ THE THREE HARES

SanjeevR:	Infinite lifetimes?
Sal_M:	Any lifetimes, all lifetimes!

There was a brief lull during which the three's thoughts returned to their everyday lives.

SanjeevR:	So, you going to the dojang today, Salma?
Sal_M:	Later, yeah.
DeadStone:	What you up to, Sanjeev?
SanjeevR:	Dr Hansen's extracting a spaniel's back tooth and she's allowing me to observe.
DeadStone:	Cool. You'll make a great vet.
Sal_M:	@DeadStone Did you go to the Wing Chun class Lily recommended?
DeadStone:	Not yet, but I will.
Sal_M:	@DeadStone What you doing now?
DeadStone:	Got some HW. Then I'll go see my granny. What time is it in NJ?
SanjeevR:	Just after 8 am.
DeadStone:	Just after 8 pm here. How abt you, @Sal_M?
Sal_M:	Around 1 pm.
SanjeevR:	Amazing, don't you think?
DeadStone:	What is?
Sal_M:	That Sanjeev can read the time?
DeadStone:	LOL

Sanjeev tickled Jigsaw's ears, which made Jigsaw groan in ecstasy.

SanjeevR:	Very funny. What I mean is as we sit and talk, we're circling the sun at 67,000 miles an hour, rotating around our axis at 1,000 miles per hour, which means it's morning for me and evening for Sara.

Salma shook her head. Trust Sanjeev.

SanjeevR:	Hey, did I tell you I looked up Lin Dan?
DeadStone:	No!
Sal_M:	No
SanjeevR:	Well, I did. He's back at Shanghai Jiao Tong University, still researching genes, still interested in fingerite.
DeadStone:	You know, he could corroborate our story.
Sal_M:	He could. But would he? Respectable scientist says three kids used a piece of silk to cut through the solid wood and metal door of his prison cell? Resurrected a thousand-year-old corpse in a Jade Suit? Disappeared through a solid wall? It would blow people's minds. If they could stop laughing at how ridiculous it sounded.
DeadStone:	I guess you're right.
SanjeevR:	OK. Well, here's something to totally blow *your* minds.
Sal_M:	I can hardly wait.
DeadStone:	Give us a hint.
SanjeevR:	I've been thinking about what Zang Guolao said just before we were transported. Been thinking about it a lot, actually.

In Beijing, Sara pulled her fingertips through her long hair wondering what Sanjeev was going to say.

In London, Salma heard her neighbours close their flat's door. She couldn't remember anything that Zang Guolao had said that was any stranger than anything else that had happened.

Both leaned a little closer to their mobiles.

DeadStone:	OK, I'm officially intrigued. Go on.

Just then, Sanjeev's mother called up the stairs. Breakfast was ready and his mother hated it when he didn't come to the table at once.

SanjeevR: Oh! Oh! Breakfast time. Gotta go.
DeadStone: Hey, you can't do that!
Sal_M: TELL US WHAT YOU'RE THINKING OR I
                 WILL JUMP ON THE NEXT FLIGHT TO NY
                 AND MAKE YOU SEE STARS!
SanjeevR: LOL. OK.

"Sanjeev!" his mother called again, "your breakfast is getting cold."
"Be down in a minte, Mom," he cried back.

SanjeevR: What exactly did Zang Guolao say when they took
                 back the Hands of Fate, the triskelion, and the
                 Jade Dragonball and we asked how we were going
                 to get home?
Sal_M: Basically, he said we didn't need the triskelion,
                 right?
SanjeevR: Yes, but do you remember his actual words?
DeadStone: I think so.
SanjeevR: Go on.
DeadStone: "When you put them together, you will be
                 transported."
SanjeevR: Zackly!
DeadStone: Oh!
SanjeevR: Yup!
Sal_M: I have no idea what you're on about.
SanjeevR: Don't you get it?

"Sanjeev! I won't tell you again!" Jigsaw, ears up, dashed from the room.

"I'll be right there!" Sanjeev called. He reckoned he was two minutes away from being in deep trouble with his mother. Eyes locked on his mobile, he texted as he shuffled out of his room.

Sal_M:	Don't get what?
SanjeevR:	The Immortals didn't say anything about it being a one-time deal.
Sal_M:	Still not with you.
SanjeevR:	We've got the power to transport ourselves anywhere! All we need to do is put our tattoos together.
Sal_M:	Oh…OK. Got it. But if we do that, we could end up any place, any time.

At the bottom of the stairs, Sanjeev stopped, catching his mother's eye as she slipped a plate onto the breakfast table and sat next to his father. Practically, with his chin on his father's leg, Jigsaw, tail swishing, eyes on the plate, was behaving himself…for the moment.

In Beijing, Sara stood and gazed from her window at the dusky sky and the lights shimmering in the distance.

In London, Salma finished her tea, rinsed her cup, and stood with her back leaning against the sink, surveying the tiny kitchen.

DeadStone:	@Sal_M has a point. We might end up 500 million years in the past—in the Palaeozoic era.
SanjeevR:	The Cambrian explosion!
Sal_M:	That's what I mean. Could be dodgy.
SanjeevR:	Er, yeah. I suppose so.
Sal_M:	But …
DeadStone:	Hmm?
Sal_M:	What if we went somewhere really cool.
DeadStone:	Like?
Sal_M:	Like ancient Korea around 50 BCE, when the earliest Korean martial arts appeared.
SanjeevR:	Or the 1927 Solvay conference: Einstein, Bohr, Marie Curie, Heisenberg, Schrodinger.
DeadStone:	Going to 1791 when Mozart composed his Clarinet Concerto.

There was a pause of several seconds before the conversation continued once again.

DeadStone:	It would be *such* a bad idea.
SanjeevR:	Terrible!
Sal_M:	The worst.
SanjeevR:	What was I thinking?
Sal_M:	What *were* you thinking?
DeadStone:	He wasn't thinking.
SanjeevR:	I wasn't thinking…but you know what I'm thinking?
DeadStone:	I know *exactly* what you're thinking.
SanjeevR:	Are you both thinking what I'm thinking?
Sal_M:	That depends on what you're thinking. What are you thinking?
SanjeevR:	I'm thinking…it's time I had breakfast.

List of Characters in Order of Appearance

Salma—15 years old, dedicated student of taekwondo. Originally from Syria but now living in London with her mother. Her father passed away from a 'broken heart'. Her Hand of Fate is the every-changing map (of Yggdrasil).

Lee Arnott—Salma's taekwondo instructor.

Grandmaster Cho—Grandmaster at Salma's Dojo.

Shan Wu—Was called Shan Mu but changed his name when he went over to the 'dark side'. His brother was Shan Tuo. In Book 1, a monk took Shan Mu from his home and he never saw Shan Tuo again. Shan Tuo has the degenerative disease that Chan, a relative of the brothers, has. Shan Wu tried to steal the Elixir of Immortality from the Immortals but was caught and imprisoned in the Jade Dragonball. Chan managed to find the Jade Dragonball after it was dropped into the ocean by the Immortals. Chan has extracted Shan Wu from the Jade Dragonball, but Shan Wu is not fully corporeal. He is regenerating inside the Jade Suit which was stolen from the Met Museum in Book 2.

Salma's mother—Works at the British Museum.

Tuyen—Salma's best friend at school.

Sanjeev—15 years old American of Indian descent, likes sci-fi and has a dog called Jigsaw. His Hand of Fate is the Gold Monkey Key.

Sara—15 years old of mixed Scottish-Chinese heritage, likes classical music; esp. Martin Frost. Her Hand of Fate is the silk dagger.

Byrhtnoth—Leader of the East Saxons. He wears a heavy black tunic, black trousers, and a deep brown cloak with a distinctive red cap.

Wistan—East Saxon, son of Wurstan responsible for keeping watch over Salma.

Wurstan—East Saxon ealdorman. Father of Wistan and close companion of Byrhtnoth.

Dunnere—East Saxon ealdorman, also a close companion of Byrhtnoth.

Godric—East Saxon within this inner circle of Byrhtnoth.

Olaf Tryggvason—Viking chief who has sailed up the River Blackwater along with 3000 Viking warriors.

Zhongli Quan—Immortal 1. When he first meets Salma after the battle, he is clean-shaven and a has a wild, black thicket on his head. He is bare chested. His skin is covered with inky-black tattoos of animals that seemed to writhe like living beasts. Has a huge belly. When he meets the teens in the Jade Palace, he has a gold fan. He has a quick temper and is impatient with Salma.

Lan Caihe—Immortal 2. Wears a yellow robe on first meeting Salma after the battle. Has sleek, black hair. Later, he is wearing a blue, tattered gown and only one shoe. His voice alternates between deep and high-pitched. He carries a basket of flowers.

Li Tieguai—Immortal 3. An old man who uses a crutch to walk. He wears a filthy, torn robe barely covering his body and a large gourd hanging on a piece of rope around his waist. He and Lan Caihe have a fractious relationship. Li Tieguai wore the silver amulet that was struck by Shan Wu's magic and broke into three pieces becoming the three pieces of the triskelion.

Lu Dongbin—Immortal 4. Dressed in a flowing blue robe, he has a sword that hangs at his waist.

Han Xiang Zi—Immortal 5. Slim, dressed in a wheat brown robe, his dark hair pulled tightly into a knot tied with a ribbon of red silk on the crown of his head. He was the messenger in Bk2. He plays a flute. Tries to maintain harmony in the group. Politest of the Immortals.

Zhang Guolao—Immortal 6. An old man Sara met and befriended in Book 1. He has a soft, dreamy expression and wears a white robe when he meets them for the first time in the Jade Palace.

He Xiangu—Immortal 7. Princess Li Mei in Book 1. She is dressed in a bright yellow, red, and white robe and is usually carrying a flower.

Cao Guojiu—Immortal 8. He carries a jade tablet and as a scholar is dressed in a red scholar's outfit with a tall hat.

Qin Shi Huang—The First Emperor of a unified China. He is fierce with a sword at his side, wearing a yellow robe whose gold border was richly embroidered with intertwining dragons. Two long curtains of beads fall from the tall cap on his head, reaching down to his sturdy shoulders, framing his solemn, black-bearded face and dark, penetrating eyes.

Shan Tuo—The brother of Shan Wu. Shan Tuo is told of Shan Wu's fate by Gong Wei.

Chan—Head of a crime syndicate, he is a distant relative of Shan Wu and Shan Tuo. He has the same degenerative disease that Shan Tuo had, giving him the appearance of being much older than he is. He is also an acolyte of Shan Wu. Shan Wu is his master who he is determined to bring him back to life fully.

Lin Dan—A brilliant Chinese scientist who is a world-famous bio-engineer. Under duress, he helps Chan develop the Elixir of Immortality that Chan wants to bottle and sell.